Push Back

(The Act of Forcing an Enemy to Withdraw)

James E. Merriman

iUniverse, Inc.
New York   Bloomington

Push Back
(The Act of Forcing an Enemy to Withdraw)

iUniverse books may be ordered through booksellers or by contacting:

iUniverse
1663 Liberty Drive
Bloomington, IN 47403
www.iuniverse.com
1-800-Authors (1-800-288-4677)

ISBN: 978-1-4401-8142-9 (sc)
ISBN: 978-1-4401-8144-3 (dj)
ISBN: 978-1-4401-8143-6 (ebk)

Printed in the United States of America

iUniverse rev. date: 11/2/2009

Fay, once again this book would not have been possible without your love and support.

Prologue

THE AXIS OF EVIL

"[Our goal] is to prevent regimes that sponsor terror from threatening America or our friends and allies with weapons of mass destruction.... North Korea is a regime arming with missiles and weapons of mass destruction, while starving its citizens.

"Iran aggressively pursues these weapons and exports terror, while an unelected few repress the Iranian people's hope for freedom.

"Iraq continues to flaunt its hostility toward America and to support terror....

"States like these, and their terrorist allies, constitute an axis of evil, arming to threaten the peace of the world. By seeking weapons of mass destruction, these regimes pose a grave and growing danger. They could provide these arms to terrorists, giving them the means to match their hatred. They could attack our allies or attempt to blackmail the United States. In any of these cases, the price of indifference would be catastrophic."

George W. Bush
2002 State of the Union Address

James E. Merriman

THE BUSH DOCTRINE

"Finally, the United States will use this moment of opportunity to extend the benefits of freedom across the globe. We will actively work to bring the hope of democracy, development, free markets, and free trade to every corner of the world. The events of September 11, 2001, taught us that weak states, like Afghanistan, can pose as great a danger to our national interests as strong states. Poverty does not make poor people into terrorists and murderers. Yet poverty, weak institutions, and corruption can make weak states vulnerable to terrorist networks and drug cartels within their borders."

The National Security Strategy of the United States of America
September 20, 2002

"The Bush Doctrine is the name given to a set of foreign policy guidelines first unveiled by President George W. Bush ... that would place a greater emphasis on military preemption ... unilateral action, and a commitment to 'extending democracy, liberty, and security to all regions.'"

Wikipedia, the free encyclopedia

SUCCESSOR TO GEORGE W. BUSH

"The United States of American stands as an example of what free people can accomplish. The greatness of this country comes with an obligation to support basic human rights for all people. All people yearn for the ability to speak their minds and have a say in how they are governed; confidence in the rule of law and the equal administration of justice; the freedom to live as one chooses. Our foreign policy will adhere to a single standard for those who would hold power over others. You must maintain your power through consent and govern with tolerance and compromise. You must respect the rights of minorities and place the interests of the governed and the legitimate workings of the political process above your personal power. In short, we will work for true democracy for all peoples.

President Janet Sampson
Successor to George W. Bush
Inaugural Address

Chapter 1

2009

Banafrit Amisi's brown eyes narrowed and her brow furrowed as she skillfully guided the remotely controlled mini helicopter through the hot and humid air of Gulfport, Mississippi, toward the Ajax Chemical Plant. She had not mastered this skill during her studies at Tulane University; it had come at a Wahhabi training camp in the desert of Saudi Arabia.

The tiny helicopter weighed eighteen pounds but was capable of carrying a twenty-five pound payload. Today it carried only four one-pound blocks of Iranian-manufactured C-4 plastic explosives.

From her vantage point on a low hill about a half mile from the plant, she could see the Ajax Chemical Plant's massive storage tanks of highly pressurized liquefied chlorine gas. Her hands were moist inside latex gloves, and sweat slid down her face. As the helicopter cleared the fence surrounding the plant, she stopped breathing.

This was the moment she had trained for. She detonated the C-4 just before the helicopter crashed into one of the massive storage tanks. This triggered a chemical reaction in which the C-4 decomposed and released a variety of gases which initially expanded at 26,400 feet per second. The explosion, which could be heard for miles, demolished the tank, releasing a cloud of toxic gas.

Gulfport is Mississippi's second largest metropolitan area with over seventy thousand residents, most of whom were located downwind from the explosion. During her training, Amisi had read the Homeland Security–published statistics that this type of incident could result in a toxic cloud extending as far as twenty-five miles, exposing 5 percent of the population to a lethal dose of gas, half of whom would die. An additional 15 percent would require hospitalization, with many others treated and released.

Amisi stood, mouth open, eyes wide, staring at what she had done. Planning was one thing, but seeing the result was unbelievable. Then her training kicked in. She smashed the control device into bits with a rock and flung the pieces around as she walked back to her rental car. There she stripped off her gloves, removed the size 10 men's tennis shoes she had been wearing, and replaced them with size 5 Adidas running shoes. The tennis shoes were destined for a nearby Goodwill drop-off bin. Amisi sported stylishly cut short dark hair, trendy sunglasses, jeans, and a T-shirt; she looked like any other college student.

She exhaled slowly, and self-satisfaction tugged at the corners of her mouth as she drove away, marveling at what one could purchase over the Internet. Not the C-4, of course, but the mini helicopter. She had another helicopter and two remote-controlled model planes hidden near a chemical plant outside New Orleans and two refineries near Houston, Texas.

Abdul Fahd was lying flat on the ground at the top of a grassy hill overlooking the parking lot for Memorial Hospital in Birmingham, Alabama. From his position behind two low bushes, he was invisible to those below who were streaming in and out of the main entrance.

His hands were dry; the heat didn't bother him, even in his khakis and blue button-down oxford shirt. This was nothing compared to the desert in Afghanistan, where he had spent hour after hour on a remote firing range, preparing himself for this moment and for those to come. For the first time in his life, he was in control. He would choose who would live and who would die. His only regret was that he could not target those who had bullied him during his teenage years in Washington DC.

Fahd's dark eyes smoldered as he picked up the Remington Model 7400 hunting rifle, purchased for cash at a Tucson, Arizona, gun show with his counterfeit driver's license. Later he visited ten different sporting goods stores, each time purchasing two boxes of shells, fifty shells to a box.

The rifle was solid in his hands; it belonged there. It had become an indispensable part of who he was. Fahd made his decision and carefully placed his eye to the scope. His heart rate was its usual sixty-five beats per minute. He sighted in on a woman in purple floral scrubs, probably a nurse hurrying to work; a perfect target.

He slowly inhaled and then, exhaling, gently squeezed the trigger. The top of the nurse's head exploded in a spray of pink mist.

Without waiting to see the reaction below, Fahd slithered backward until he was off the crown of the hill, stood, and strolled back to his rental car. Hit and move. Hit and move. It had been drilled into him time and again during his months of training for this mission. He put the rifle in its case and laid it in the trunk. As he drove off on the way to his next stop, he whispered, *"Allahu Akbar."*

For the briefest of moments, a picture of the nurse's exploding skull flashed before his eyes—an innocent caregiver whose life he had taken.

He shook his head sharply. *No. She was an infidel, no better than a cow.* No infidel was innocent. This was his jihad; many would die, but that was Allah's will.

The two hundred thousand residents of San Bernardino were enjoying another sunny California morning as the regular freight train entered the city's outskirts and braked to a crawl. Mohamed Alrifi, a Sudanese dropout from Chino State, sat in his rental car and observed the slow-moving train with cheap binoculars. When he saw what he was looking for, he exited the car and eased down the incline to the train. The gravel crunched under his Nike running shoes as he nonchalantly walked alongside the train track, glancing from time to time at the passing tank cars. Only a trained observer would notice that the pockets of his cargo pants sagged and bumped against his legs as he walked. There was no one to observe him, however, for there was no security, and the half-mile-long train was manned by three employees who hadn't slept all night.

When the first of two silver tank cars with large black lettering boldly proclaiming HAZMAT pulled abreast of him, Alrifi, in one smooth, practiced motion, reached into his left side pocket and extracted a one-pound block of Iranian C-4 encased in synthetic webbing. With his right hand he ripped off a strip of tape, exposing an adhesive, and in the same motion stuck the packet to the side of the passing tanker. Next came the C-4 block from his other side pocket, and the process was repeated on the next car. The whole process had taken less than ten seconds.

Alrifi turned away from the train and jogged back to his rental car. When he was a mile away from the train, at about the time it should have been in the center of the urban area, he dialed a cell phone number. The signal detonated the C-4, exploding both tank cars and producing a massive chemical cloud.

Alrifi knew only that his mission was to blow up two tankers of some kind of hazardous material. An hour later, he heard a news report on the radio that he had hit the jackpot. The tank cars contained methyl bromide, a colorless gas with practically no odor. It was used as a fumigant to control insects and was poisonous at room temperature. The gas would soon be causing the good people of San Bernardino headaches, dizziness, and nausea. Many in the immediate vicinity might receive a fatal dose.

Transportation of this and other hazardous material through urban areas was perfectly legal and happened thousands of times a day all across the country. Alrifi had maps of the routes used by Hazmat carriers which he had found on the Internet and printed out. His plan was off to a better-than-expected beginning. He had charted a dozen stops on his way to Interstate 40 in Asheville, North Carolina, where unescorted trucks of Quad State Trucking regularly carried uranium hexafluoride bound for Global Nuclear Fuels–Americas in Wilmington, North Carolina.

––––––––––––––––––––––––––

Paeng Aquino drove his rental car up the narrow, winding Going-to-the-Sun Road in Glacier National Park, Montana. Each time he rounded a sharp bend in the road and saw no oncoming traffic; he lit a Molotov cocktail and tossed it out the window. The bottle disappeared over the edge and plummeted several hundred feet before crashing into the dense undergrowth below. No one was witness to this desecration of one of the most magnificent places in America. As he topped the pass, smoke was billowing up from below.

Aquino pulled into a parking area at the top of the highway and visited the restroom. He returned to his car with a cup of tea and opened his map to check the highlighted route to Yellowstone National Park one more time. As he pulled out of the lot, he turned up the radio, which was playing Toby Keith's "How Do You Like Me Now?" When the chorus came to "now that I'm on my way …," he pumped his fist and prayed to himself, *"Allahu akbar."* He no longer served infidels on cruise ships. Paeng Aquino, small, bastard son of a US sailor and a Philippine woman, was now *mujahidin*. He was somebody to reckon with.

Chapter 2

2004

Ali Alwaleed, foreign policy adviser to the Crown Prince of
Saudi Arabia, stood on the lushly landscaped balcony of the
Buckingham Suite in London's Dorchester Hotel savoring the last
of a Cohiba cigar. From his vantage point high above Mayfair, he
looked across London to Westminster, the dome of St. Paul's, and
beyond to Canary Wharf. Over the years, the four-room suite
had been a refuge for many heads of state and celebrities. Today,
still lavishly decorated in Queen Anne antiques, it would host a
meeting that would change the course of history.

Alwaleed, trim and just over six feet tall, wore a Savile Row
navy pinstriped suit and a Turnbull & Asser white shirt with a red
paisley patterned silk tie. An eggshell pocket square and gleaming
Guccis completed his attire. He looked every bit the Oxford-
educated sophisticate that he was. Alwaleed had been working
on this project since George W. Bush had promulgated his Bush
Doctrine.

Democracy in Saudi Arabia ... American military forces permanently stationed in the Kingdom or anywhere in the Middle East ... the Crown Prince was apoplectic. When he calmed down, he tasked Alwaleed with developing a plan to prevent America's intervention in Saudi internal affairs and to get its forces out of the Middle East.

Formulating a plan was difficult enough, but the problem became much more complicated when the United States invaded Iraq and upset the balance of power throughout the Middle East. Iraq was no longer a buffer between Sunni and Shiite power; worse, the country and its oil were up for grabs. The mix of ancient, religiously fueled sectarian hatred, oil, money, politics, and people seeking personal power was more than enough to start another world war.

Today's meeting had one purpose: to finalize how to put the Americans in their place. They were going to get the Americans out of the Middle East and stop their attempts to dictate policy and morality to the rest of the world.

The two men waiting for Alwaleed had arrived separately. General Ri Chan-bok, the chief of staff to North Korea's Kim Jong Il, had arrived first, followed an hour later by Sher Tabrizi, head of the Quds Force of the Iranian Revolutionary Guard.

Alwaleed pushed up his French cuffed sleeve and checked his Rolex. He had kept them waiting just long enough to establish that he was in charge of the meeting. He left his cigar on the balcony and, crossing his bedroom, stopped at the full-length mirror and adjusted his tie. Satisfied with his appearance, he opened the tall polished mahogany double doors and entered the spacious living room. Both his guests stood as he crossed the plush carpet. He shook hands with Ri and nodded to Tabrizi, saying, *"Assalaam alaikum,"* before settling in a comfortable wing chair, crossing his legs, and tugging at the sharp crease in his trousers. His servant handed him a Laphroaig single-malt scotch and left the room, quietly closing the door.

Tabrizi, a Harvard graduate, was a member of the Mensa organization which only accepted those whose IQ was in the top two percent of the population. He was short, with blazing black eyes separated by a large nose. A cowlick poked out of his dark hair, which needed cutting. When in London, he preferred the Brooks Brothers look: gray suit, white button-down shirt, and striped tie. As if preparing for battle, Tabrizi had removed his suit coat and loosened his tie. Perspiration beaded his forehead as he unbuttoned his cuffs and rolled up his sleeves. As he sat forward on the sofa which, along with several chairs, was grouped around a large coffee table, his ample love handles caused his shirttail to pull loose.

Ri had a round head with a small button nose on a concave face that gave him the look of someone who was burdened with a birth defect; however, one look from his cold, penetrating black eyes evaporated that notion. He sat ramrod straight in the other wing chair, impassively sipping green tea. He was of average height, dressed in an ill-fitting gray suit, wash-and-wear white shirt, and plain black tie. Ri's polished black shoes were obviously part of his military uniform. His gray hair was short, cropped as short as any recruit's. While not a fashion plate, Ri was an accomplished military strategist with the job of formulating a plan to deal with the diplomatic and armed pressure being applied to North Korea by the United States.

"Gentlemen," began Alwaleed, "we come together today in a common cause: put an end to the Bush Doctrine and with it the American Empire. Our governments and our way of life are not secure so long as the Americans attempt to rule the world. It is perfectly clear that they intend to establish a permanent military presence in Iraq and, if necessary, Afghanistan from which to dominate the Middle East. Cheney and Rumsfeld made that clear as early as 2000. Removing Hussein was merely a pretext for their long-range military goals. As for their attitude toward North Korea, nothing further need be said."

Tabrizi interrupted. "You are right, of course, but the problem is more than military. Everything America stands for is an affront to Allah. Under Islam, our rulers derive their power from Allah, not the people. Western-style democracy turns this immutable principle on its head. It rejects any political theology based upon Allah and replaces it with a political philosophy based on man. This is blasphemy, pure and simple."

"You are both right," said Ri, "but let us be clear about something else: our governments have no intention of allowing the United States to interfere in how our countries are governed."

"Yes, of course," said Tabrizi with a nod, "but we must stop the invasion of Western culture. It is immoral, degenerate, and anathema to Muslims. Ayatollah Khomeini understood that Satan is not an invader, imperialist, or exploiter, but a tempter and seducer who whispers in the ears of men. The very idea of women …"

Alwaleed let him drone on while he savored the smoky flavor of the scotch. It was a taste he had acquired during his years at Oxford that was denied him in his native Saudi Arabia. Like most Saudis who were able to get to London, he took advantage of the sensory and fleshly pleasures that were unavailable in the Kingdom. As Tabrizi pounded the table, spilling his untouched coffee from its cup, Alwaleed's mind wandered toward the evening, when he would again experience the delights of Cordelia Nightingale.

Alwaleed had already brought Ri onboard. They just had to reel in the Iranian to make it work.

After several more minutes of telling Alwaleed and Ri what they already knew, Tabrizi seemed to be winding down or at least running out of breath.

"I think we are all agreed," said Alwaleed, "that once we get rid of the Americans, we will create an Iraqi federation of three states, Shiite, Sunni, and Kurdish, with a central military government to keep peace and allocate oil proceeds."

Tabrizi interrupted Alwaleed once again. "I am here with authority to propose a four-step plan to deal with the Americans.

"First, we enter into a treaty stating that an invasion of any of our countries will be considered an act of war against all of us. Second, Saudi Arabia will cut off their oil. Third, Iran will send five hundred thousand ground troops into Iraq at the request of our Shiite allies. Fourth, North Korea will threaten the Americans with their nuclear weapons. We must keep democracy from taking hold in Iraq at all costs. It is vital to our survival." Tabrizi stopped talking and looked around.

Neither Alwaleed nor Ri had any intention of enabling Iran to flood Iraq with ground forces. If the Americans were forced out, Iran and their Shiite allies would control Iraq and its oil.

Ri took a sip of tea and delicately set down his cup. With his elbows on the arms of his chair, he folded his hands with his index fingers pointed directly at Tabrizi and fixed him with an unblinking gaze. In an emotionless voice he said, "Half a million men will do you no good. If you attack their forces in Iraq directly, they will destroy you and use it as a pretext for regime change in your country. It is a fool's game, and we will not play."

Tabrizi looked at Alwaleed, who responded in a conciliatory tone, trying to ease the harshness with which Ri had rejected the Iranian plan. "I must concur with General Ri, Sher. The United States only imports about 20 percent of its oil from us. Furthermore, as a practical matter we cannot cut off the flow of oil to the United States. We need the money, and we need the leverage to keep ourselves in power. If we cut off their oil, they will just get it somewhere else, and we have slit our own throat."

The pitch of Tabrizi's voice rose in frustration. "You must agree that the Bush Doctrine threatens all of us. We must do something. Propose an alternative."

Alwaleed put down his drink, placed his elbows on the arms of his chair, and steepled his fingers. In a professorial tone, he asked, "Sher, what is the genesis of the Bush Doctrine?"

"Why 9/11, of course," snapped Tabrizi.

Alwaleed remained patient. "What is the Bush Doctrine intended to prevent?"

In a voice filled with growing impatience, Tabrizi said, "Terrorist attacks in America, of course. What is the point of this Socratic exercise?"

"Please bear with me for a moment, Sher. How can one tell if the Bush Doctrine is a failure?"

Tabrizi thought for a moment and said, "If there are terrorist attacks in the United States."

General Ri interjected, "How many men and women can you muster who are willing to die or at least risk death for Iran? They must—"

Tabrizi interrupted. "Why, thousands upon thousands."

Ri held up his right fist, index finger extended, toward Tabrizi and sternly lectured the Iranian. "Do not interrupt me. I don't mean illiterate brainwashed children, I mean English-speaking men and women who have lived in the United States or are at least familiar with its customs and can fit into the flow of life in the United States."

Tabrizi thought for a moment before answering. "I don't know, surely many hundreds."

Alwaleed leaned forward, pointed at Tabrizi, and said, "The means to get the Americans out of the Middle East and end their attempt to export democracy is not to be found in the Middle East. It is in their country. We must take the battle to them in their homes, in places where they work and take their pleasure. What I am suggesting is that we play on American self-absorption and lack of patience. A plague of disasters such as forest fires, car bombs, poisoned food, bombed bridges, blown-up trains, and random sniper attacks will completely demoralize them. It will become clear that the only way they can hope to have life in the United States return to normal is to get out of the Middle East and forget about meddling in the internal affairs of other countries.

"If we start with one hundred operatives and assume that 90 percent get into the United States, that will leave us with ninety. Assume that another 10 percent are picked up before they can do any damage; we still have eighty. Assume that the remaining operatives average ten disasters before they are finished. That is eight hundred separate disasters that the Americans have to deal with.

"Just imagine the uproar when they figure out what is happening to them. No one will feel safe. They won't be able to enjoy their beer and football. As the disasters mount, as they suffer damage in their communities, the complacent ones will rise up and align themselves with the pacifists. When that happens, the Americans will be out of the Middle East for a generation or more. They will stop trying to export democracy and return to a sensible foreign policy like that of Kissinger where the goal is stability, not democracy. The American Empire will come to an end. They may even revert to isolationism, as they did after World War I."

Tabrizi said, "I am not convinced such a small number of people can accomplish enough to cause the Americans to withdraw from the Middle East, much less abandon the Bush Doctrine. General Ri, what about you? Where does North Korea fit in?"

The corners of Ri's mouth turned up in the approximation of a smile. "We will give you two nuclear bombs to detonate in two large cities, perhaps Los Angeles and Miami. The FBI and local law enforcement will be running around like beheaded chickens trying to figure out what is going on and find those causing the terrorist incidents. Even if the bombs are discovered before detonation, there will be a massive impact on the American psyche. Their people will demand an end to foreign intervention when they see the price they are going to pay if they continue."

Tabrizi was visibly stunned, clearly unprepared for the enormity of what Ri proposed. With evident uncertainty, he asked, "What if they retaliate?"

Alwaleed was ready for the question. "Against whom? We already have identified recruits for this project from Pakistan, Iraq, Indonesia, Syria, Lebanon, Jordan, Palestine, Egypt, Sudan, and the Philippines. We only need twenty people from Iran. These people will all be separately trained; they will not know one another. All they will know is that Allah has selected them for a special mission. The Americans cannot drop bombs on the rest of the world. They will be helpless and unable to retaliate."

Tabrizi held up his hand. "How many people know about this plan? What if one of these recruits drops out or talks? How do you know one of them is not a spy?"

General Ri's robotic voice answered the questions. "First, all recruits are members of families with impeccable Muslim credentials. They will be aware that their families are in essence hostages. Second, the recruits will not be trained together, and each will act alone. Third, we expect a dropout rate of 50 percent. Those that drop out or are mustered out will be killed. Fourth, all recruits embarking on this mission will have an encapsulated microchip embedded in their heads which allows us to track their whereabouts. The capsules also contain an explosive compound which can be detonated by satellite transmission. Each operative will be required to check in on a precise schedule. If they miss a check-in or we know they have been captured, the explosive will be detonated."

Alwaleed could sense that Tabrizi was still hesitating. "Sher, the coup de grâce is that we have two imams who are American citizens, one living in Phoenix and one living in Detroit, who are willing to place the bombs once we get them into the country. If they are caught, they will have poison capsules to martyr themselves. If they are not caught, the Americans may never know who set off the bombs. Even so, what if they do find out? The imams are American citizens."

Alwaleed sat back, crossed his legs, tugged at the crease in his trousers, and picked up his glass of scotch. He was certain Tabrizi had bought into the program.

"Wait, let me think," said Tabrizi. "How do you propose to get all these people into the United States along with two nuclear bombs?"

"The Mexican border," said Ri in his flat voice.

"Precisely so," said Alwaleed.

"Why the Mexican border?" Tabrizi asked.

General Ri said, "That two-thousand-mile border is an open door into the United States. Thousands of trucks, trains, buses, and cars are crossing the border daily. There are tunnels under the border. One can merely step across a three-strand wire fence."

Tabrizi hesitated for only a moment. "What about the border fence the Americans are installing?"

Again Alwaleed was ready. "We intend to use Mexican professionals to move our people across the border. The fence only runs along part of the border. The Mexicans are already cutting it and tunneling under it; they have even developed ramps to drive trucks over it. A twelve-foot fence only requires a thirteen-foot ladder."

Tabrizi thought about the idea for a few moments. Then he spoke very slowly. "We can give you the people, we can use camps in Sudan and Lebanon as well as our own to train people, but I am not sure about the training program itself."

Alwaleed put down his glass and said, "Don't worry, we already have plenty of American-educated trainers who will take care of that."

Tabrizi sat silently for almost a full minute before struggling to his feet and pacing the room. He stopped several times and started to speak, seemed to think better of it, and resumed pacing.

Alwaleed knew that Tabrizi believed Islamic law, the *sharia,* was the only valid system for regulating human life; however, Tabrizi was not a subscriber to jihad and martyrdom as preached by the Wahhabi sect. At heart Tabrizi was a politician. Alwaleed also knew that for Iran to achieve its political goal of dominating the Middle East, it needed to get rid of the United States. He expected Tabrizi to conclude that if religion could be harnessed to achieve a political goal, so be it. Dead Americans wouldn't bother him at all.

Tabrizi returned to his seat and fixed Ri with eyes that blazed with excitement. "Tell me about the bombs."

"They weigh less than sixty pounds and are designed to fit in a normal-size suitcase," said Ri. "With the power of ten kilotons, each one is equal to the bomb the Americans dropped on Hiroshima."

Tabrizi's eyes widened as the consequences of what was being proposed became clear to him. "All right," he said, "I will recommend this plan to my superiors. I am sure they will agree, and I will start to recruit our people. What is the timetable?"

"ASAP," said Ri.

Sher Tabrizi left first. Alwaleed and Ri shared a drink.

Alwaleed knew Ri had purchased the bombs in Pakistan through a now-deceased intermediary using dollars received from the United Nations Development Program. North Korea required and UNDP acquiesced in making all grant payments in cash; the funds became untraceable. There was a certain irony in using American contributions to the UN to buy bombs for use in their own cities. If this plan worked, he knew Ri would be well positioned in the struggle for succession that was sure to follow the death of Kim Jung Il.

As the door closed behind Ri, Alwaleed sent a coded text message to the Prince and immediately dialed Cordelia Nightingale.

Chapter 3

2009

Arturo Ramirez lit another cigarette as he waited in traffic to cross the Bridge of the Americas from El Paso, Texas, into Juárez, Mexico. He was of medium height and, at forty-eight, kept fit and trim with regular exercise. With his wavy black hair and light olive complexion, he looked more Castilian than Mexican. In his new Range Rover, dressed in blue jeans and a white open-necked shirt with Maui Jim sunglasses, he exuded the confidence of a man who was sure of his place in the world.

Arturo was on the way to the funeral of his grandfather at Carlos Sanchez's one-hundred-square-mile ranch south of Nogales, Sonora, across the border from Nogales, Arizona. The ranch was named Los Lobos, which always caused him to chuckle when he thought about it. *Wolves, coyotes* … He traveled with a black suit hanging in the back of the Range Rover and a lifetime of memories from his grandfather, Pepe, custodian of the Sanchez family's oral history.

When the Mexican War ended in 1848 with the Treaty of Guadalupe Hidalgo, there were many Sanchez family members living in modern-day California, Arizona, New Mexico, Texas, and parts of Colorado. Together with parts of modern-day Nevada and Utah, this land constituted almost half of Mexico's territory. It was taken from Mexico for $15 million in compensation.

His grandfather had often said, "We didn't cross the border, the border crossed us. The Americans stole our land."

He was historically accurate. Article 10 of the treaty stated the United States government would honor all land grants awarded to citizens of Spain and Mexico in the territory being ceded to the United States. The version of the treaty ratified by the US Senate eliminated Article 10. Members of the Sanchez family had valid land grants from both the Spanish and Mexican governments for vast tracts of land in the American Southwest which were taken from them.

Arturo had spent the last week buying two more ranches along the Texas side of the Rio Grande from disgruntled ranchers who were fed up with the constant flow of illegal immigrants from Mexico. What the Texans failed to realize was that the Sanchez family, through a maze of Mexican and offshore entities, owned the land opposite these ranches on the Mexican side of the Rio Grande and had funneled illegal alien traffic across the ranchers' land until they were ready to pull up stakes.

Fifteen minutes later, when Arturo finally reached the border barrier, he was greeted by Jorge Dias, a proud ten-year member of ICE (US Immigration and Customs Enforcement), who was a graduate of Texas A&M and a Marine Corps veteran. Jorge had the primary responsibility for ensuring safe passage for family drug shipments at this border crossing. He was married to Maria Sanchez.

Jorge gave him a big smile. Arturo grinned and said, "Next week the Longhorns are going to trample you worthless Aggies."

"No way, brother. The Longhorns are heading for the slaughterhouse," replied Jorge, waving him across the bridge. Arturo had played cornerback for the Longhorns, and some years later, Jorge had been a second-string running back for the Aggies. The banter went with the territory.

Arturo turned his thoughts to the border ranches owned or controlled by the family. This was his area of responsibility, and he would have to update Carlos Sanchez, his distant cousin, after the funeral.

More than two hundred Sanchez family members had attended Pepe Ramirez's funeral early that morning when it was relatively cool. Now it was hot, well into triple digits. At least it was a dry heat, mused Jamie Ruiz as he crossed the deep veranda that circled the ground floor of the Sanchez hacienda and entered the two-story library though French doors. This was his first time inside the massive twenty-thousand-square-foot hacienda. The library had French doors on the opposite wall which led to the back veranda and the huge swimming pool. Oil portraits hung on the walls between bookcases. The high ceiling, tile floor and the minimal lighting gave the room a cavelike feel.

Jamie could feel the sweat running down his sides to his waist. It wasn't the heat that was causing saddlebags to develop under his armpits; it was his nerves. His black hair felt damp, his olive complexion greasy, and he could feel the thirty extra pounds of fat he was carrying around his waist. At five and a half feet tall, he was ruthless with subordinates and competitors but very nervous around his superiors. He had been surprised when Carlos Sanchez had ordered him to attend this meeting. Something was up, and since he had no idea what it was, he feared the worst, which in his business meant that he could be made to disappear.

Jamie, fifty-two years old, had been running the family coyote operation which guided illegal immigrants across the border for five years. The current charges were five thousand dollars for Mexicans, seven thousand for Central and South Americans, and thirty thousand for Chinese, Arabs and others from outside the Western Hemisphere. In 2008, gross revenue from his operation was over three billion dollars. All of it in cash. If the Mexicans did not have the cash, they were held in US safe houses until stateside relatives paid up. There was no such thing as credit.

Carlos Sanchez, still in his dark funeral suit, sat behind his desk. He was an older version of his older son Hector, who had recently been elected President of Mexico. At sixty-four Carlos retained a full head of jet black hair curling over his collar; only a few wisps of gray surrounded his ears. His smooth olive complexion would have been the envy of a fashion model. He was a handsome man until one looked into his empty, bottomless black eyes. The eyes were a Sanchez family genetic trait.

On the sofa to Carlos's right sat Ramon, his younger son, who had changed from his suit into white slacks and a black Tommy Bahama short-sleeved shirt. He stood and walked across the room to shake Jamie's hand. Jamie quickly wiped his palm on his suit pants and shook hands. Ramon's grip was firm and his palm dry.

Jamie looked down as they shook hands. It was an unconscious act of deference. He was a Harvard Business School graduate and had worked ten years for a major accounting firm in Mexico City, becoming a well-respected partner before the family business called for him. Still, he could not look either Carlos or Ramon Sanchez in the eyes.

Arturo Ramirez, who had been standing in front of Carlos, shook Jamie's hand, and they both sat in the guest chairs in front of the desk.

After a nod of greeting, Carlos said, "Jamie, what is our revenue situation so far this year?"

Jamie sat up a little straighter as he answered, though he dared look no higher than Carlos's hands on the desk before him. "Revenue is up twenty percent over the same period last year."

"That is excellent. What do you think is causing the increase?"

"In my opinion the increase is due to the two factors. First, at Ramon's suggestion, I arranged to have the US Border Patrol capture three coyotes who had built up substantial businesses. The Border Patrol needs to catch coyotes and illegal immigrants, and what better ones to catch than those who were stupid enough to set themselves up in competition with us?

"The second reason is compliments of the Border Patrol: with increased enforcement, more people have to use us to successfully cross the border."

The Sanchez system involved much more that sending a group of hapless peasants into the desert with a bottle of water and a teenage guide. The family moved more than a million people a year across the border with a combination of techniques. In urban areas, there were tunnels under the border. In other places the family owned the land on both sides of the border. In remote areas vehicles picked up and delivered those who stepped across the three-strand barbwire fence that marked the border.

False Border Crossing Cards, known as Laser Visas and false visas, were used for highly valued people. For truly special people, the family had access to valid Mexican passports. The family trucking company moved cattle, meat, produce, and people across the border in some of the more than four and a half million trucks that crossed into the US each year. Less than five percent of the truck traffic was checked. and with a little help from well-placed ICE and Border Patrol agents, Sanchez trucks were almost never checked. The family operation also used some of the nine thousand trains and three million buses that crossed the border every year. With over three hundred and fifty million people crossing the border annually, the statistics were overwhelmingly in favor of the Sanchez family's well-oiled smuggling machine.

Carlos wasted no more time on preliminaries. "One of our people in Mexico's London embassy has been approached by someone that wants our help in crossing one hundred people into the United States within a one-week period. Each of these people must be crossed separately. The fee is ten million dollars."

Jamie could not help himself and exclaimed, "That would be our highest fee ever." He looked around the room, but no one's expression had changed; there was no response from anyone.

"We can do the math," snapped Carlos. "The question I have for you is, can you do it?"

Jamie thought for a moment and said nervously, "Our success rate is ninety-two point five percent. We could probably improve on that by using our cross-border ranches. But it would not be prudent to guarantee a hundred percent success rate."

Carlos turned to Arturo, who, in contrast to Jamie, was visibly relaxed, and asked, "What do you think?"

"From my perspective, this proposition brings with it a very high degree of risk. These people may be terrorists. If even one of them is picked up, it will not be the usual catch and release or a bus back to the border. They will be interrogated, and if it is discovered that they used our ranches to cross the border, the US government will be all over us. The ranches are too valuable to our drug trade to put at risk for a few million dollars."

Carlos leaned forward and took a Cuban cigar from the humidor on the corner of his desk. He said nothing while he clipped and lit the cigar with a gold Dunhill lighter. He drew on the cigar and exhaled smoke toward the ceiling.

"Señor Sanchez," asked Arturo, "if I may, where are these people from? Are they terrorists?"

"That is not your concern," snapped Carlos. "Since we will not be using the ranches, you may go."

As Arturo left the room, Jamie thought any fool could figure that sooner or later the terrorists were coming to the United States.

"Jamie, how do you suggest we get these people across?" asked Carlos.

"There are thirty-five legal border crossing ports of entry. I will prepare a precise plan using tunnels in Nogales, Calexico, and Tijuana, and trucks in El Paso, Brownsville, Del Rio, Presidio, and Laredo. We can walk the rest across in New Mexico. I figure we will get at least ninety of them in, spread over a week," said Jamie.

"All right, get the specifics together tomorrow. I will be in touch. You can leave," said Carlos, waving Jamie out of the room.

Chapter 4

When the door closed behind Jamie, Carlos turned to Ramon, who was standing by the French doors looking out at the pool. "All right, Ramon, what's bothering you?" he asked in a soft voice.

Ramon turned from the door, put his hands in his pockets, and looked into his father's eyes. "I assume these people are Muslim terrorists. I am not comfortable with unleashing them inside the United States. We have a lot of family there who could be hurt. Smuggling workers and drugs is one thing; terrorists are quite another matter. We don't really need the money."

Carlos looked at his son with a benign expression, which was unusual for him. He would never admit it, but in addition to loving his son, he had great respect for his intelligence and common sense.

"If we don't do it, they will just go to someone else. The end result will be the same, except someone else will have our money. I don't particularly like it either, but we are not the world's policemen." Carlos crossed the room to a tea cart and poured himself a glass of white wine from the bottle in an ice bucket. Ramon joined him and poured himself a glass. They wandered out of the library and crossed the veranda, heading for the arbor on the far side of the pool, Ramon saying nothing, Carlos smoking his cigar. Father and son sat down at the small stone table under the flowering bougainvillea vines of the arbor.

Ramon took a sip of wine, set his glass on the table, and looked into his father's face. "I would like to think we have some principles. We help people who want to work get to a place where they are needed and can get work. We supply a product the Americans are desperate for. The drugs kill fewer people than cigarettes and alcohol. We supplement the pitiful salaries of politicians, police, and the military. If we help the terrorists, do we not become terrorists ourselves? How big a risk would we be running?"

Before Carlos could respond, their conversation was interrupted by the arrival of a Mexican government helicopter at the helipad about a quarter mile from the back wall of the hacienda. A few moments later, Carlos and Ramon watched Hector walk toward them from the hacienda with his latest mistress, Stephanie Chambers, by his side.

Hector was a little over six feet tall with the trademark Sanchez jet black hair, neatly barbered, and black eyes. He was extraordinarily handsome in a sexual way. Fawning magazine articles often compared his looks to the movie star Antonio Banderas. Hector had had a playboy reputation until he decided to move from governor of Sonora to the presidency. Since then he had toned things down a bit.

He was dressed in a dark blue Hickey Freeman business suit with a striped shirt and red tie. Holding his arm, Stephanie smiled beautifully. The American was a tall, athletic-looking woman who, before withdrawing, had been on the short list for the US Olympic heptathlon team. In a simple black Armani dress and short black hair, she was striking, not beautiful.

Both Carlos and Ramon stood and exchanged greetings with the couple.

"We are on our way to Phoenix," said Hector. "I have a meeting with John Lawton, the new DEA head, and Stephanie has some serious shopping to do. I thought I would stop in and say hello."

Carlos smiled and said, "Your timing is excellent; we need your opinion on some business matters. Perhaps Señorita Chambers could occupy herself in the hacienda for a few brief moments."

"No problem," said Stephanie as she turned and started toward the house. The three men stood and watched her walk gracefully away from them.

"I love the way she moves," sighed Hector.

No one responded, and the three men sat.

Carlos spoke first. "We have been asked to move one hundred people across the border separately over the course of a week. The fee is ten million dollars. Ramon thinks these people are probably terrorists and is not sure we should assist them. He's probably right about them being terrorists, but to my way of thinking, if we don't do it, someone else will, and we will be out ten million dollars. What do you think?"

Hector reached into his inside jacket pocket and withdrew a Cohiba cigar, a shared family vice. He bit off the end, and Carlos lit the cigar. Hector took a puff and inspected the end of the cigar to be sure it was properly lit. Then he crossed his legs, took another puff on his cigar, and began.

"I can see terrorist attacks within the US potentially working to our advantage. Like it or not, the Americans meddle with everyone in the world. Whether it is Iraq, Iran, Somalia, China, North Korea, Venezuela, or Mexico, it is the same. France and Germany are fed up with them. They are always telling others what to do and making threats if their wishes are not followed. I had to send troops to temporarily disarm the Tijuana police and pretend to investigate the entire force for corruption to keep the Americans off my back. What a joke. Their demand for drugs is a massive growth industry that they blame on us. Bullshit; if they didn't use the stuff, we wouldn't be able to sell it. Personally I am sick of them trying to run the world. I don't agree with Chavez or that moron in Iran on much, but I do agree that the Americans need to be put in their place."

Hector paused and took another puff on the cigar before resuming. "The Democrats in Washington are solidly against the Iraq War. A few bombs in America's backyard would put the entire country behind them. It could be that it will be a long time before they do anything outside their country but spew hot air. Anything that can get the Americans to stop meddling in foreign countries would work to our advantage."

No one spoke for several moments, and then Ramon began. "I'm not so sure. What if the Americans retaliate?"

Hector put his cigar in the ashtray and leaned toward Ramon with his forearms on the table. Carlos leaned back and watched his sons with pride that he kept from showing on his face.

"Against whom, brother? I assume these are Muslim terrorists, certainly not Mexicans. We are totally insulated from the coyotes that will move these people, and our government is not involved. If things get too uncomfortable, we can arrest some of the Fuentes coyotes and throw them in jail until things calm down. There is little if any downside, and the upside is huge. This could bring an end to American meddling."

Both sons looked at Carlos. Decision time.

Carlos began without any hesitation. "The only downside I can see is that there could be some danger to our family along the border. However, I think these people need large population centers to do their mischief.

"We do it. If any of our people get hurt, we will compensate their immediate families."

Stephanie crossed the veranda, intent on getting some water from the kitchen. As she passed the library, movement from the exercise room caught her attention. She stopped and looked in through the French doors. Carlos's only daughter, Margarita "Boots" Sanchez, was jogging on a treadmill with her back to Stephanie.

Boots was five eight with shoulder-length wavy black hair which was now in a ponytail. In her mid-twenties, she had a classic hourglass figure, and her round derriere remained firm as she jogged. Perspiration made her skin glow. Stephanie stood transfixed; she could not bring herself to move. Boots stopped the treadmill and turned toward Stephanie but did not appear to see her. The workout suit accentuated her flat belly and jutting breasts. The woman was magnificent. Boots began a series of slow, sensual catlike stretching exercises. To Stephanie, the stretches

31

were almost sexual. Boots ended her routine sitting on the mat with her legs spread wide and her upper body bent forward, arms extended. She lifted her head, looked directly at Stephanie, and smiled. Then she stood and began toweling off. She gestured for Stephanie to enter.

Stephanie slowly put her hand on the door handle, turned it, stepped tentatively just inside the door, and stopped. Boots walked over and stood so close that their breasts were almost touching. Stephanie couldn't step back; she was mesmerized by deep, lustrous ebony eyes. Boots said very softly, "I am so glad to see you again."

Before Stephanie could say anything, the silence was shattered by Hector calling, "Stephanie. Come on, we've got to go." He appeared at the door. "Oh, here you are. Hello, Margarita," he laughed, "are you after my woman again?"

Boots just smiled, touched Stephanie lightly on her upper arm, and said, "Off you go. I'll look forward to seeing you again."

"Come on, Stephanie, we've got to get to Scottsdale, can't keep the DEA waiting," Hector said as he took her hand and led her from the room.

Chapter 5

2009

There was only an hour of daylight left in the clear, Colorado fall day when Grant Meredith splashed across the Pine River on his horse and loped across a recently cut pasture to the main barn. He had spent the afternoon on horseback touring the Durango Land & Cattle Company, his four–thousand-acre ranch, filling a small notepad with projects that would take years to complete.

The barn boom box reverberated with the sounds of the Delbert McLinton and Tanya Tucker duet, "Tell Me About It." That meant Tommy was somewhere nearby.

Tommy Taylor, ex-guitar player for Stevie Ray Vaughn and ex-professional team roper, was currently Grant's only ranch hand. He emerged from the shaded barn interior and shot a brown stream of tobacco juice in the general direction of a sleeping barn cat. Tommy was a short bowlegged man who started every day with a clean pair of Wrangler jeans and a long-sleeved snap-button shirt topped by a grimy, sweat-stained Stetson hat of indeterminate color. By the end of the day, ranch work left his clothes looking like his hat. Today was no exception.

Grant dismounted, and when Tommy reached to take the reins, Grant put them behind him and handed Tommy the notepad with a big smile and said, "Just a few little things to get done before the snow flies."

Tommy glanced at the pad, shook his head, smiled, and drawled with his south Texas accent, "Grant Meredith, I knew when you were gone that long, you were up to no good. Your little things make a man wish for a long, cold winter by the fire."

Before Grant could continue the repartee, the afternoon FedEx truck pulled up to the barn trailing a cloud of dust. He knew what was coming: the briefing materials for today's teleconference and next week's BlackRock board of directors meeting. Grant excused himself, took the package, and walked fifty yards to the rambling two-story ranch house that sat among a stand of hundred–year-old ponderosa pine trees.

He settled his long, lean frame into a tooled leather desk chair and filled his favorite pipe. As he drew on the pipe, he sighed in satisfaction at the view of the river and a long pasture running south. He had been building and developing the ranch since he sold BlackRock, the private military contracting company he had founded after leaving the army, to a private equity firm. Blood, sweat, and money was creating his vision of a twenty-first-century working ranch. A long scar on his right forearm rose as a testament to the blood he had spilled working with ranch equipment, horses, and cattle. As for money, he no longer chuckled at the old joke that the way to become a millionaire rancher in Colorado was to come with ten million and ranch until there was a million left.

The book-lined ranch library was his personal sanctuary. A Remington bronze sculpture, paintings of Western scenes, and a hand-woven Navajo Two Grey Hills rug gave the room a comfortable Western ranch ambience. The ranch was eighteen miles from Durango, three and a half hours from Santa Fe, and five hours from Flagstaff, Arizona. Put another way, it was a remote part of flyover country. Fortunately, Grant had been able to install state-of-the-art telecommunications equipment provided by Cisco Systems which made possible today's teleconference.

Grant put his feet up on the desk and began reading the memorandum addressed to the BlackRock board members from Reggie Brown, the chief operating officer, entitled "Saudi Contract Concerns." He had been dreading this memo for a week.

BlackRock had been created to fill the void left by the downsizing of the US military after the end of the Cold War. Former members of the Delta Force, Rangers, and SEALs were handpicked as "military contractors" to train military and police forces for foreign governments. These contractors also provided security for US civilian personnel in highly dangerous places such as Iraq and Afghanistan. Earlier this year, BlackRock had been awarded a five-hundred-million-dollar contract to provide security services for the Saudi oil fields and royal family.

Grant finished the memo just before Reggie Brown, at BlackRock headquarters in North Carolina, opened the teleconference.

"Gentlemen, we are in a mess. Bush had no idea what he was going to unleash when he deposed Saddam. Despite the way it looks now, as soon as our troops pull out, Iraq will descend into chaos that does not bode well for the Saudis and by extension BlackRock. There will be a Shiite/Sunni bloodbath and a Kurdish revolution for independence; the whole mess may spread throughout the Middle East."

The former president of the United States, Homer Johnson, interrupted Brown. "Excuse me, Reggie, I can't keep this Sunni/Shiite distinction straight. Explain, please."

"Mr. President, the Sunni Muslims follow one descendant of the Prophet Muhammad, and the Shiite Muslims follow another. This rift was made permanent in AD 680 with the Battle of Karbala. Seventy percent of Arabs are Sunni, but in Iraq 65 percent are Shiites.

"I know this is difficult to follow, but please bear with me.

"Iranians are Persians, not Arabs; moreover, Iranians are Shiites. Therefore, when Bush deposed Saddam, who was Sunni, he gave voice to the Shiite majority. Many are calling Bush the father of the first Arab Shia state. The significance here is that you get an alignment of Persian Shiites and Iraqi Arab Shiites, who are more loyal to their religion than their country. This is perfect for the Iranians who have been proselytizing in Sunni countries since Ayatollah Khomeini came to power in Iran in 1979."

Grant said, "Reggie, a lot of people in the government think that even if there is fighting in Iraq, it will be limited to a civil war. Why do you think the fighting could spread, and how would the Saudis be impacted?"

"Grant, the Shiite Muslims are also in parts of Syria and Lebanon. The Sunni Muslims are found in Saudi Arabia, part of Iraq, Jordan, Egypt, Qatar, and the United Arab Emirates, not to mention much of northern Africa. Iran will finance the Iraqi Shiites in a purge of the Sunnis. This will confirm the Saudis' nightmare that Iran wants to dominate a Shiite government in Iraq and control the oil as a precursor to domination of the Middle East. The Saudis will fund Sunni resistance. Both sides may send troops into Iraq. But that is not all.

"Jordan is afraid it will be overrun with Sunni refugees.

"The Kurds in the north of Iraq are already moving toward declaring an independent state. Turkey is absolutely against Kurdish independence because they have a Kurdish separatist movement in their own country. Even more troubling is the Turkish Kurds using northern Iraq as a sanctuary from which to launch attacks into Turkey. The Turks have had enough and are sending troops into northern Iraq to root out the Kurdish separatists.

"Overlaid against this scenario is the fact that Al-Qaeda is Sunni, and Hezbollah and Muqtada al-Sadr and his Mehdi Army are Shiite. These guys want nothing but chaos.

"We are being told that the Saudis and other Middle Eastern governments are scared that fighting in Iraq will spill over into the entire Middle East. They want a new military government in Iraq, democracy be damned, and they want stability ASAP.

"If this isn't confusing enough, add the Iranian push for nuclear weapons and Israel's need to protect itself. If Israel nukes Iran … well, I just don't know. It's way above my pay grade."

Paul Brandt, head of BlackRock personnel and operations in Saudi Arabia, spoke for the first time. "On another level altogether, most of the Middle East, including Saudi Arabia, is upset about the encroachment of Iran into the Arab world. Iran is supporting Hezbollah in Lebanon, Hamas in Gaza, and the Mahdists in Iraq. According to my sources, the Saudis are convinced that the US does not have the will to prevent Iran from finishing its development of nuclear weapons. That is why the Saudis along with the UAE are in the market for the technology to develop nuclear reactors. My sources tell me that they will soon be joined by Egypt, Algeria, Turkey, and even, for God's sakes, Yemen.

"Why? They claim reasons that range from energy-intensive desalination plants to reliable electric power. Why do the Saudis and Algerians, with plenty of oil, want nuclear power? The only answer that makes sense is as a hedge against Iran. If you recall, it was 'civilian' nuclear technology that served as a springboard for Israel and India to develop nuclear weapons. They could all have nuclear weapons in a decade.

"Two-thirds of the world's proven oil reserves are in Iraq, Iran, Saudi Arabia, and Kuwait. If they want to fight among themselves, the first thing to attack is oil production facilities.

"I think the Saudis saw this coming when they hired us."

Homer Johnson said, "What do you guys want to do?"

"Either withdraw," said Brown, "or quadruple the number of personnel we have on duty in Saudi Arabia."

"Thank you, gentlemen," Grant said. "We will have an answer for you after the board meeting."

He closed the video screen, went to the bar, and pulled a bottle of vodka from the freezer, added three olives to a martini glass, and filled it with the chilled vodka. He walked to the French doors and stared out at the darkness.

What a god-awful mess. BlackRock had about a thousand men and women in Saudi Arabia. There were another two thousand in Iraq and Afghanistan providing security to diplomats and others under the auspices of the State Department. They were all sitting on a powder keg. If things really blew up, the Saudi royal family and United States civilian personnel would be prime targets, and BlackRock was the only protection they had. The military focus would be on restoring order; they did not have time to babysit civilians.

It was perfectly clear to Grant that BlackRock had to either give their people appropriate resources or else pull them out of danger.

Chapter 6

BlackRock's board of directors meeting to discuss the Saudi security contract was held at the Phoenician Resort in Scottsdale, Arizona. BlackRock had been acquired by Integrated Security Services in 2003. Integrated provided a wide variety of contract work to private clients, including foreign governments. Both companies realized almost immediately that the military simply did not have the manpower to provide security for all the private companies rebuilding the Iraqi infrastructure. There were fortunes to be made, but BlackRock needed Integrated's capital to expand and hire more ex-military contractors, and Integrated needed BlackRock's personnel both in the field and in Washington.

What Grant had failed to appreciate at the time was that, although Integrated was run by a former head of the DIA (Defense Intelligence Agency) and had several retired generals on its board, the power was held by The Plaza Group, a New York City merchant bank that owned Integrated and many other companies in the defense industry. The chairman of The Plaza Group was former President of the United States Homer A. Johnson. A key partner was Lawrence Kammerer, a seventy-two-year-old former Secretary of Defense.

Kammerer and a retired general kept arguing about the administration's Afghanistan policy, which had little to do with the Saudi security contract. Grant kept bringing them back to the subject at hand, the request to either withdraw from the contract on the basis of changed circumstances or else increase BlackRock personnel in Saudi Arabia. After four hours of wrangling, it was finally decided to double in-country personnel and make up the cost when the contract came up for renewal in six months.

"Grant, thank you for keeping things focused in there. If it wasn't for you, I think Kammerer would have decked Schwartz," said Homer Johnson, putting his arm across Grant's shoulders in a friendly way as they left the meeting.

Grant left President Johnson in the lobby and headed for his bungalow. He needed a steam bath and a drink in the worst way. When he got to the bungalow, his girlfriend, Cat Rollins, wasn't there, so he went to the health club steam room.

For the last several months, Grant had been spending time with Cat, as he tried to forget Stephanie Chambers. Some time back, Grant's feelings about Stephanie were becoming serious when she abruptly told him she had killed his brother Ricky. She did not know Grant or Ricky at the time and had done it on orders from her CIA superior, who was paid by the GateKeepers, also known as the Sanchez family. Grant could not get past it, and he didn't think she could either.

Cat was a celebrity of sorts in Durango. She had just missed making the 1984 Olympic team as a downhill racer. After the Olympics, she had married Greg Wingate, who had made the team, and they moved to Durango to run the Purgatory Ski

School. Long story short, her tenure at Purgatory and as Mrs. Greg Wingate did not last long. It didn't take Cat long to find her next husband, Dan Rollins. He owned two square blocks in downtown Durango. That had lasted until the late 1990s, when the good Mr. Rollins traded her in on a new model. That was the bad news for Cat. The good news was the divorce settlement, which left her not wealthy but financially independent.

Cat consoled herself with a boob job in Beverly Hills, a facelift in Phoenix, and a little liposuction here and there, keeping her forty-something body in prime condition. At five six and one hundred twenty-eight pounds, she still made her blue jeans look good. Cat had given up the slopes and taken up horses. Fast horses. Barrel racing had hooked her, and she was in every rodeo within striking distance of the Four Corners. If a fifty-eight-year-old woman had won the National Finals Rodeo barrel racing competition, surely Cat in her forties could do the same. She bought the best horses. She trained harder than she ever had for skiing. She won some money from time to time but not nearly enough to qualify for the NFR.

Like many male athletes, Cat was having a hard time realizing that her competitive athletic career was on its way downhill. Now and then she consoled herself with tequila and a cowboy. Grant was the current cowboy. He knew where he stood but liked her; she was fun and absolutely unbridled in the sack.

Cat was emptying shopping bags on the bed when Grant got back from the steam room. She looked great. No hat hair, no dirty shirt, no dirty chipped fingernails, and no windblown red skin. Her short blond hair was nicely styled. She had on makeup in addition to lipstick and was wearing a clingy red sundress with a scoop neck and four-inch high heels. She turned to Grant for a moment and said, "Oh, there you are. Fix us a couple of margaritas. You aren't going to believe who I met today."

One thing about Cat, it was definitely all about her. She had no interest in the BlackRock board meeting. Grant went to the small wet bar in the bungalow living room and mixed the drinks. The bungalow was on a small rise between the massive swimming pool and the main hotel building, commanding a view of the pool below and Scottsdale's lights stretching into the distance. Grant sat on the sofa facing a wall, and Cat took the club chair facing the view. He thought that this seating arrangement said something about their relationship. As Cat picked up her drink, he noticed that she, once again, had rings on nine of her ten fingers. The third finger of her left hand was the orphan. He had no intention of asking her what significance, if any, should attach to the missing ring.

She took a long swallow of her margarita, leaned eagerly forward, and started right in. "Well, you just won't believe what happened today. I went to Nordstrom, like I said I would, and there in the shoe department was this tall dark-haired woman, mid-thirties, I would guess, with two Mexican-looking hunks in dark glasses. Now these guys were paying no attention to her or the shoes but stood looking around the store at everyone else. I figured these guys had to be bodyguards, I mean how cool is that? Right there in Nordstroms, a movie star or something."

She had a mischievous gleam in her eyes that Grant had seen on more than one occasion. There was a surprise in store, probably a shocking surprise, and since he was the only one there, he waited to be surprised. Cat's voice, which was normally high-pitched and breathy, rose an octave.

"Well, so anyway," said Cat, pausing for quick sip of margarita, "this woman and I were looking at boots and sat next to each other to try some on. So, you know, I started talking to her, and she was really nice. She was living in Mexico and had come up with her boyfriend who was on a business trip. I asked her about the guys with sunglasses, and you won't believe it, she said her boyfriend was the president of Mexico, and they were two of his bodyguards."

Grant was sipping his margarita when she uncorked this revelation. He swallowed wrong and started coughing. He quickly excused himself and went into the bathroom to regain his composure. He knew what was coming. When he returned to the living room, Cat was standing at the bar mixing herself another margarita. Actually, she was making two.

"Here," she said with a huge smile on her face. "We both know you need this." She turned and leaned against the wet bar. "Well, when I said I was from Durango, and she said she had been there several times, I thought we were becoming new best friends, so we introduced ourselves. She said she was Stephanie Chambers and asked if I knew Grant Meredith. Well, I was too stunned to say anything right away, so she said you were about six feet tall, very fit, and looked like a cross between the young Omar Sharif and the Marlboro Man.

"Well, you know, when I said I was here with you, I mean, you should have seen the look on her face. You would have thought

I'd told her the Pope died or something. She couldn't wait to get out of there."

She handed him his drink and said with an air of victory, "I bet she is one of your old girlfriends, and by her reaction, it ain't over for her."

Grant could only smile crookedly and raise his glass to hers. Then he gulped down half the margarita, hoping it would help him regain his composure.

Chapter 7

Stephanie slipped into the backseat of the stretch limousine along with one of her bodyguards. The other sat in front with the driver. As they pulled away from Fashion Square, she glanced in the driver's rearview mirror and saw a black Suburban with heavily tinted windows pull in behind them. Even the Mexican president's mistress was entitled to Secret Service protection while visiting the United States. How ironic that a former CIA assassin was entitled to such security precautions. How many times had she killed others who had such protection?

"Driver, please take me to the Biltmore Fashion Park," she said and leaned her head back against the seat.

That woman called herself Cat. What a ridiculous name. What a piece of work. All those rings and enough perfume to require fumigation of any room she left. The poor shoe salesman couldn't make up his mind whether to look at her silicone-enhanced boobs, which were about to flop out of that flimsy sundress when she bent over, or at her crotch, which had to be plainly visible just beyond the hem of her short dress as he knelt in front of her to help her try on boots. What in the hell was her Grant doing with that kind of woman?

Her Grant? Well, the Grant she had known would never be seen in public with that slut. Grant was—well, he had been a pleasing blend of worldly sophistication and cowboy unpretentiousness. He was kind without being weak, the kind of man a woman could depend on, could trust. He couldn't be serious about some oversexed, over-the-hill broad with fake boobs and air between her ears. It had to be the sex. Yeah, that must be it. She was probably a good lay.

She and Grant had made love only once. Well, to be honest, not love; they'd had sex in that line shack on his ranch with a fire roaring in the fireplace and the rain pounding the metal roof. She knew then, as she had often thought since, that he wanted more than the sex, but all she had wanted was the sex. One of life's missed opportunities?

Grant had drifted away at the end of her CIA career and the end of her obsession with killing terrorists. After her father had been killed in Beirut, she had educated and trained herself to assassinate terrorists, and getting the chance to do it for the CIA had been a God-sent opportunity. The problem was that killing those people—and they needed killing, she didn't doubt that— had not made her feel better. It hadn't filled the space her father had occupied.

She knew a lot of people in New York and around the world, but she had no friend in whom she could confide. After resigning from the CIA, she had wandered aimlessly around the country. A friend living in Tucson had suggested a weekend trip to Puerto Peñasco, Mexico, which Americans called Rocky Point. After dinner and too much tequila, they had run into Hector Sanchez at a beachfront nightclub called Manny's.

She hadn't seen Hector since they attended the Sorbonne together over fifteen years ago but recognized him instantly. Though they had been lovers during his semester there, they had lost touch after he returned to Brown University. At Manny's, Hector told her he was attending a meeting of the US and Mexican border governors. Coincidentally, they were both staying at the Las Palomas resort.

Stephanie was drunk enough and unhappy enough to confront him about his family's involvement in smuggling drugs into the United States.

Instead of getting into the public screaming match she was trying to provoke, Hector quietly said that if she would go with him for coffee, he would explain everything.

Stephanie could see that her friend, a gay hair stylist, had found another companion for the evening, so she went with Hector back to Las Palomas. A full moon illuminated the ocean while they sipped coffee on the balcony of his oceanfront penthouse. Hector patiently explained that some members of his family were indeed in the business of transporting people into the US to supply its need for low-wage workers. Others, he said, did arrange to supply drugs for the continually expanding US demand for a product that was demonstrably less lethal than cigarettes and alcohol. That, however, was not what he did. He was a politician and was readying his run for president of Mexico.

He was, as he always had been, smooth and persuasive. He denied nothing and deftly sidestepped the whole issue of legality.

The next morning, he asked her to come and stay with him. Having nothing else to do, she went—and now here she was, mistress of the president of Mexico. The Mexican public did not care that he had a mistress as well as a wife and children, and neither did Stephanie. She didn't think she loved Hector, but she did love the sex.

Although she wanted for nothing, there was still an empty place inside her which had been there since her father's assassination. There was the unresolved matter of Boots, which had been dormant until yesterday, and now there was Grant. Apparently she hadn't forgotten him.

Maybe she should give him a call. What would he say? For that matter, what would she say? "Hello, Grant. Sorry I kind of disappeared for a while, but I met that bimbo you are dating, and ... Yes, I am the mistress of the president of Mexico, but ..." But what? No, that wouldn't do.

Chapter 8

The sheets were twisted and damp. Grant lay beside Cat, who was facing away from him, gently snoring. Their lovemaking, if you could even call it that, had been more like an aerobic athletic event than shared intimacy. Grant had been trying to sleep for the last hour but just could not turn off his mind. He gave up, slipped out of bed, and pulled on the hotel terry-cloth robe before letting himself out onto the moonlit bungalow patio.

Stephanie. He thought he had moved past her but obviously had been deluding himself. *Here I am, forty-five years old, financially successful, never married, no kids, and no serious romantic prospects. Sport fucking lost its glamour fifteen years ago. I am a monogamous kind of guy and have spent a meaningful amount of time with several interesting women over the years but never someone with whom I wanted to spend the rest of my life.*

He hadn't been all that comfortable lately. His reaction to hearing about Stephanie was causing him to wonder if his uneasiness flowed from the fact that he wasn't really sharing his life with anyone. Maybe; but if that was it, things weren't going to get any better soon.

If Cat was right, Stephanie hadn't forgotten about him either, even if there was no likelihood their paths would cross again. But if he was honest with himself, the passage of time had almost healed the wound and filled the gap Ricky's death had left in his life. While Ricky was fading, Stephanie had reappeared. He could again see her face clearly, see the way she moved, the way she laughed. Grant thought, *I would slap myself if it would do any good.*

Chapter 9

Hector Sanchez met with John Lawton, the new head of the Drug Enforcement Agency, in Sanchez's suite at the Biltmore Hotel. For both security and secrecy, it was a better meeting place than the DEA Phoenix offices.

Sanchez studied Lawton while they exchanged pleasantries. Lawton was a powerfully built man who wore a tailored blue suit, white shirt, and red tie. With a shaved head and bushy mustache, he looked like the ex-Marine he was. Before being appointed to head the DEA, he had been chief of police in Yuma, Arizona. Not much of a résumé for a DEA administrator. It probably reflected the lack of importance the DEA had in the current administration.

Lawton got down to business at once. "Mr. President, the purpose of this meeting is to insist on behalf of the United States of America that Mexico get serious about stopping the flow of illegal drugs into the United States. Almost all of the marijuana and a high percentage of other illegal drugs enter this country from Mexico. We put the dollars involved at twenty-five to thirty billion dollars a year. Put simply, you people have got to slow down the flow of illegal drugs."

It wasn't what Lawton said that infuriated Sanchez; he'd expected something like it. It was Lawton's condescending tone. Hector Sanchez was not the man's servant; he was the president of Mexico. The way Lawton's lips seemed to twist into a sneer when he said "you people" made Sanchez's blood boil. The man's racism hung on him like body odor. If not for the self-control of a professional politician, he would have shot Lawton on the spot.

"Might I suggest, Chief Lawton, that Mexico has as much chance of stopping the flow of drugs into the United States as you do of bulldogging a tornado."

"President Sanchez, I am not a police chief, I am the Administrator of the Drug Enforcement Agency of the United States of America and am most certainly not a cowboy. I consider your remark impertinent. We are not asking you to stop the flow of drugs; we are realists. We just want you to slow it down."

"Administrator Lawton, the real problem is the demand for drugs in the United States. As long as your people put the stuff up their noses or shoot it into their veins, someone is going to supply it. It is Economics 101. You learned nothing from Prohibition. You do not have the political will to stop drug use, so why continue the charade?"

"Mr. President, with respect, our prisons are full of drug offenders, from petty users to big-time dealers. It's the main reason our prisons are overcrowded. If the supply is reduced, prices will rise, and that will reduce demand; that is Economics 101."

"You have had a War on Drugs for decades," said Hector, "spending billions and billions of dollars, and there are more drugs at cheaper prices than ever. All you have done is create a self-perpetuating bureaucracy. The War on Drugs is simply a jobs program. Just legalize the stuff; we will all be better off. You will have room in your prisons for serious criminals, and you can tax drugs to support all your social programs."

Hector's source was a recent column in the *Wall Street Journal*. The argument made sense, but he was sure that it would be ignored. The family could profit from legal drugs but not nearly as much as from illegal drugs.

"We are not here to discuss our drug policy, Mr. President. Let's come to the point. We know who is behind the flow of drugs into our country. If you don't get with the program and slow down the flow of drugs into the United States, we will slow down implementation of the CANAMEX and NASCO highway corridors."

Hector went to the wet bar and took his time filling a glass with ice and water. Well, now at least the cards were on the table. Lawton might as well have said that the Sanchez family controlled most of the flow of drugs into the United States and had the ability to slow it down. On the brighter side, Lawton hadn't told him to shut it down; that left room for business as usual.

"Perhaps we could do more, Administrator Lawton, but the cost … we just do not have the funds."

Lawton chuckled and said, "Don't worry about money; we'll get it for you. Now what will you do with it?"

The meeting lasted another half hour before Lawton left, promising a billion dollars for drug interdiction programs in Mexico.

Hector paced the living room of his suite holding a glass of vodka, no ice. From time to time he stopped pacing and took a swallow. He had made the best of a bad situation. He had no intention of slowing down the flow of drugs. If he did, someone else would take up the slack. The problem for the Americans was their unwillingness to deal with the demand side of the equation. What bothered him the most was the threat to slow down implementation of the highway corridors. That would be bad for Mexico, bad for foreign trade, and, most of all, bad for the Sanchez family.

Most of the US trade with East Asia passes through the ports of Long Beach and Los Angeles, which are inundated with cargo. Starting in 1995 the US encouraged Mexico to develop deep-water ports to provide an alternative. The concept was that container freight could be off-loaded in Mexican ports and shipped into the US along two principal corridors. CANAMEX would run from Nogales to Las Vegas to Salt Lake City and into Canada. The other corridor would run from Laredo to San Antonio to Kansas City to Omaha and north into Canada.

Mexico had spent billions developing its deep-water ports to take advantage of the economic opportunities that would follow increased trade through its country. The increased trade would make it even easier for the Sanchez family to move people and drugs into the US. If the US slowed down implementation of these trade routes, however, the political and economic consequences for Mexico would be severe.

Hector stopped at the bar and put three fingers of vodka in his glass and resumed pacing. Goddamn Americans. He was going to have to do something.

His secure satellite phone rang. It was Ramon. Before Ramon could say anything, Hector exploded with the American demands and the injustice of it all. Ramon listened without interrupting until Hector wound down.

"Brother, what a coincidence. I have an idea," said Ramon. "I was calling about Guillen. I thought we had gotten rid of him and put an end to his smuggling drugs through Laredo when you put him in jail. It turns out he continues to run his organization from prison. The Americans want to prosecute him. Get them to take the death penalty off the table, and you can extradite him to the US for trial. That has never been done before. You will look like you are serious about stopping the drug trade, and the DEA can preen for the press about a new era of cooperation. It should buy us quite a bit of time. We can pitch them a few more of our competitors later."

"I like it," said Hector. "But someone has got to teach the goddamn Americans a lesson."

Chapter 10

Ali Alwaleed didn't need a vacation, but he did want to meet personally with the Sanchez family representative who would be responsible for getting his operatives into the United States. In his position, he could not travel anywhere in the world unnoticed, so he didn't try. With his wife and three other couples, he left Riyadh in his Gulfstream G550 and spent three days in London shopping before flying to Cabo San Lucas at the tip of Baja California. Alwaleed and his entourage were enjoying a fifteen-thousand-square-foot villa in Cabo's tony Pedregal neighborhood when he called a prearranged number for a taxi to take him to the marina. He told his guests he was going to inquire about chartering a boat for deep-sea fishing.

Alwaleed, in the traditional Cabo uniform of ball cap, sunglasses, T-shirt, shorts and sandals, practiced on the villa's putting green while he waited for the taxi. Finally an old Mercedes taxi arrived, driven by Jamie Ruiz, also wearing the traditional Cabo uniform. Alwaleed got in the cab, and they headed toward the marina at exactly the speed limit.

"Mr. Alwaleed, it is a beautiful day, what is your favorite color?" asked Ruiz.

"Green. And, sir, what is your favorite number?" replied Alwaleed.

"Six hundred sixty-six," said Ruiz. "Nice to meet you."

Alwaleed pulled an MCD-22H electronic device from his pocket and turned it on. The device was about the size of a BlackBerry and was used by the United Nations to sweep for bugs. The four lights at the top of the device remained solid green. Blinking red lights would have indicated the presence of a listening device. When Alwaleed looked up, he saw that Ruiz was holding up the same device with solid green lights. Alwaleed chuckled with a shrug. Ruiz smiled back at him in the rearview mirror.

"All our operatives are ready to go and will begin arriving in Mexico next week," said Alwaleed.

"Very well. Once payment has been received, an envelope will be delivered to your embassy in Mexico City which will tell you where and when each person will be picked up to begin their journey. How and when your people get here and where they stay prior to pickup is not our concern. They are to be at the pickup point at the precise time given, not before and not after. If they are even one minute late, my pickup man will have left. Once your people cross the border, they will be taken to a crowded place in a city and dropped off. Then they will be on their own. We guarantee that eighty of these people will be delivered. If the number is less, we will refund the fee for each of those people. Personally, I think we will lose only two or three, but the guarantee is eighty."

He reached back over the seat and handed Alwaleed an envelope. "Wire the funds in equal amounts to these accounts by the close of business tomorrow in the respective countries."

Alwaleed opened the envelope and studied the list of twenty banks. "It's none of my affair," said Alwaleed, "but none of these banks are in Mexico; why?"

"Correct, it is none of your affair. Perhaps you will tell me what your people are going to do in the United States," Ruiz countered.

"That is none of your affair. However, to put your mind at ease, they are spies with specific missions." Alwaleed knew that Ruiz would assume his people were terrorists. Silence would just confirm his suspicions, so he had decided to give him a credible alternative. He didn't think Ruiz really cared anyway; he was in it for the money.

Alwaleed had been thinking about providing some of his operatives with weapons and explosives that were not readily available in the United States. He had secured one hundred pounds of Iranian manufactured C-4 which was already in Mexico and ready for allocation among his operatives; but he wanted more. He adopted a casual manner and said, "I was reading that certain elements in Mexico have access to military munitions such as RPGs. Is that true?"

Ruiz said, "That is what one reads in the newspapers."

"I wonder what one of those would cost," mused Alwaleed.

"I have heard it said that an RPG-7 can be had for two thousand five hundred dollars but that is speculation on my part.

How many do you want?" asked Ruiz innocently, looking at Alwaleed in the rearview mirror.

"Oh, I don't want any," said Alwaleed. "I represent a small security company that wishes to acquire ten RPGs, but your price seems a little high."

Ruiz said "I may be able to get you ten for twenty thousand dollars, but you would have to take delivery in Mexico and make your own arrangements to transport them out of the country."

"If you can procure them, you have a deal. Get me a time and place, and I will have a courier exchange the money for the weapons."

"I will call you tomorrow," said Ruiz.

After Ruiz dropped him at the marina, Alwaleed enjoyed a leisurely lunch in the outdoor café at the edge of the water, paying particular attention to the young women in bikinis.

Two days later the G550 took him to Vienna.

Chapter 11

The OPEC Fund for International Development was headquartered in the most impressive of all the palaces on Vienna's Ringstrasse. This Austrian national monument was built in the Renaissance style during the 1860s. The quarterly Fund meeting in the ornate main conference room had concluded, and the delegates were milling around when Ali Alwaleed and Sher Tabrizi slipped away unnoticed, crossed the atrium, which rose five stories to the roof, and ascended the massive staircase to the second floor. From there, they followed a deserted hallway to the back of the palace, entered an empty office, and closed and locked the door.

Tabrizi flopped onto the sofa, wheezing from the climb and the short walk down the hallway. Alwaleed leaned against the edge of the desk so that he was looking down on Tabrizi.

Alwaleed spoke first. "We are finally ready to implement our plan. We have finished training all one hundred operatives and have begun moving them to Mexico. The infiltration is scheduled to take place over their Memorial Day weekend."

"I sent you fifteen men and three women. How many of them are included?" asked Tabrizi.

"Ten men and one woman."

"What about the others?" Tabrizi knew the answer but asked anyway.

"They are with Allah."

Tabrizi was silent for only a moment. "Very well, what about the bombs?"

"According to my last report from General Ri, they were placed in separate containers of electronics shipped a week apart from China. He arranged with Chinese port officials to submit false automated manifests to US Customs. Under the US Container Security Initiative, there will be no need for further inspection of the containers in Mexico or the United States. One container was off-loaded at the Lázaro Cárdenas port on Mexico's Pacific coast and placed directly onto the Kansas City Southern Railroad de Mexico. The container will be shipped on the railroad nonstop to Kansas City and clear customs at the new SmartPort.

"The other container was off-loaded in Guaymas and is being trucked two hundred miles to Nogales. There the bomb will be removed from the container and moved across the border in a tunnel. The tunnel runs 1,200 feet from the basement of a bar in Mexico to a body shop on the American side."

Tabrizi allowed himself a satisfied smile. "Where are they going to be set off?"

Alwaleed shrugged. "I have no idea. I have no need to know that. The plan is that only Ri and the imam who will detonate a bomb will know where it is going to be set off."

Tabrizi thought for a while and then said, not bothering to hide his admiration, "How perfect. Once the imam gets the bomb, the chain is broken, and even if the Americans grab the person who delivers it to the imam, there is no way they can stop it from happening."

Tabrizi realized that if the imams drew the wrong kind of attention to themselves, it was possible they could be arrested before the bombs were detonated. He decided not to share that thought with the Saudi. Such a probability was small, and even if they were caught, the publicity would have a devastating impact on the American public. If the government tried to keep it quiet, the conspirators could leak the near disaster to the press.

"Sher, the reason I wanted to meet with you is to decide when and how we are going to inform the Americans that we want them to withdraw from the Middle East and keep out."

Tabrizi stood, shoved hands in pockets, and started pacing around the room. After a full minute of pacing with his forehead furrowed, he turned, put his hands on the desktop, and leaned toward Alwaleed, who had been watching him. "Timing first; we don't want to announce anything before the imams have the bombs. I think we announce our ultimatum as soon as the bombs are in place without mentioning the bombs. Then allow some more incidents to take place and renew the ultimatum, claiming we have positioned twenty bombs. Then set off one of the bombs and announce again. They probably won't fold then, but later, when the second bomb explodes, it will give credence to our claim to have many more."

"Why not wait until after the bombs go off?" asked Alwaleed.

"After a hundred or so of our incidents, someone in the American government will probably figure out what is going on but won't be able to prove it and will have no idea how to stop it. Since they can't be sure what is happening and don't know what to do, they will investigate frantically but probably won't announce anything to the public. When we take credit for the incidents and present our demands, the press and public will go off the charts because they haven't been told anything and will begin to realize the consequences of meddling in the affairs of other sovereign nations.

"The press will certainly bring up the Bush Doctrine, and the op-ed writers will claim that the devastation will stop if the government abandons the Bush Doctrine, brings its troops home, and returns to the realpolitik foreign policy of Kissinger."

Alwaleed, who had been watching him closely, interrupted. "Surely you don't think the American government will give up that easily. In fact it may just reinforce the arguments in favor of the Bush Doctrine."

"Initially, I think you are right. Although we will get the internal debate going, the reaction of the serious leaders will be that the Bush Doctrine has not been pursued quickly enough, and the incidents are the consequences of that failure. However, once the bombs go off, the isolationists will drown out everyone else. The effect will be infinitely more powerful than the bomb that got Spain out of Iraq."

"All right, that timing makes sense," said Alwaleed. "How should we deliver our ultimatum?"

Tabrizi sat back down on the sofa. "Probably the Internet; let me think about that for a while, I don't want the release to be traced back to us.

"Ali, I want to ask you a very serious question. Why do you think the North Koreans are working with us?"

Alwaleed had recruited the North Koreans to the plan, so Tabrizi expected his ready answer. "First, Kim Jong Il is struggling to stay in power. The North Korean economy, what there is of it, is a disaster. The isolation and financial pressure being put on them by the Bush Doctrine is making it more and more difficult to feed the people. Just last week James Reed, the former American ambassador to the UN, gave a speech in Tokyo where he said that the six-party talks on North Korea's nuclear program had failed, and the only step left was to push for regime change in North Korea.

"Second, while General Ri hasn't mentioned this, they are using us and this plan to get the Americans out of South Korea. With them gone, the path to reunification with South Korea will be much easier. If they can't reach agreement, Kim will simply let his people walk south. There will be no way to stop them short of mass slaughter. Ri's army will follow, and Kim Jong Il will take over. It is really the only way he can solve his problems and remain in power."

"That makes a lot of sense. Do you trust General Ri and the North Koreans?" asked Tabrizi.

"Not in the least," said Alwaleed without hesitation. "We have a community of interest in getting rid of the Americans, but I don't trust him."

Tabrizi knew Alwaleed didn't trust the Iranians either.

Tabrizi cleared his throat. "Nor do I trust General Ri."

Chapter 12

Grant and Tommy were horseback, cutting calves from their bawling mothers in the middle of a cloud of dust, when Grant's cell phone rang and vibrated. It was Reggie Johnson from BlackRock.

"Hold on, Reggie, I've got to get away from these cattle to hear you." He loped his horse to the far gate, opened it, and trotted around the barn. "Okay, I can hear now. What's up?"

"We have a problem in Saudi Arabia," said Johnson, "and I want your advice. Our guys captured two ragheads trying to put an IED under our main barracks building. They were put in an isolation room for interrogation, and during initial questioning, one of the guys keels over bleeding from the eyes, ears, nose, and mouth. The other guy starts screaming that he has some kind of an explosive device in his head and we have to get it out before it explodes."

"What happened to the first guy?" Grant asked.

"Hold on, Grant, let me finish," said Johnson. A former Delta Force colonel, before joining BlackRock, he was not used to being interrupted.

"Paul Brandt was doing the interrogating. He called for our on-site doctor and told the raghead he could have immediate medical help if he told Paul where he got the IED and who put the device in his head. That was quick thinking on Paul's part. Anyway, the guy starts shaking his head no, and Paul tells him that he is dead if he does nothing, but if he talks, we'll get him out of the country. Guy says he is Al Qaeda, and a doc in Riyadh named Ali Al-Fulani put the implant in his head. They get this guy into the operating room, but before they can put him under, he starts leaking blood like the other guy. The doc cuts his head open and says there was a remote-controlled explosive implant in his head that killed him. Same with the other guy."

"What about—"

"Just hold on, I'm not done yet. We asked the Saudis to pick up this Al-Fulani guy for questioning, and they claimed there was no such person. Said the dead cocksucker must have been lying. Brandt asked around about the doc's name and was told a guy with that name is personal physician to the Crown Prince. At this point, I want some direction from my superiors."

What in the hell is going on? The Saudis hired BlackRock for protection, so why are they lying to us? Aloud he asked, "Are you sure the Al-Fulani you found is the same person that the dead guy was referring to?"

"I'm not positive, but the name is the same," snapped Johnson, "and the Saudis surely know the name of the Crown Prince's personal physician; they must be lying."

Grant had to agree; Johnson was probably right. "What about the explosive device?"

"Doc isn't sure, but he thinks it is the same type that the Livermore Lab patented a few years ago."

Christ, this was not good. BlackRock had almost two thousand men and women in Saudi Arabia. Grant wondered if, for some unknown reason, the Saudis were helping Al-Qaeda attack BlackRock. Why?

"Reggie, I'm going to Saudi Arabia," said Grant. "I'll fly to Scottsdale on the early flight from Durango. Have the jet meet me there. Tell Brandt to put together a plan to covertly snatch this doctor. I'll think about it on the way over, but if it's a go, I want the plan ready to implement when I hit the ground."

Grant was still mounted on his horse, thinking, when Tommy rode up.

"Sorry, Tommy, I got hung up on the phone. I've got to take a trip overseas. I'll be gone for a week or so."

"Okay. Anything special I can do while you're trottin' around the globe?"

"No." Grant smiled and dismounted. "You've got the list."

Tommy groaned and whined dramatically and said "Kemosabe, have you forgotten 'A fiery horse with the speed of light, a cloud of dust and a hearty Hi-Yo Silver' and all that stuff?"

"No, but your horse isn't named Scout," Grant said with another grin. "However, I do remember 'A cowboy's work is never done.'"

"Who said that?"

"Sonny and Cher." Grant handed Tommy the reins and headed for the house.

"Not my kind of music," Tommy hollered after him.

Chapter 13

A few minutes before 6 a.m. on a rain-soaked, foggy Monday morning, Ed Bailey sat with his size thirteen feet propped on his desk at the FBI's National Security Branch. He was drinking his third cup of coffee, staring out through a drenched window while waiting for his daily report of incidents around the country potentially related to terrorism. He was already tired; borderline exhausted was more like it. Since he had become executive assistant director of the NSB in October 2005, fourteen-hour days, six and seven days a week had become routine. It wasn't the hours that were wearing him down, it was the responsibility. The NSB was tasked with preventing terrorist acts within the US. They had thwarted ten potential terrorist attacks which had not been publicized; however, 9/11 was never far from his thoughts.

Bailey loved his wife and two teenage daughters, but the situation at home was becoming impossible. Their patience with his long hours and lack of involvement in the family had been exhausted long ago. He knew his marriage was on the rocks but felt helpless to do anything about it. With some modest loans there was enough set aside to get the girls through college. He would have put in thirty years with the government next month, and with the hassles of a new administration, he was seriously considering retirement. It was time to give the job to someone much younger—someone who would thrive on the pressure, at least for a while.

His reverie was interrupted when his computer beeped and its screen filled with the report. The first item read:

"A train carrying nitric acid and other presently unidentified hazardous materials derailed and caught fire just outside Richmond, Virginia, at 4 a.m. this morning. A chemical cloud drifted over a 5 to 7 mile radius, prompting an ongoing evacuation of about 100,000 residents. Firefighters and a response team from EPA have been unable to get close to the blaze, even with protective suits and breathing equipment. Although no fatal injuries have been reported thus far, Richmond traffic is gridlocked and a political firestorm is brewing. Tentative cause of the accident, according to railroad officials, is a wrongly positioned manual track switch which diverted a main line train onto a side track where it collided with tank cars filled with the chemicals. Each tanker was clearly marked with the HAZMAT warning symbol. There was no security in the area of the switch. At present how the switch became wrongly positioned is unknown and, due to fire, we are unable to approach switch at this time. Updates to follow."

Bailey made a note to call the Agent in Charge on this one. Chances were this mess would ultimately be attributed to vandalism, but he had to be sure. That was his job.

His screen blinked, and an emergency e-mail appeared.

"A CXS freight train carrying highly radioactive nuclear fuel rods as well as hydrochloric acid and other hazardous materials derailed inside the 1.5 mile Howard Street Tunnel in downtown Baltimore and caught on fire an hour ago. It is possible that flammable chemicals on board may drive the temperature in the tunnel above 1,500 degrees Fahrenheit. The nuclear containers are only designed to withstand 1,475 degrees for thirty minutes. A major catastrophe is brewing.

"Smoke is billowing out of the tunnel over downtown neighborhoods. Several city blocks have been evacuated and highways are blocked. Cause of derailment unknown and will remain so until fire is under control and track cleared. Updates will follow."

Bailey pulled his lanky six foot six inch frame out of his chair and scratched his short, kinky, graying hair. This could be a coincidence but his job was to assume the worst and act accordingly. He turned on the television set built into his bookcase to see if there were any pictures of the fires and listen to how the news media were reporting them.

On the screen, the reporter was covering another incident. "Here in San Bernardino, less than an hour ago, a Union Pacific train carrying hazardous materials jumped the tracks. There are unconfirmed reports of an explosion, but it is not known if it was before or after the derailment. Two tanker cars of deadly methyl bromide have been ruptured, spreading a cloud of gas. Evacuation within a five-mile radius from the accident has begun, causing absolute chaos on the roads. People are leaving this highly populated area any way they can: ATVs, bicycles, some mothers are jogging with infants in strollers. Authorities have asked us to move further away from the scene. I will update you as soon as we are repositioned."

Bailey's phone rang. He picked it up. "What the bloody hell is going on?" demanded FBI Director Howard Meyers.

"We don't know what caused any of these incidents," said Bailey. "It may just be coincidence, or it could be the beginning of our worst nightmare. Howard, it's simply too soon to have any concrete information on the causes and whether they are related."

His office door opened, and his assistant Cheryl stuck her head in. "Senator Little of Mississippi is on the phone, and he insists on talking to you immediately."

"Okay, tell him to hold, I'm talking to the director," said Bailey in an exasperated tone. "Look, Howard, this stuff just started coming in. Give me a little time to sort things out."

"Okay, Ed, I've got to go. DHS is on the line," said Meyers as he hung up.

Bailey sat down at his desk, put the TV on the Fox News channel, and hit the mute button. Then he pulled down his tie, rolled up the sleeves of his blue oxford button-down shirt, and punched line two on his phone.

"Hello, Senator—"

Little rushed to interrupt. "I know about the trains, I just got a call from the Gulfport TV station. The Ajax chemical plant had a huge chlorine tank blow. The airport and several miles of the Interstate have been closed. Five hotels are being evacuated, for Christ sakes. What is going on?"

Bailey paused, took a deep breath, and said in a carefully controlled voice, "We are evaluating the data now. Was there any security at the plant?"

"About as much as your friendly 7-Eleven," snapped Little.

Bailey's computer beeped, and another report flashed on his screen.

"Within the last three hours, gasoline tanker trucks have exploded in Miami, Bismarck, Trenton, Sacramento, and Portland; damage being assessed. None of the explosions were caused by a collision. Causes unknown; will update."

"Senator, I've got to go. More data is coming in," said Bailey as he hung up without waiting for a reply.

He got up and paced the floor, hunched forward with his hands clasped behind his back. He was an analytical man who had an undergraduate degree in chemical engineering followed by a law degree. In the no longer rare flare-ups he had with his wife, her consistent complaint was that he needed to think less and feel more.

The trains could be an unfortunate coincidence. The chemical plant explosion could just be another industrial accident. He had no idea why five different gasoline trucks might explode in five different locations on the same day. If these incidents were deliberately caused, a minimum of nine people were involved and probably more. The fact that they'd all happened on the same day probably meant the perpetrators were organized in some fashion. If these were organized terrorist attacks, it was probably just the beginning, and the public needed to be warned.

However, at this point, since he did not know for sure what had caused the incidents, he did not want to alert the press. Besides, in this age of 24/7 cable news, the talking heads would put things together quick enough. The last thing he wanted to do was be responsible for needless panic. Jumping to conclusions could disrupt people's lives and hand the terrorists a psychological victory as a bonus.

He stopped in front of the only window in his office and looked out. The rain had turned to a thundering downpour, and with the fog swirling outside, he could not see anything. Decision made.

Bailey crossed his office in four long strides and yanked open the door. Cheryl looked up at him with an expression that was uncertain and verged on fear. He stopped, took a deep breath, and said just loud enough for her to hear, "Cheryl, implement Code Red. Get the Code Red Team in the War Room immediately. This is not a drill."

Chapter 14

The War Room was the NSB command center. It was a three-tiered room with two levels of cubicles containing state-of-the-art computers and communication equipment. Huge screens on every wall displayed television, security camera, and satellite images from around the world. On the bottom level was a long rectangular conference table with twelve chairs, one for each regional head who reported to Bailey. Within two minutes, all the chairs were occupied and the communication stations manned.

Bailey, standing, hands on hips, spoke into his headset. "Bob, any updates on the prior incidents?"

"No sir, but I have a compilation of reports that have just come in," Bob said.

The main screen on the front wall filled with data.

Jacksonville, FL:	Unidentified man shot and killed in west side Wal-Mart parking lot. Unknown sniper suspected.
Orlando, FL:	Unidentified woman shot and killed in Disney World parking lot. Unknown sniper suspected.
Birmingham, AL:	Unidentified woman shot and killed in hospital parking lot. Unknown sniper suspected.
Memphis, TN:	Twenty-five-year-old university student killed in Memphis State University student parking lot. Unknown sniper suspected.

Before any of the people around the conference table could speak, Bailey held up his hand and jabbed the line one button on the speakerphone on the table in front of him.

"Assistant Director Bailey, this is Ron Johnson, ICE San Diego. Yesterday, we were trying to question a man who the San Diego PD arrested trying to buy a rifle with a forged driver's license. He had no other identification, and there was nothing in the system on him. They called us in because the guy wouldn't answer questions and there was no record of him being a US citizen. While he was being questioned, he fell over with blood coming out of his ears, eyes, and mouth. I just got the preliminary autopsy report. The tentative finding is that he died from some kind of small explosion inside his head."

Bailey interrupted, "Did the guy say anything at all? Did he speak or seem to understand English?"

"Yes sir, the cops who arrested him told me he asked in perfect English to call a lawyer. They didn't let him. Also, now don't take this the wrong way, but this guy looked foreign, Philippine or something, not like an American."

Bailey resisted the temptation to ask this man what an American looked like and said in a businesslike tone, betraying no emotion whatsoever, "Thank you, Agent Johnson. Please get us the preliminary autopsy report as soon as possible, and put a rush on the final; I want it ASAP."

He pushed the disconnect button and leaned forward with his hands on the table. "All right, people, assuming we are dealing with a group of terrorists, what is the takeaway from what has happened so far?

The people around the table were silent, looking at the table; only Warren Jackson made eye contact with Bailey. Jackson had moved to NSB from the Defense Intelligence Agency, where he had been a Middle East specialist. Bailey nodded at him.

"Many terrorist incidents are the result of a suicide bomber," said Jackson. "The guy in San Diego was in custody, so he was probably not involved in perpetrating any incident. There were no known suicides in the reported events. My guess is that they will strike again and again and again until they are eliminated."

No one said anything.

Bailey broke the silence. "Each of you knows what your job is when we are Code Red, so get to it."

The only sound was the clicking of twelve keyboards as each regional supervisor instant-messaged his regional office.

Chapter 15

Howard Meyers came through the door into the NSB War Room like he was shoving aside a troublesome offensive lineman. He was a tall, heavy man whose belly had stopped creeping over his belt years ago and now just hung there. His meaty face sported a large nose that had been broken several times and a high forehead with wispy gray hair. Meyers had been an organized crime prosecutor in the Justice Department before being appointed FBI Director. His head swiveled from side to side as he marched to the bottom level of the room. There, he pulled Ed Bailey aside.

"Ed, the president called. What can I tell her?"

"Look," said Bailey, pointing to the large screen in the middle of the front wall where a new field report was displayed.

> A New York City Department of Environmental Protection technician has reported the following: Bluegill fish used in a 1090 Intelligent Aquatic Biomonitoring System have detected an unknown toxic substance in NYC water supply treatment plant. Tests are being run to determine nature of substance. Decision pending to suspend water

supply until substance identified and potential threat quantified. Potentially, nine million people will be affected by water shut off. MAYOR NYC WANTS ADVICE ASAP.

FYI: IABS developed by US Army. Electrodes mounted in aquarium monitor bluegill respiratory system. Software analyzes fish behavior and when abnormality detected computer sends warning to tech on duty. This system has been monitoring NYC drinking water since 2002.

Bailey and Meyers looked at each other without speaking. Meyers took Bailey by the arm and pulled him toward a small glass-walled conference room across the floor. Inside were a battered rectangular wooden table and six swivel chairs with dirty yellow upholstery. A single speakerphone sat on the table. Once the door was closed, Meyers punched a button on the phone and ordered the operator to get him the mayor of New York City, immediately. Thirty seconds seemed like forever, as the two men stood waiting, until the connection finally came.

"Mike, this is Howard Meyers. I've got Ed Bailey with me. What is the significance of this report, and how reliable is it?"

"The report itself is accurate. There is an unknown toxic substance in the water supply at the Bronx treatment plant. Since we don't know what it is, we don't know if chlorine will get rid of it. It killed the fish, and they are being tested along with the water. We won't have the results until tomorrow. We just don't know what we are dealing with."

"If the water is shut off, what do you tell people?" asked Meyers.

"If you don't shut it off and people get sick or die, what do you tell them?" replied Bailey.

"We don't live in a cave up here, I know about the train wrecks, the chemical plant in Gulfport, and the gasoline trucks. Given that context, I think the safest approach is to shut off the water. At a minimum we have to put out an alert to boil and purify drinking water. Either way we are likely to get a panic. I am already getting calls from reporters, and local TV news is all over the story. Please remember that fear is contagious, and there are only so many ways out of Manhattan."

The supervisor for California opened the door and handed Bailey a field report from the San Francisco NSB field office. Bailey scanned the report with Meyers reading over his shoulder.

> A terrorist who attempted early this morning to drive a van filled with explosives to the base of the Castaic Dam, forty-one miles northeast of downtown Los Angeles, was shot and killed by security guards. Castaic Lake is held in place by a 425-foot-high earth-fill dam with a capacity of 325,000 acre-feet. It is used to supply drinking water and electric power to the western portion of the Greater Los Angeles area.

"Mike, I'm going to contact Homeland Security and the president. Keep yourself available," said Meyers, dismissing Bailey, as he punched the phone button.

Chapter 16

Ed Bailey sat with his head in his hands. It was all he could do to keep from screaming in frustration. DHS had declared NSB Code Red, the highest terrorist alert, two hours ago. The mayor of New York City had issued an alert that citizens should avoid consuming tap water that had not been boiled. Over the last six hours the regional supervisors had given him multiple reports which he was trying to summarize for Meyers. The press office was being inundated with calls from media outlets of every description. Things were happening so rapidly that all they could say was that the incidents were being investigated and that a formal statement would be made as soon as possible.

There had been explosions in shopping malls in St. Louis, Nashville, and Omaha. Deaths and injuries were being tallied. There was no apparent motive, and no one had claimed responsibility.

There had been thirty sniper attacks on police cars in twelve states, resulting in sixteen deaths. There was no apparent motive, and no one had claimed responsibility.

Forty-three letter bombs had exploded in twenty-two states, with twenty deaths and twenty-three serious injuries. There was no apparent motive, and no one had claimed responsibility.

Fifty letters had been received in forty-eight states containing a white substance which may have been ricin. Recipients were being tested. There was no apparent motive, and no one had claimed responsibility.

Bombs had exploded in two Las Vegas casinos. One hundred and thirteen people had died, and almost one thousand had been injured. Security cameras had not picked up any suspicious activity. There was no apparent motive, and no one had claimed responsibility.

There had been two more explosions at chemical plants with another twelve deaths. There was no apparent motive, and no one had claimed responsibility.

There had been an explosion at a New Jersey refinery, and a major fire was out of control. Eight people had died, and twenty had been hospitalized. There was no apparent motive, and no one had claimed responsibility.

All of this was frightening, but what sickened Bailey were more than sixty reports of children being shot all across the country, at soccer and baseball games and even in school yards. Thirty had died, and twenty were in critical condition.

Not one perpetrator had been captured.

Local law enforcement across the country was swamped. The FBI was inundated.

The country was in complete chaos. They simply were not prepared for an all-out terrorist assault.

Chapter 17

The White House Situation Room was manned by communications personnel 24/7. The walls in the five–thousand-square-foot room held six flat-panel screens. Secure technology enabled the room to receive data from around the world and communicate with military operations and foreign governments. A central conference table had seating for eight people. There were an additional eight chairs along the wall for other participants. This seating area was surrounded by watch officers arrayed on two tiers of curved tables with computer terminals.

Seated at the head of the table for this hastily called meeting was President Janet Sampson. A former gynecologist, she was a plain-looking fifty-two-year-old with shoulder length gray hair who shunned makeup. Stocky but fit, she was attired in her trademark black pantsuit with a white ruffled blouse and sensible black lace-up shoes. Dr. Sampson had been appointed US Senator from Washington State to finish her husband's term after he died of a heart attack. She had no children and no political experience—and therefore no baggage when she took office.

While her husband had been a hail-fellow-well-met, baby-kissing, old-time politician, Sampson proved herself to be an articulate and persuasive point woman for the Republican Party. She had been asked to run for president by a number of feminist organizations who envisioned her as vice-presidential material. Sampson had reluctantly joined a broad, evenly matched primary field of men who, as the campaign wore on, destroyed each other's hopes and dreams. As the candidates dropped from the campaign, rather than help the men who had savaged them, they gave their delegates to Sampson, who had managed not to offend any of them. She ended up with the nomination by default.

As the election drew near, she was so far behind in the polls that the media pundits had written her off. Not enough foreign policy experience, pro-choice, not enough experience inside the Beltway, didn't appeal to male voters, ad infinitum. The handsome young New York governor, John O'Reilly, was a shoo-in. One month before the election, the *New York Daily* published three pages of sexually explicit e-mails the governor had sent to three teenage interns who worked in his office. His homosexuality was out of the closet, his wife filed for divorce, and his two daughters denounced him publicly.

Senator Janet Sampson, MD, got 90 percent of the votes with a turnout of 20 percent of eligible voters and had been in office exactly sixty days.

Seated to President Sampson's right was Omar Watson, who had been confirmed as the Secretary of Homeland Security the preceding Thursday. He was still moving into his office. Watson's appointment repaid the Missouri Republican machine for its successful turn-out-the-vote effort. The thirty-eight-year-old light-skinned African American congressman had leaped at the opportunity to fill out his résumé. He and his Missouri mentors were grooming him as presidential timber.

Seated to the president's left was CIA Director Charles Milberg, a silver-haired retired federal appeals court judge who had been appointed by President Bush with one year left in his administration. Milberg's replacement had not yet been announced.

Seated next to Judge Milberg was Rear Admiral Bart Deforest, DHS liaison to the Joint Chiefs of Staff. The diminutive Deforest was a desk jockey with no command or combat experience.

Howard Meyers rushed in, with Ed Bailey in tow. Meyers took a seat at the end of the table opposite Sampson. Bailey took a chair along the wall near Meyers and two chairs down from the chiefs of staff for Sampson and Watson, who sat next to each other.

"Madame President, before we get started, my people tell me that the FBI has not shared any of their information with DHS," said Watson, turning toward Meyers. "We are supposed to vet the data, compare it with what we have from other sources, and then, and only then, bring it to you. This is a serious breach of protocol which needs to be addressed immediately. I have a flow chart which my chief of staff has put together that demonstrates how this information should be flowing."

Judge Milberg cleared his throat and said in his bass voice, "Madame President, the CIA is not involved directly in internal affairs, but we would like to have some input into the flow of information because there will undoubtedly be many instances where there are overlapping areas of responsibility."

Meyers sat at the end of the table drumming his fingers on the tabletop. Under the table, he was tapping the toe of one foot. Ed Bailey leaned forward, put his forearms on his thighs and looked at the floor. Everyone else in the room was focused on the discussion.

President Sampson cut off Milberg and said "Howard, what do you have to say?"

"Madame President, I will be pleased to discuss the flow chart with Secretary Watson as soon as he has finished moving into his office. In the meantime"—he looked at Watson—"with all due respect, I want to discuss what we believe to be a series of terrorist attacks around the country."

President Sampson's eyes blinked involuntarily as she jerked slightly in her chair. "You are right, of course. Go ahead."

"Ed Bailey is running this for us, and I will turn it over to him," said Meyers.

Bailey stood and walked over to a lectern behind Meyers, put a disk into a hard drive built into the lectern, and pushed the remote control. The screen filled with data.

#	Nature of Incident	Deaths	Serious Injuries	# of States
3	Shopping Malls	unknown at present	3	
3	Hazmat Trains	"	3	
3	Hazmat Plants	"	3	
5	Gasoline Trucks	5	3	5
1	Refinery	unknown at present	1	
2	Casino Bombs	113	1,000	1
43	Letter Bombs	20	23	22
50	White Powder Envelopes	unknown at present	48	
1	Attempted Dam explosion	1		
30	Sniper Attacks Police	16	12	
34	Sniper Attacks Adults	20	24	
60	Sniper Attacks Children	60	30	
342	Food poisoning	76	25	12

Bailey turned to face the group. "Madame President, these attacks have taken place across the country. If we assign the food poisoning, letter bombs, and white powder envelopes to the people who perpetrated the other attacks, that leaves one hundred and nine incidents that may have been carried out by separate individuals. The most likely scenario is that these types of attacks will continue until the perpetrators are neutralized.

"As you know, New York has told us that its monitoring system is reporting an unknown toxic substance in its water supply. The mayor has issued an alert that consumption of tap water should be avoided or the water boiled. He is thinking about turning off the water supply until the substance is identified and is waiting for our advice. If the water supply has been compromised, New York City will have to be evacuated. I don't have to tell you what that would mean.

"These are the facts. This is obviously a well-organized attack. What worries me even more than these horrors is a 'Dark Winter' scenario."

"What is a 'Dark Winter' scenario, Mr. Bailey?" asked President Sampson.

"It was a political-military exercise conducted just before 9/11 which simulated the effect of a smallpox attack in the United States. The report was titled 'Dark Winter.' The exercise scenario postulated an outbreak of smallpox, a contagious, disfiguring, and fatal disease, in Pennsylvania, Georgia, and Oklahoma. The disease quickly exhausted the US government's vaccine supplies. People tried to flee from one place to another, and the National Guard was called out to keep people from moving around and transmitting the disease. Foreign countries banned US air traffic and anyone entering their countries from the United States.

"The spread of the disease was devastating. Three thousand cases in mid-December increased tenfold by early January and tenfold again by late January. By early February, the projection was three million people infected and one million dead.

"These people may have brought the disease with them either in containers or by infecting themselves and hanging out in crowded places. As bad as things are, it could get much, much worse."

Bailey sat down. No one said anything. There was complete silence except for some background humming of communications equipment. One by one each head turned toward President Sampson.

She took a deep breath, raised her right arm, bowed her head and said, "Let us pray for guidance."

Watson quickly looked around the table and bowed his head.

Milberg folded his hands on the table and bowed his head.

Rear Admiral Deforest bowed his head.

Meyers's eyes widened, and he turned to look at Bailey.

Bailey raised his eyebrows and shrugged.

"Lord God in heaven, we, your humble servants, come this day to ask for your help and blessing in dealing with the crisis facing the American people," said President Sampson.

Meyers watched Watson raise his head and glanced furtively around the table before fixing his gaze back on the tabletop. Watson must think they needed all the help they could get.

President Sampson continued, "Though we walk through the valley of the shadow of death, we will not fear this evil, for thou art with us and wilt show us the way." She raised her head and said, "Suggestions, anyone."

Bailey stood, took two steps to Meyers's elbow, and whispered in his ear, "The New York water supply, for Christ sakes."

The corners of President Sampson's mouth were turned up slightly as she looked from one man to the next. Meyers could not tell if it was a smile or a grimace.

"Madame President," Meyers said, "the first order of business needs to be the New York water supply. The mayor is waiting and needs our advice now."

"You simply cannot turn off the water," said Milberg. "There will be panic in the streets."

"What if thousands are poisoned—what then?" asked Watson.

President Sampson looked at Bailey and said, "Mr. Bailey, you have been thinking about this longer than we have. What do you think?"

Bailey looked at Meyers, who nodded slightly. "I think the mayor can hold off for a while. People can drink and cook with bottled water. He should reemphasize boiling for those who cannot afford bottled water. If the water must be shut off, the city will have to be evacuated. We all need time to prepare for that. New York has an evacuation plan, but they need time to get ready. In any event, the news reports are that traffic is already gridlocked and public transportation swamped. Shutting off the water will turn the situation from panic to pandemonium."

President Sampson had been leaning forward with her forearms on the table and her hands clasped. She sat back and looked around the table. No one said anything. "Until we know more, I am not prepared to risk pandemonium in New York City. I cannot even imagine what an evacuation would mean. Jon," she said, turning to her chief of staff, Jonathan Krebs, "call the mayor, and tell him to hold off the water shutdown until we determine what the substance is. If he refuses, let me know." Krebs crossed the room and entered a secure phone booth to make the call.

"Omar, how are we going to allocate our personnel?" she asked.

Watson's eyes widened, and his knuckles showed white as his hands gripped the arms of his chair. He looked at his chief of staff.

Rear Admiral Deforest, lips compressed into a thin line, leaned forward, put his elbows on the tabletop, and pointed at Watson with narrowed eyes.

"If I may interject, Madame President, Secretary Watson and his chief of staff are just moving in, and they have no clue how to deal with this situation. The director of operations has been relieved of his duties and is cleaning out his office. Three quarters of the DHS headquarters staff has been on the job less than two years. The so-called Homeland Security Network which is to allow states and major urban areas to communicate with each other and local authorities to communicate with federal and state antiterrorism authorities simply does not work. This is going to be much worse than the communications mess during either

9/11 or hurricane Katrina. I think you must rely on Howard and Ed to run things for the time being."

Watson leaned back like he had been slapped, and his chief of staff rose halfway out of his chair before President Sampson raised her palm toward Watson.

"Don't take it personally, Omar; he is just stating the obvious," she said.

Watson's features relaxed, and he sat back in his chair and exhaled slowly. He turned toward Meyers and held out his hand palm up. "It's all yours, Howard."

Meyers hadn't had any time to think about this issue, but he did not hesitate. "Our people will investigate the incidents. Local law enforcement will be alerted to watch infrastructure. State police will watch truck traffic. Governors will be alerted to mobilize the National Guard and keep them on standby. The National Guard units along the Mexican border will be moved to the closest nuclear power facilities. The Coast Guard will be put on high alert. The Border Patrol will be pulled back into urban areas and assigned to any gaps in coverage. Finally, all stateside military personnel will be put on full alert."

"What about posse comitatus?" asked Watson.

"There is an exception for domestic emergencies," said Judge Milberg, "but I suggest a simple congressional bill be prepared suspending the act. If you want to use the troops, you will have it ready for Congress."

President Sampson stood and said, "All right, gentlemen, get to it."

They all marched from the room at double time.

Chapter 18

Sayed Suleiman's mouth was so dry he could not swallow. His heart was racing, and his head swiveled constantly; he could barely sit still as his Chevy Tahoe, with darkly tinted windows, inched along in heavy southbound traffic on Lexington Avenue in New York City.

The fourth son of a former Syrian ambassador to the United Nations, he had received all his education in Islamic schools that preached hate. The high school textbook used in his New York City Wahhabi school taught that jihad was the reaction of pious Muslims to the decadence of democracy and modernity. Today he would strike the necks of the infidels.

He had stolen the SUV two hours ago from the long-term parking lot at Newark Airport. The air conditioner was on full blast, but he was still sweating freely. His undershirt was soaked. He knew the city as well as anyone and had been given New York as the place to make his jihad. When he was issued an RPG-7 upon arriving in Mexico, he almost jumped for joy. During his training, he had fired a dozen of these rocket propelled grenades and had become quite adept in their use. One was lying fully assembled and armed on the backseat.

Suleiman had given a lot of thought to maximizing the impact of this terrorist weapon of choice and had decided on Bloomingdale's, one of New York's most famous department stores. It was Saturday at noon, and people were swarming in and out of the store. He timed it perfectly, and his SUV came to a stop in traffic directly opposite the main entrance. He slid across the seat to the passenger door and stepped to the street, turning to open the rear door through which he extracted the RPG-7. Shielded behind the big SUV, he calmly turned toward the main entrance and pulled the trigger.

A percussion cap ignited the primer, building up gases in the launcher's chamber. The force of the built-up gases hurled the grenade out of the tube at three hundred and eighty-four feet per second. The abrupt acceleration of the grenade leaving the launcher triggered a fuse that ignited a squib of nitro which activated the rocket propulsion system. The grenade hit the front entrance before the stabilizing fins had the chance to deploy and before the telltale trail of smoke emanating from the RPG could be observed by anyone.

The exhaust gases exited to the rear of the launcher so there was no recoil. Suleiman dropped the tube and walked through the smoke and screaming to the corner, where he descended into the subway and took the first train that came by. He wanted to pump his fist in the air. He wanted to yell praise to Allah at the top of his lungs. He was so excited he was ready to explode. But months of training prevailed. He took a paperback book from his pocket, sat down, and read as the train hurtled down the tracks to Wall Street where his presence would be felt very soon.

The body count was twenty-three dead, sixty-two hospitalized, and eighty-nine treated and released.

Chapter 19

Grant weathered a heat-induced bumpy descent into Riyadh's King Khaled International Airport where he was met by Paul Brandt, a former Special Forces colonel who was in charge of BlackRock's security forces in Saudi Arabia. Whenever Grant saw Brandt, he involuntarily thought of the old Tennessee Ernie Ford song about Big John, broad at the shoulder and narrow at the hip. Brandt had flaming red hair and a bushy handlebar mustache, but his most distinguishing feature was his hands; huge, rough, and callused. Bottom line, he gave one the impression that he could tear you apart before breakfast. Grant loved the guy. They piled into an armored BlackRock Hummer and headed for company HQ.

The BlackRock headquarters building was in an undistinguished industrial office park just outside the airport complex. The cramped reception area had only one door into the rest of the building. The receptionist's station was behind bulletproof glass and staffed by a woman dressed in desert camouflage fatigues with short brown hair and no makeup. She was expressionless as she very slowly looked Grant up and down while he waited for Brandt to have his fingerprint and eyeball read by the scanners next to the door. The door opened after the scanned data was accepted, and they passed into a large linoleum-tiled room filled with folding tables holding computers and sophisticated communications equipment. Wires ran all over the floor, held down by duct tape. Brandt gave Grant a quick tour before they settled into his ten-by-ten office just off the main floor.

The coffee they had picked up in the small kitchen was hot and good.

"Well, Paul," Grant said, taking a sip of coffee, "it doesn't look like you're exceeding your facilities budget around here." Brandt merely nodded. *Okay,* Grant thought, *no small talk.* "What's your thinking about the good doctor?"

Brandt pulled a cigar from his pocket and took his time peeling off the cellophane wrapper. He bit off the end of the cigar and spit it into a trash can. Then he lit the cigar with a kitchen match and inhaled deeply. Finally, from inside a cloud of smoke, he said, "There are a number of problems that need to be addressed. Off the record, I asked the embassy military liaison if they would pressure the Saudis to be more forthcoming, and he said it was our problem, not his. Picking up the doctor is no problem; we've got that worked out. The problems are how long are you going to be able to keep him, how are you going to get him to talk to us, and what do we do with him when we're finished? Solve those, and we're home free."

Grant's jet lag vanished as his brain kicked into gear. "I don't think we can keep him very long. The Saudis know that guy died from an explosive capsule at the base of his brain, and they know we know it. They also know that we know about the doctor. If they think he has disappeared, they will think of us first. I think we have an hour or less if we time it right.

"We have to be able to persuade him to talk to us almost immediately. There will not be enough time to motivate him with pain, sensory deprivation, or any of those techniques. Most important, when we let him go, he has to keep his mouth shut. We can't make him disappear."

They sat, silently drinking coffee. Grant started to say something and stopped. Some more time passed in silence. Then he said, "I don't … like this very much, it's not my style, but according to our surveillance, the doctor and his wife have a six-month-old baby that stays alone with a French au pair from about eight in the morning until three in the afternoon while the wife is at work; she's a lawyer.

"We put two men in the house with the au pair and the baby and pick up the doctor. If he doesn't tell us what we want to know, we have him call the au pair, who tells him about her visitors. Then we tell him what is going to happen to his baby if he doesn't tell us what we want to know. We tell him no harm to the baby if he talks to us and keeps his mouth shut afterwards. When our men leave, we give the au pair ten grand in francs. She's French; she'll take the money to keep quiet."

Grant's plan addressed the key issues. But threatening to harm a baby didn't sit well with him. He was glad that the baby would not be aware of anything and that the au pair would get a sizable sum of money for her fright. The doctor was a bad guy, and he didn't care about his feelings. Someone had tried to blow up the BlackRock barracks, and there was a connection with this doctor.

His priority was to protect his men. What if the doctor called their bluff? That was the unknown element. They certainly weren't going to harm the baby or the au pair.

"Paul, you put the file together," Grant said. "Tell me about the au pair."

"About twenty, medium height, medium build, not bad-looking but not a head-turner. Spends a lot of time with her iPod," Brandt replied.

"Okay, how does this sound? If he calls our bluff with the baby, you take him inside the house, take some lurid photos of him and the au pair, and threaten him with exposure."

"Now, I like that, but to cover our asses, I think we should get approval from Operations," said Brandt.

"Paul, you're right, but we just don't have time. If we get Operations involved, it will take a week for them to vet the caper. We can be done with this by lunch tomorrow. We need that information to determine what is going on. I am concerned that some faction of the Saudis has turned against us."

Chapter 20

At 7:30 the next morning, Dr. Ali Al-Fulani, a corpulent middle-aged man in a wrinkled khaki suit, emerged from the elevator into the parking garage below his apartment building. No one else was in the garage when two men completely in black, down to their gloves and ski masks, grabbed him, shoved a cloth into his mouth, put a black hood over his head, and threw him roughly into the back of a windowless telephone company repair van. Inside the van, two other men jerked him to his knees and expertly tied his arms behind him and to the bar running down the side of the van. Then they looped a short rope around his ankles and secured it to the same bar. All of the doctor's weight was on his knees.

Paul Brandt reached out with a gloved hand and lifted the hood just enough to jerk the cloth out of the doctor's mouth. He replaced the hood and slapped him. Hard. Using a voice synthesizer, Brandt said in flawless Arabic, "Ali, keep quiet and listen, and you will not be hurt. I want information which you will give to me. If you do not, the men in your apartment will kill the au pair before they blind and cripple your baby. If you tell anyone about today, we will kill your wife and baby. If you understand, nod, do not speak."

The doctor opened his mouth beneath the hood, and Brandt slapped him again. Harder. The doctor's head bobbed up and down.

"What is your baby's name?"

"F-Fahad," stuttered Al-Fulani.

"What is the name of your au pair?"

"Aimee," said Al-Fulani in a somewhat firmer voice.

"You implanted explosive capsule devices into the heads of two men," Brandt's electronic voice announced. "One died from the device, but the other told us about you before the capsule in his head exploded. Do not deny that you did it. How are the devices detonated?"

Al-Fulani hesitated.

"Think your baby's name, and then answer me."

"A radio wave on a certain frequency will detonate the capsule," whispered Al-Fulani.

"On whose order were the capsules implanted?" demanded the synthesized voice.

Al-Fulani's body began to shake uncontrollably.

"I will not ask you again. I will have your baby blinded in two seconds," said the implacable voice.

"Alwaleed, Ali Alwaleed," said Al-Fulani, dropping his head to his chest.

"Into how many people did you implant these capsules?"

"One hundred," said Al-Fulani in a barely audible voice.

Silence. Brandt didn't think this man would know anything else that could help them.

"We are going to open the door and put you out. You will count to one hundred and then remove the hood. If you remove it too soon, the man watching you will kill you."

Dr. Ali Al-Fulani was untied and helped out of the truck so that he did not fall. There was a wet stain on the front of his pants. The truck left the garage at a normal speed. Elapsed time: three minutes and thirty seconds.

Later the watcher reported that Al-Fulani must have counted to four or five hundred before removing his hood.

———————————

Grant was sitting at Brandt's desk when Brandt came in with two cups of coffee and a frown on his face. He had been gone less than two hours.

"Did everything go all right?" Grant asked as he got up and gave Brandt his chair.

"This mission went exactly the way we planned it. We snatched him in the parking garage and had our information in less than four minutes. When the guy pissed in his pants, I knew we had him. We have three pieces of information. First, Ali Alwaleed ordered him to do the implants. Second, he did one hundred of them, and third, they can be detonated by a radio frequency."

"Who the hell is Ali Alwaleed?"

"Chief troubleshooter for the Crown Prince. Kind of a minister without portfolio. A very powerful behind-the-scenes player," said Brandt.

This situation made absolutely no sense to Grant. "Do you have any idea what is going on here?" he asked Brandt

Brandt slowly shook his head.

Chapter 21

Grant was exhausted. The BlackRock jet had satellite television which he tuned to Fox News to find out what was going on in the world. Brent Bixby was in the middle of one of his Special Reports.

"New York City's water supply was restored earlier today after tests revealed that an unknown substance that was found in a water supply test station would be neutralized by routine chlorination.

"In other breaking news, it has been determined that the train accident in Richmond involving hazardous chemicals was caused by a manual track switch that was out of alignment. A train derailment and resulting fire in a Baltimore tunnel was caused by failure of a damaged section of track. In San Bernardino, the tanker explosion which released toxic gas was the result of an explosive device of some kind.

"In Bismarck, Trenton, Sacramento, Portland, and Miami, gasoline truck explosions were caused by similar explosive devices.

"There have been sixty reported sniper attacks killing thirty children across the country. Many schools are closing.

"There are reports of sniper attacks on police across the country.

"Now we go to Laurie Dawn in Las Vegas for an update on the casino bombings … No, wait, this is just coming into our newsroom. There are reports of explosions at the General Motors assembly plants in Flint, Michigan, and Oklahoma City … Now there has been an explosion at Ford's massive Rouge manufacturing plant in Dearborn, Michigan. We are being told that the explosions have severely damaged these plants, and it may take months to repair them.

"The collateral effect of these plant shutdowns will ripple throughout the economy. Peter Benson, our chief automotive reporter, estimates as many as three hundred thousand people could be out of work as a result of these plant closings.

"We are trying to get comments from the White House and expect a statement shortly."

Grant had no children and no close relative, so he did not pretend to imagine how the parents of the slain children felt. It was simply unimaginable that children would be slaughtered while they were playing in a school yard. How would parents deal with the horror that had come into their lives like an unexpected tsunami? He felt anger and the desire to lash out at someone or something, but who or what?

He was used to soldiers dying; it came with the territory. Drunk drivers and accidents robbing people of their lives was an everyday occurrence that one took for granted—unless, of course, random death took a member of your family. What he was not prepared for was an organized attack on his country that was not a direct attack on authority figures but an attack on innocent civilians. While 9/11 had been unexpected and truly horrible, it happened, and the killing was over. This time the killing was just beginning.

It was one thing to read in the newspaper about terrorists killing innocent people in another country or see pictures on television, but now the terror was loose in the United States, and he had no doubt that it was going to continue. He wasn't prepared for this, and neither were his fellow citizens. Most frightening of all, he did not think any level of government was prepared to deal with a small army of trained terrorists rampaging around the country.

As the return flight drew interminably to its end, he wondered if he had lost any friends who were in the wrong place at the wrong time. When his plane touched down, he had calmed enough to wonder if there was any connection between the failed attack on BlackRock and the terror attacks at home.

Chapter 22

Stephanie stood transfixed in the living room of Hector's new ten-thousand-square-foot villa just outside Puerto Vallarta. The villa was perched on a hillside several hundred feet above the Bay of Banderas, offering Stephanie a 180-degree view up and down the coastline. Water in the negative edge pool seemed to drop off the cliff to the ocean below. Hector put his arm around her as they stood watching the sunset.

"I am glad you like it, darling," he said. "We have it all to ourselves tonight. Margarita and her new boyfriend will be joining us tomorrow for the weekend. We should have a splendid time."

Late the next morning Boots, stunning as usual in short white shorts, a red halter top, and sunglasses atop her luxuriant black hair, arrived with her new boyfriend. Stephanie was surprised to see a very fit looking fortyish Korean man in jeans and a T-shirt. Boots introduced him as Kim, a Korean diplomat attached to the North Korean embassy in Mexico City. After watching him move about, talk, and sit at lunch, Stephanie decided he seemed more of a soldier than a diplomat. When she mentioned this to Hector, he dismissed her comment by saying that all Korean diplomats probably had a military background.

The next day, Hector and the Korean went to visit a friend of Hector's, leaving Boots and Stephanie alone. Boots went shopping. Stephanie went through her ritual one-hour workout with light free weights and ran three miles in under twenty minutes. Then she donned her blue bikini, went for a swim, and settled in beside the pool.

The afternoon sun was warm and pleasant. Stephanie flipped through a *People* magazine, looking at the pictures while sipping margaritas from an icy pitcher left by the housekeeper. After a while, she lowered the magazine and turned on her stomach, dozing as a warm breeze wafted over her body.

Slowly, very slowly, she regained enough consciousness to feel soft hands sensuously caressing the backs of her legs from her ankles to her bikini bottom. Stephanie sighed softly and made no effort to move. She let herself stay half-asleep, absorbing the pure pleasure of the touch.

At some point the hands untied her bikini top and continued the caress up and down her back. Stephanie groaned softly. She had never experienced such pleasure and had no desire to move or come fully awake. She could feel long hair around her face and lips next to her ear. She barely opened her eyes and saw the hair was a luxuriant black. The lips breathed "turn over" ever so softly in her ear, and she knew it was Boots. She rolled over slowly without opening her eyes.

She could feel lotion being applied to her body as the hands caressed her stomach and moved to her breasts, which had come free when she turned over. As the soft fingers gently teased her nipples, she moaned softly.

Boots took Stephanie's hand and slowly drew her to her feet. Stephanie opened her eyes and saw Boots wore nothing but a miniscule white thong. Boots, without any resistance, led Stephanie across the patio and into her room.

Boots stood very close to Stephanie and slowly lifted her chin. She softly pressed her lips against Stephanie's.

Before Stephanie could react, there was a commotion in the living room as Hector and Kim returned. Hector was calling for margaritas and Stephanie. Boots placed her hands firmly on Stephanie's waist and gently pushed her away. "Go. There will be another time."

That night Stephanie woke with a start; she had been dreaming of Boots caressing her naked body. Unable to get back to sleep, she put on a light robe, went out onto the balcony, and stared at the moonlight reflecting off the ocean.

Who was this person in her body? The Stephanie Chambers she knew was an army brat, an Olympic caliber athlete, an honors student at the Sorbonne, a successful public relations executive who mingled with movers and shakers of American business and politics—and, of course, a CIA assassin. Grant Meredith had been a bright spot until they found out she had killed his brother. That ended her tentative romance with him and her career with the CIA.

She had wandered aimlessly back to Hector. This was an exercise in self-pity. She was free to do anything she wanted, and she had chosen this life. She had let herself become the mistress of a Mexican politician who, at the very least, provided political cover for his drug-smuggling family. Yes, she had whatever she wanted and had no responsibility except to keep Hector sexually satisfied, which was hardly a burden. But she didn't read anymore. She didn't pay any attention to current events. Other than exercise and shop and fuck, she really did nothing. Now, here she was about to have an affair with Hector's sister. *Who, in God's name, am I?* she wondered.

She was still standing with her hands on the balcony railing as the sun came up behind her.

Hector and Kim had lunch in an oceanfront restaurant and took a long walk on the beach.

As soon as they were out of hearing distance, Kim said, "Our packages have arrived. One was put on the railroad, and the other is ready to be transported across the border. My superiors want to know when and how they will be delivered so that we may arrange for pickup."

"We will move one package through a tunnel in Nogales," Hector answered. "We are using a tunnel which was prepared with the help of mining engineers. The Border Patrol found the tunnel several years ago and poured cement into its opening on the US side. The tunnel is otherwise intact and very serviceable. We have diverted the tunnel around the sealed opening for a short distance and will break through and deliver the package into the US.

"A diplomatic message will be delivered to your embassy tomorrow with the precise time and locations where your people may pick up the packages in Nogales, Arizona, and at the SmartPort in Kansas City."

Kim considered this. "As I understand what you are telling me, the Americans discovered this sophisticated tunnel and did not destroy it. They just dumped a load of concrete in the tunnel mouth. I have trouble believing that."

"I can't explain the Americans; I can only tell you the facts," said Hector.

"What if you are discovered when you break the new opening?"

"The Border Patrol will be there to protect us when we open the tunnel. These Border Patrol officers are part of our family. Nothing will go wrong. Just have someone there to take your package at the appointed time. If they aren't there, we will not be responsible for the package."

Chapter 23

Ed Bailey had not left the NSB War Room since he returned from his meeting with the president at the White House. Food came from the Bureau kitchen, and there was a small bunk room with a shower just off the War Room. Things were going from bad to worse so quickly he couldn't keep track of the bad news.

He had just finished pushing purple pins, signifying sniper attacks, into the big map at Albuquerque, Dallas, and Minneapolis.

Earlier he had put yellow pushpins, signifying Hazmat incidents, in Ardmore, Oklahoma, for a refinery fire and in Philadelphia where another refinery fire had released 400,000 pounds of hydrogen fluoride. The explosion triggering the Oklahoma refinery fire wasn't too bad; only twenty people had died. There was total chaos, however, in Philadelphia, where the hydrogen fluoride had asphyxiated thousands of people and thousands more were still at risk.

Bailey was juggling six red pushpins in his hand which, when placed, would signify forest fires. There were forest fires raging in the Sawtooth National Forest in Idaho, the Bitterroot and Helena National Forests in Montana, the San Juan National Forest in

Colorado, and the Angeles National Forest outside Los Angeles. The most immediate danger to property was the Malibu fire, which had already destroyed fifty homes. Each one of these fires had begun in the last few days, and each one was listed as arson, caused by a series of Molotov cocktails. He pushed himself to his feet and walked to the map, taking his time to place each of the red pins.

The simple fact was that although the FBI had twelve thousand special agents, after taking into account their ongoing workload, it did not have enough trained agents to aggressively investigate all these incidents. Local law enforcement was torn between investigating the incidents and providing increased security. Bailey had suggested bringing home military investigative personnel from around the world to help. Meyers had floated the idea, but it was dead on arrival. The president did not want to feed a nationwide panic that was on its way to pandemonium.

The phone on the conference table buzzed, and Bailey returned to his seat to take another call, probably about another disaster.

"Mr. Bailey, this is Special Agent John Klinger in Baton Rouge. Your assistant said I should speak to you immediately and put me through."

"Okay, go ahead," said Bailey

"Early this morning, a doctor at the local hospital was shot and killed by a sniper while entering the hospital."

Oh no.

"A few minutes later, a few blocks away, a traffic officer stopped a young woman for rolling through a stop sign. She had a fake driver's license, so he searched her car and found a Savage 110 hunting rifle with a Nikon scope in the trunk. She wouldn't talk to the locals and asked for a Legal Aid attorney. They kept her alone in a holding cell until the attorney arrived. When they went to the cell, she was dead. There was blood leaking from her ears, eyes, and nose. The ME preliminary finding is that some kind of explosive device inside her head went off," said Lawton in a matter-of-fact, flat voice.

"Any idea as to her nationality?" asked Bailey, leaning back and running his hand through his hair.

"She's black, kind of African looking to me," said Lawton, "but I'll ask the ME if they can determine that for us."

"Okay," said Bailey. "Send me a picture and the autopsy report, which I want done right now, and call me if they can pinpoint nationality."

Shit, thought Bailey as he hung up and sat with his head in his hands for a moment. Then he took another purple pin from the box and pushed it into the map at Baton Rouge.

Before he could sit down, the phone rang again. He picked it up tentatively. "Bailey."

"Mr. Bailey, Agent Lawton again. We got a fingerprint hit on this woman. She is, was, Acai Al-Azhari, Sudanese, age twenty-four. Until last year, she was a student at LSU."

Chapter 24

The War Room door burst open, and in rushed Omar Watson and Howard Meyers. Bailey stood and noticed that both Watson and Meyers had dark circles under their eyes and lines in their faces he had not seen before. He didn't need to look in the mirror to know that he had acquired those characteristics himself. No one thought about shaking hands.

As the three men were sitting down at the conference table, Meyers said, "Ed, give us a review of where we stand."

Bailey sat up straighter and said, "Gentlemen, things are bad and getting worse by the minute, and I mean literally by the minute." He stood and went over to the map full of different-colored pushpins.

"The incidents span the country. The thirteen yellow pins in this map each represent a Hazmat incident, train derailment, gasoline truck explosion, refinery or chemical plant explosion followed by fire, and so forth. I am including the NYC water incident in this category. None of these incidents was an accident.

"There are six red pins representing forest fires started by multiple Molotov cocktails.

"There are fifty purple pins representing sniper attacks, including those on children. Thirty of these children were killed.

"There is one white pin where someone tried to blow a hole in the Castaic Dam north of LA.

"There is one green pin representing the RPG attack at Bloomingdale's.

"The death toll is in excess of 9/11 and rising.

"The explosions at the GM and Ford plants did not kill anyone, but it will take months to get those plants up and running again. Layoffs are being calculated, and the ripple effects on the economy will mean losses in the billions.

"Three of the perps have been eliminated. They all had explosive devices in their heads. One was a Philippine Muslim wanted in connection with several terrorist incidents in the Philippines. Another was a former LSU student from Sudan. The last one's country of origin is unknown at this time.

"Given all this information, in my opinion, the United States is under attack by an unknown group of at least fifty terrorists. I think they will continue to conduct their operations on a small scale, so that without a lot of luck or a big mistake, we won't catch very many of them anytime soon. I assume they all have these explosive capsules implanted in their heads which can be detonated remotely. Even if we could keep one alive, I doubt they could tell us very much because each one is probably an individual cell."

Watson and Meyers were both slumped in their chairs as Bailey sat down.

Watson spoke first. "We don't know who sent these people, so we have no way to retaliate."

"There has to be a point to all of this," mused Meyers. "Terrorists always want something ..."

Watson pushed himself up from the table very slowly and said, "Howard, let's go see the president."

As they were leaving the room, the phone rang, and Ed Bailey snatched it up. "Bailey," he said and instantly held up his hand for Meyers and Watson to stop. He listened for a full minute before slowly hanging up the phone and dropping like a sack of potatoes into his chair.

"We have accumulated over fifty incidents with thirty-five deaths from food poisoning in ten states so far. All the incidents involved food purchased in major chain grocery stores in the last three days. Twenty-five of the dead are children under age fifteen."

As he was delivering the news, Bailey's eyes had moistened. He suddenly slammed his palms on the table top. "As God is my witness, I want to kill these people with my bare hands."

Watson looked at his shoes. Meyers walked over to Bailey, put both big meaty hands on his shoulders, and said, "Ed, all you can do is the best you can do. That is all any of us can do. Keep pushing your people. You have got to keep control; don't let them feel you are panicking."

Watson looked up and said, "Maybe we should ask the people to form neighborhood watch–like groups to surveil their surroundings and call in anything suspicious."

Meyers turned and said, "The problem with that is we will get so many calls that the phone systems won't be able to handle it, and we will waste too much time checking out worthless reports. Come on, let's go."

Chapter 25

The west wall of the main conference room in The Plaza Group's New York City headquarters was floor-to-ceiling glass overlooking Park Avenue. Today curtains were drawn across the east wall of soundproof glass with a view into the reception area. Thick burgundy carpeting covered the floors, and a fourteenth-century tapestry towered over a credenza that held a silver coffee service. Grant sat at one end of the polished mahogany conference table.

Representing The Plaza Group and sitting at the other end of the table was Homer Johnson. Lawrence A. Kammerer and James R. Brown, former Secretary of State, also representing The Plaza Group, sat on either side of him. Empty chairs separated these men from General (Ret.) Arnold Schwartz from Integrated Security Services. Across from Schwartz was A. Charles Litton IV. Four, as his friends called him, had recently resigned as chief counsel to the Department of Defense.

Grant had arranged this meeting on the flight back from Saudi Arabia. He spent thirty minutes bringing everyone up to date on events in Saudi Arabia, including the brief interrogation of the Crown Prince's doctor. Now it was time to raise the issue that was troubling him the most.

"Setting aside for a moment the safety of BlackRock personnel, I am deeply concerned about a brief AP wire story that I read on the plane. According to the story, the Border Patrol picked up an illegal alien in San Diego who died in custody from an exploding head implant. The two men who tried to blow up our barracks in Saudi Arabia died from exploding head implants. We have the Crown Prince's doctor having put one hundred of these implants in people on the orders of the Crown Prince's chief troubleshooter, Ali Alwaleed. I see a clear relationship between Saudi Arabia and the terrorist attacks taking place here. I wanted to get your input before taking any further action."

President Johnson spoke first. "Grant gave me a heads-up about this, and I asked Wally Richards to see what he could find out."

Richards was an Integrated Security Services board member and a former director of the CIA.

"Wally tells me that these incidents are probably related," said President Johnson, "but there is a blackout on information while an evaluation is going on. However, he did find out that a terrorist tried to blow a hole in the Castaic Dam north of LA and was killed by a guard. During his autopsy, a device inside his head was detonated. This guy was identified as a Philippine Muslim with a terrorist background. That was all the information Wally could get."

Kammerer, always a quick study, had the first question. "Grant, what was the nationality of the two men who tried to take out our barracks?"

"I don't know for sure. We—excuse me, *I* just assumed they were Saudis. We did not ask the doctor about the nationality of those getting the implants."

Oh no. Jesus H. Christ, Grant thought, *I am such an idiot. I didn't think beyond the implications for Saudi Arabia/BlackRock relations.*

"All right, son, don't worry about it," said Kammerer in an uncharacteristically mild tone. "It seems important now, but I'm sure it didn't then."

James Brown, whom Grant hardly knew, had been frowning ever since Grant told them about interrogating the Crown Prince's doctor. He was a career diplomat whose tenure as Secretary of State had been during the Clinton years. He was only sixty, but with sparse gray hair, eyes set deep into a heavily lined face, and a wattled neck, he looked considerably older.

Now he said, "Four, can you give Mr. Meredith some insight as to his legal position at this time?"

A. Charles Litton IV was a graduate of Oberlin College and Georgetown Law School. Despite the warm weather, he wore a three-piece suit with a gold watch chain stretched across his vest. His face was thin with a prominent beak of a nose. Self-confidence was definitely not his problem. He sat up a little straighter and seemed to preen.

"Criminal Law 101, you deprived the doctor of his freedom, if only for three or four minutes. That was kidnapping, for which you can be beheaded or stoned to death in Saudi Arabia … That was just meant to get your attention. I doubt, given the penalties, that you would be extradited. That being said, even if the United

States did not prosecute you for kidnapping, you could get twenty years in prison for violating USC 2340A for committing an act of torture."

"Now, hold on, Mr. Litton," Grant said. "With all due respect, the doctor was not tortured. We didn't hurt him, we just scared him."

Litton looked down his nose at Grant. His thin lips looked like he had just taken a bite of a lemon. "Please, Mr. Meredith, allow me the courtesy of finishing before you instruct me on the law. The statute was intended to implement the United Nations Convention against Torture and the Detainee Treatment Act of 2005. Under these Acts, your United States Senate has defined mental torture in part as prolonged mental harm resulting from threatened infliction of severe physical pain and suffering or threatening imminent death or severe physical suffering to another.

"You see, Mr. Meredith, the only issue is whether what you did resulted in prolonged mental harm to the doctor. 'Prolonged' doesn't mean that you threatened harm to him and his family for a long period of time. The test focuses on the state of mind of the person being questioned. I think it fair to say the doctor will never forget what you did to him, and that will satisfy the legal test of prolonged mental harm."

Litton sat back in his chair, folded his hands in front of him, and crossed his legs. He looked around the room, but no one said anything.

Grant found himself at a loss for words.

General Schwartz finally said, "I told those assholes at State not to do this."

"Wait just a minute here," said Kammerer. "Four, if you are right, any detainee could claim that he was threatened with, oh, say, waterboarding and suffered mentally. That would require a trial to determine if he suffered prolonged mental harm. In essence we do not know what 'prolonged' or 'mental harm' means until some judge or jury makes an after-the-fact decision. That is absurd."

Litton unfolded his hands palms up and shrugged before saying, "I don't make the law. I just read it for others."

Homer Johnson cleared his throat, and everyone looked his way. "Gentlemen, this is all very interesting, but it seems we have information that President Sampson and her team should be given immediately, regardless of how the information was obtained. I will set up a meeting with them and take Grant with me. I can't imagine that, under the circumstances, Grant has much to worry about. Anything else?"

"Yes sir," Grant said. "I think it would be a good idea if General Schwartz could work with Paul Brandt on a security plan for our people in Saudi Arabia."

Schwartz responded without hesitation. "You've got it."

Chapter 26

The container of electronics equipment shipped from mainland China had been off-loaded at the Mexican port of Lázaro Cárdenas with preclearance documentation from a Chinese electronics company. This meant that under the US Bureau of Customs and Border Protection protocols designed to "extend the zone of [US] security outward," the container was not subjected to X-ray and gamma-ray inspection upon arrival in Mexico or the United States. It then moved by train directly to the CTY customs bonded public warehouse in Kansas City's foreign trade zone. Here the container was scheduled to be stored until it was picked up by a nonexistent trucking company, whose president on paper was one Mohamed Ali Yusef.

The same day in Dearborn, Michigan, Imam Mohamed Ali Yusef received a cell phone by DHS courier. Included in the package were instructions to drive to a specific Marriott hotel in North Kansas City and await further orders.

Yusef was a true believer. The prior evening during services at his mosque, he told the young men before him, "We don't make a distinction between civilians and non- civilians, innocents and non-innocents; only between Muslims and unbelievers. And the life of an unbeliever has no value. It has no sanctity. We will use democracy to destroy the United States."

He embraced the opportunity to strike a nuclear blow for Islam in the belly of the beast.

The second suitcase bomb had a similarly easy entry into the United States. It took exactly fifteen minutes for the suitcase to be pulled though the Nogales tunnel in a wagon. Two Border Patrol officers took the suitcase three blocks, where it was handed to Imam Mohamed Khomeini. Khomeini drove straight to downtown Los Angeles where he checked into the Bonaventure Hotel and ordered a sumptuous meal from room service.

Khomeini was dying of cancer. He knew the bomb blast would seal his trip to Paradise.

Chapter 27

Grant Meredith and Homer Johnson were met at the West Wing entrance to the White House by Jonathan Krebs, President Sampson's chief of staff, and immediately taken to the Situation Room. Grant had never been in the White House before; they were moving so fast, however, he had no time to look around.

Seated at the conference table were President Sampson, Omar Watson, and Howard Meyers. The president's freshly pressed black pinstriped pantsuit and crisp open-necked white blouse were in stark contrast to the sagging flesh of her face and the dark half moons under her eyes. Watson and Meyers looked like they had slept in their clothes, if they had gotten any sleep at all.

After the introductions, Grant summarized what he had found in Saudi Arabia, skipping over the methods of interrogation used on the doctor. Fortunately, the president's people were too distracted to focus on the omission.

Watson looked at President Sampson and said, "Madame President, I am unaware of current security clearances for former President Johnson and Mr. Meredith."

President Sampson raised both her hands off the table palms up, briefly closed her eyes and said, "Omar, under the circumstances we need all the help we can get; we'll worry about the technicalities later. Howard, give them a brief update."

In a tense voice, Meyers said, "We have a dead Sudanese woman sniper, a Philippine male bomber, two dead male bombers who are likely to be Saudi, and a presently unidentified man, probably an illegal alien, who died in Border Patrol custody; each of whom died from an explosive head implant.

"Your piece of the puzzle gives us a Saudi doctor who implanted these capsules in one hundred people. We now have ninety-five people with explosive head capsules unaccounted for. Based on what we know now, it is reasonable to assume that we are under siege by these ninety-five people. Unless they make mistakes, it will take a considerable while to identify or apprehend them, during which time they are likely to continue these random attacks.

"Finally, I cannot find the words to describe what the murder of innocent children in their school yards is doing to the country. People are either staying home with the shades drawn or running for areas that they consider safe. However, the attacks are across the country in big and small communities. No one is safe anywhere. Schools are closed; flights are cancelled; highways out of any size city are clogged. The media is fanning the panic. I don't want this repeated, but we are not prepared for this type of attack.

"Am I missing anything?"

The room was silent. Meyers was looking at each person, silently prompting for questions. Watson was staring at the tabletop. Finally, President Sampson voiced the thought that was on everyone's mind. "Is this a Saudi government operation?"

No one said anything, so Grant volunteered, "Quite possibly. However, at this point one cannot be positive. It could be a frame-up by Al Qaeda or another organization. We have multiple nationalities involved. Alwaleed could be acting without Saudi government approval. The linchpin is Alwaleed. Is he carrying out government policy or setting up a scenario to overthrow the monarchy?"

Watson interrupted. "We have Sudanese, a Filipino, and maybe Saudis involved. Thus far, in my opinion, it is more likely action by Muslim extremists, rather than the Saudi government."

President Sampson said, "It is clear to me that nothing is clear. The involvement of Saudi nationals does not mean this is a politically motivated attack by the government of Saudi Arabia. It could just as well be part of a Wahhabi jihad. "

Homer Johnson ended his silence. "Wahhabism is the official religion of Saudi Arabia. Is the government distinguishable from its religion?"

Grant: "I know you have experts on the subject, but it seems to me that we have been pushing the Saudis to move in the direction of democracy. Perhaps they are enabling the extremists to carry out these attacks."

Watson again: "I cannot believe they could be so stupid as to attack us."

A communications officer quietly descended from the top of the room and whispered in the ear of the president's chief of staff. Krebs nodded and then said, "We have just taken a message off the Internet which will appear on the middle screen in just a moment.

The message appeared on the screen:

> Your country is under attack. As your government knows, we have conducted multiple operations in almost all of your states. More of your people have died thus far than during 9/11, and we are just getting started. No one and no place is safe. You can avoid the devastation of your way of life by publicly stating within forty-eight hours that you will immediately redeploy all military personnel stationed outside the United States to your own country. All weapons, equipment, and other military supplies will be left where they are. You will leave unarmed and empty-handed. This must be completed within thirty days of this date. Our attacks will continue until you make such a public commitment. We will remain poised to continue our attacks if you do not complete your agreement in timely fashion. This demand is not subject to negotiation.
>
> The Rest of the World

The room was silent.

Krebs broke the silence. "We have just received a report that two minutes ago there was an explosion at the Mormon Tabernacle in Salt Lake City. Casualties and damage are presently unknown." He paused and put his hand over his earpiece. "A sniper has just killed three people at Wal-Mart headquarters in Bentonville, Arkansas."

"Gentlemen, your attention please," said President Sampson, snapping everyone to alertness. "Omar, what is the likelihood that this message is from the people causing these incidents?"

Chief of Staff Krebs interrupted by holding up his hand again. All eyes turned toward him. He inhaled slowly and said, "A hijacked gasoline tanker truck just exploded under the downtown Phoenix highway stack. Those bridges are steel reinforced, but the heat was so intense that the structural integrity of the bridges has been compromised. Two of them collapsed. Deaths are ten and counting. There will be total traffic chaos in the downtown area of Phoenix for at least eighteen months. There were several eyewitnesses who saw a man stop the truck under the bottom of the stack and get into a car that had stopped in front of him. Less than one minute later, the truck exploded, probably from a block of C-4 attached to the tanker and detonated from a safe distance. The getaway car had been stolen and was later found at an exit on Highway 51. They probably switched cars."

Watson ignored the Phoenix disaster and said, "Madame President, I think the message is credible, but we cannot be absolutely positive."

"Assuming it is genuine, the United States is not going to withdraw within its own borders," roared Meyers.

President Sampson stood, pressed both palms on the table, leaned forward, and snapped, "Howard, I am the commander in chief. You are Director of the FBI."

"Now look here …," said Meyers, rising from his chair with a crimson face.

Omar Watson's head was swiveling back and forth between Sampson and Meyers.

"Please, please, stay calm," said Homer Johnson, raising both hands.

Grant was stunned. He had never envisioned that this was how the United States government actually worked. They were in a situation where decisions would be made on no more information than was available in the media. All the intelligence apparatus was useless. Police procedures had little chance of early success. A military response had no target. The country seemed to be shutting itself down, just sitting still. In these circumstances, it would be more difficult for the terrorists to move around unobtrusively. However, at some point, life had to go on. Grant thought they could use some advice from the Israelis but wasn't sure if he should suggest it.

Krebs whispered in the president's ear, and the Fox News feed appeared on the center screen. Bret Bixby was in the middle of a Special Report:

"Given the number of incidents, their timing and location, our military analyst, General Peter Robertson, concludes that the United States is under siege by terrorists.

"General, it seems to me that DHS is not responding to these incidents very well. What has that massive department been doing since it was established?"

"Good question, Bret. Our viewers should understand that no fewer than eighty-nine, yes eighty-nine congressional committees and subcommittees have oversight of DHS. Senior DHS officials have spent vast amounts of time preparing and testifying before congressional potentates. Moreover, DHS has been under a constant state of reorganization since it was created. The local pork in DHS funding is obscene. Why should DHS have to prepare and fund antiterrorism programs in Podunk, Wyoming?

"The most depressing aspect of the DHS lack of preparedness is its failure to implement any system to scan shipping containers for terrorist weapons. We have no meaningful programs to scan maritime cargo for nuclear materials, and we still transport Hazmat through major urban areas. Entirely too much DHS time and money has been spent dealing with Congress and trying to organize itself."

Once again the room was silent. Next the Fox business reporter, Neil Campbell, appeared on the screen and announced: "An hour ago the NYSE instituted its automatic program trading curbs when the Dow dropped 3,000 points from yesterday's close. The Dow has now dropped 50 percent from yesterday's close, and trading has been halted for the day. The CBOE has also halted options trading for the day. The situation here is likely to be much worse than the credit market collapse of 2008. Back to you, Bret."

"Breaking news, there is a posting on the Internet from the terrorists demanding that the United States withdraw its military forces inside its borders. Here it is on your screen. Our Capitol Hill reporter, Jenny Atkins, has just reported that Nancy Coulter is calling the House of Representatives into a special session to discuss the terrorist demands."

"Pardon me, Howard," said President Sampson. "We are all under a lot of stress. You are right, of course; we cannot give in to such an ultimatum. I will have the attorney general draft a bill for Congress suspending the Posse Comitatus Act. Omar and the secretary of defense will draft a plan to utilize the military for homeland security. In the meantime, Howard, keep on with what you are doing. I will hold a full Cabinet meeting and will schedule a press conference.

"Homer, I would like to thank you and Mr. Meredith for coming in today," said President Sampson. "You have been most helpful."

Chapter 28

Grant was looking out the window of the BlackRock suite in the Willard Hotel a few blocks from the White House. He wasn't at all sure President Sampson had the experience or temperament to deal effectively with this crisis. Omar Watson was in way over his head. In the background, CBS interrupted its programming with a special report by Eric Jones from Joplin, Missouri where two more elementary school children had been killed by sniper fire:

"With me is Mary Peters, grandmother of seven-year-old Patricia Peters, who was murdered by an unknown sniper earlier this morning. Mary, how do you feel?"

The camera zoomed in on a woman standing outside a modest one-story house. Her hair was disheveled, her moist eyes were surrounded with smeared mascara. She bit her lip and began.

"I feel..." She took a deep breath. "I feel ... anger, and I feel helpless. I feel ... deserted by God ... I want to know how my government could allow this to happen to us, to the others ... These are ... were ... children. The government sends soldiers all around the world but cannot protect our children at home ... I feel ..." Her chest began to heave, and tears began to stream down her face before she covered it with her hands.

The camera continued to focus on her while Jones said, "Mary, the terrorists have said that they will stop the killing if we bring our troops home from overseas. Do you think we should bring them home or keep them overseas?"

Mary Peters slowly removed her hands from her face. Her moist raccoon like eyes flashed. "Bring them home, bring them home now. My God, we need protection for our children here, now. I don't care about the rest of the world; I want protection for our children."

"That's the feeling in the heartland, Chad. Now back to you," said Jones.

The screen then switched to Las Vegas where a reporter stood among fire trucks and hoses outside a casino from which smoke was drifting. The reporter, standing next to big-bellied man in plaid shorts and a golf shirt said, "Chad, I'm here with Peter Fleming who arrived at the casino just as the explosion took place. Peter, how does it feel to have come so close to death?"

Fleming's face was tight. His eyes narrowed as he said, "I am a Gulf War One vet. I say put the National Guard on the streets, get the army out there, go door to door, and hunt down these mother ... (beep). Find out where they came from, and blow the hell out of the place."

"That is a common sentiment around here Chad," said the reporter.

"I have on the line Tom Valero, former Assistant Secretary of DHS," said Chad. "Tom, can you make any sense out of these events for us?"

"Chad, in my opinion, the demand posted on the Internet is from those responsible for the carnage going on right now," said Valero. "When I was with DHS, our efforts were focused on prevention of major incidents such as airplane hijacking and the like. Frankly, we never had time to develop plans to deal with an onslaught such as we are presently experiencing. My sources tell me that DHS has no plan in place to deal with the situation. It is clear to me that conventional law enforcement is also unprepared."

"Tom, what significance do you attach to targeting elementary school children with sniper attacks?"

"These attacks are meant to impress on us that these terrorists are merciless and will destroy anything they can, including what is most precious to us: our children. It was too difficult to mount a major attack, so the terrorists have focused on our most tender spot."

"Excuse me, Tom, the White House has just issued a statement that all incidents are under investigation, and the president will speak at a press conference scheduled for 4 p.m. We will be back after a short break."

Grant turned down the volume on the television. *If these terrorists were infiltrated into the US, how did they do it? The 9/11 hijackers came in with passports, but there weren't very many of them. If they came in illegally, it was probably across the Mexican border. People or drugs, the Sanchez family might be a good place to start trying to backtrail the terrorists. Would they help? Should I contact them? How can I contact them? Should I let Watson know what I have in mind?*

The Sanchez family's rise to power in Mexico began in the aftermath of the Mexican Revolution. Jose Sanchez was a leading businessman in Sonora and had been a primary adviser to Pancho Villa during the Revolution. During the chaos that followed the overthrow of General Díaz in 1911, Jose was able to amass vast tracts of land in Sonora. It was rumored that when Villa objected to his activities, Jose masterminded his assassination. He had been one of the founders of the PRI political party which controlled Mexican politics until the election of Vicente Fox of the PAN party in 2000. By the time of Jose's death in 1930, the Sanchez family was one of the richest in Mexico. Family interests included land, banks, newspapers, mines, factories, and liquor distribution.

Carlos was a grandson of Jose. He took over the family after his father was assassinated and moved the family into smuggling people and drugs into the United States. It was Carlos who saw the opportunity in drugs when the DEA disrupted the flow of Colombian drugs into the US through Florida. He was the first to forge a connection with the Colombian drug lords.

At the press conference, President Sampson did little more than catalog incidents, say they were under investigation by all available resources, and announce that Congress would be asked to temporarily allow domestic use of military personnel to assist with the investigations and provide security. She took no questions and did not mention the terrorist demand.

Thirty minutes after the pressconference, a White Plains, New York, school bus full of kindergarten children ran off the road and burst into flames after its driver was shot by a sniper. All thirty children died.

Grant decided he was going to contact the Sanchez family.

Chapter 29

Grant's prior dealings with the Sanchezes had taught him that the family watched at least the Nogales border crossing and had some connection with the Casona del Patron bar in Nogales, Sonora. His best guess was that he would be on their watch list.

Grant came through the border turnstiles into Mexico at the DeConcini Port of Entry. He stepped to the side and looked around. In a doorway about fifty feet away sat two men in lawn chairs who were watching people as they came through the turnstiles. One of the men had a camera with a telephoto lens in his lap, and the other had some kind of a notebook open on his lap. These men had to be the Sanchez spotters.

Grant walked straight at them. The man on the left put his hand under his shirt where he probably had a gun. *"¿Hablan inglés, señores?"* Grant asked.

"Yes," said the man on the right. "What do you want?"

"I want to see Ramon Sanchez," Grant said while watching the man on the left.

"We do not know such a man," said the man on the right.

Grant knew it was not going to be easy, so he said, "I will be in the Casona del Patron courtyard," and walked away.

Grant threaded his way along the chaotic sidewalks crowded with tourists, beggars, flea-bitten dogs, and shills for the little shops selling souvenirs to the tourists. There were lots of dark, cool-looking bars with tubs of beer and ice on the long wooden bars.

The Casona del Patron was across a busy street which served as a de facto divider of the tourist area from the town proper. He passed through the dimly lit high-ceilinged front room with a flat panel screen above the bar, down a narrow hallway, and out onto a brick patio. Under the shade of a giant sycamore tree, tables were set up in front of a small stage upon which a guitar player was strumming a Mexican tune. Grant went to the stone bar in the corner and ordered a Corona with a wedge of lime and settled in at a small side table to wait. With a nod to Wild Bill Hickok, he put his back to the wall.

As the sun drifted lower, the shadows on the patio deepened. The walls surrounding the courtyard were made of brick covered with plaster which had been chipping off for years. A decorator would give her soul to produce this look in an artist's loft. The guitar music was soothing, and Grant began to relax with his second beer.

His reverie was broken by the arrival of a man with a mechanical right arm, at the end of which was a clawlike hand.

"Señor Meredith?" he asked.

"Sí," Grant replied.

"Be here tomorrow at 2 p.m." The man's English was flawless. "Señor Sanchez will see you then."

Chapter 30

Grant spent the night in Nogales, Arizona, at a Motel 6 and was back at the Casona del Patron at 2 p.m. the next day. The man with the mechanical arm arrived on time and escorted him through the opening in the back wall and into a dark blue minivan with heavily tinted windows. Two men were in the front seats and two more in the back. Grant sat in the middle row. As the door closed, his arms were pinned to his sides, and a black cloth hood was pulled roughly over his head. His hands were secured to something with plastic restraints. No one said anything.

As the van bumped along, Grant started to sweat. Maybe he had made a mistake. Maybe a fatal one. He was certainly not a coward, but he didn't consider himself a superhero either. He had planned to be sitting across a table from Ramon Sanchez on the comfortable tree-shaded patio of Casona del Patron. Instead, he was completely at the mercy of the most ruthless family in Mexico. What had he been thinking when he came across the border? The question answered itself.

About fifteen minutes later, the van pulled to a stop. Grant's hands were released. He was pulled from the van with the hood still in place, marched thirty paces, and pushed into what he thought was a helicopter. His hands were again secured with plastic restraints, and a few moments later they were airborne.

Grant's best guess was that they had been flying for less than an hour when he felt the craft descend. His restraints were removed, and he was pulled from the copter, marched under the blades, and led away from the rotary wash. The hood was jerked from his head. He could feel the sun beating down on him as he was momentarily blinded by the incredibly bright concrete landing area.

As Grant blinked his way to eyesight, he could not believe what was in front of him. There stood Boots Sanchez, hands on hips. Her five foot eight inch hourglass figure was crowned with lustrous shoulder-length wavy black hair. She was dressed in an aquamarine camisole, white jeans and tan ostrich boots. Her ebony eyes were frankly appraising him. At that moment he knew what a horse must feel like at the sale barn.

"Well, well … I have heard so much about you, I just had to see for myself," said Boots as she raked Grant up and down with her eyes. While he had seen Boots before, she had never seen him.

Grant stood there in jeans, cowboy boots, and a white linen shirt with the hot Mexican sun beating down on him and had no idea what to say.

"Turn around," she said.

When Grant did not move, the men on either side of him spun him roughly around.

"*Muy bien*," she murmured almost to herself. "I like a man with a good ass in tight jeans." Then she spoke up. "Uncuff him and load him up."

Boots drove the Jeep Wrangler, which had no top or doors. Grant had the passenger seat, and two men were in the backseat. One held a Glock easily in his lap pointed at Grant. A quarter of a mile later, guards in white wearing pistol belts waved them through the wall which surrounded the biggest hacienda Grant had ever seen. They got out of the Jeep, and Boots led him up the front steps into the shade and around the veranda to French doors which opened into the library.

Seated at a large desk, dressed in a light brown linen shirt, was Ramon Sanchez. His black hair gleamed. He was smoking a cigar and watching Grant with a blank expression as Boots led him in front of the desk. She disappeared behind Grant and left him facing Ramon, who continued to smoke and study him. The room had a tile floor and was dimly lit, with dark shadows in the corners to both sides. Grant did not look around but stood watching the other man.

After what seemed like an eternity, Ramon nodded slightly and leaned back in the desk chair as if it was just another day at the office.

"You wanted to see me, Mr. Meredith," he said.

"Yes, I have come to ask for your help, since you are a US citizen, "Grant said.

Ramon leaned forward with his elbows on the desk, fingers interlaced. He did not ask Grant to sit down.

"I am also a Mexican citizen, Mr. Meredith, and have several other passports. What do you want?"

"I am sure you know that the United States is under siege by terrorists. I want to follow their trail back to their sponsors. I consider it likely that they entered the US from Mexico. I know what your family does, and I hoped you would help me verify that they crossed from Mexico. Perhaps you might even identify them."

Ramon's expression did not change. He picked up his cigar and drew on it thoughtfully. "What makes you think I would know anything about a couple of terrorists?" he asked.

"There are at least ninety individuals involved, maybe more. I think they came from a variety of countries, but all are Muslim. If such a large group crossed the border, I think you are likely to know about it and may have helped them. I would like to think you did not know at the time that they were terrorists."

Ramon sat smoking and said nothing. He just looked at Grant with a blank expression.

"They are murdering little children in their school yards, for Christ sakes," Grant exploded. "Have you no humanity?"

Ramon's expression did not change. He examined the tip of his cigar. "Tell me, Mr. Meredith, have no children been killed in Iraq, Palestine, Bosnia, and other countries in which you Americans have intervened? Historically speaking, did you not slaughter Native American women and children? Has your mighty army intervened in Africa to stop the slaughter of children? What is so special about your children?" Ramon said all this while contemplating the tip of his cigar.

Grant was not expecting such a response.

Ramon did not wait for him to speak. "Your answers are collateral damage, retaliation, and your army only acts in your national interests. Most unsatisfying answers, don't you think?"

Grant started to speak, but Ramon held up his hand to silence him. "Don't bother. I know nothing of these terrorists. You will stay the night while I make some inquiries. Margarita will show you to your room."

He opened a file folder on his desk. Grant was dismissed. Boots glided back in, took his arm, and led him from the library.

Carlos Sanchez rose from a comfortable leather reading chair in a dark corner of the library with a brandy snifter in his hand. As he approached the desk, Ramon stood and moved around the desk to one of the guest chairs, while Carlos reached into the humidor on the desk and removed a fresh Cohiba cigar. He said nothing until he had clipped the cigar, lit it, and settled into the desk chair with easy familiarity. After a sip of brandy, he asked, "Well, my son, what do you think about this man?"

"We deny everything," said Ramon. "We cannot be sure whether he is here on his own or on behalf of the American government, so we send him back to the States."

"I don't like this American," said Carlos. "He cost us a small fortune when our cocaine distribution channel was disrupted, thanks to his meddling. If we hadn't had a contingency distribution method in place, it could have cost us even more. I think he should disappear."

Ramon raised his hands and said, "Father, if the American government sent him here, they will cause us a lot of trouble if he disappears. Hector will be here very early tomorrow; let's wait and ask him."

Carlos drew on his cigar and slowly expelled the smoke toward the ceiling where the exhaust system removed it from the room. He took a sip of brandy, set the glass aside, and stood up.

"All right, we will confer with Hector."

Chapter 31

Boots led Grant from the library onto the veranda. As they circled the hacienda without talking, she held his arm against her breast. Grant was enveloped in the scent of her perfume. When they reached a door, she stopped and turned to him, rubbing her breast across his arm. She stood very close.

"This is your room," she said, and her quiet voice had a husky edge. "There are beverages and a light supper on the sideboard. Use the pool if you wish, but it is best if you do not wander around unescorted." Then she turned and walked away.

For a moment, Grant followed the sway of her hips. *Speaking of an ass that looks great in tight jeans.*

Grant's room was the size of three normal bedrooms. There was a high king-size bed with a canopy. Along the left wall of the room was a sideboard with liquors, ice, fruit, bottled water, cold cuts, and bread. The room had a tile floor, high ceilings, and a seating area on the right surrounding a television set. A door beyond it led to the bathroom.

He hadn't eaten since breakfast but wasn't particularly hungry. He poured some Patron Silver tequila over ice and squeezed some lime over it. Very smooth. He could feel the tension caused by his transportation and meeting with Ramon start to ease. They might not help, but at least they weren't going to kill him. As the tension eased, exhaustion set in. He watched the sun slip below the horizon as he sipped his third tequila. He should have stopped after two brought a mellow glow, but he didn't.

After the third tequila, Grant knew that he should eat something, or he would regret it in the morning. It was still hot, probably well over ninety degrees. He opened a drawer in the dresser and saw a swimsuit. Why not? It would help clear his head, and Boots had said it was okay to use the pool. The underwater lights were on, and the pool looked very inviting.

Grant had been in the pool about ten minutes when the underwater lights went dark, leaving only a few down lamps in the grass. The perfect silhouette of a woman appeared at the far end of the pool; it was Boots. She dove in and slowly swam toward him underwater in a classic breaststroke. She surfaced in front of him. She was naked.

She stood so close to him that her breasts almost touched his bare chest. She put her hands on his waist and said so softly that he almost couldn't hear, "I thought you might like some company."

Grant, whose head was fuzzy from the tequila, didn't know what to say. Boots wrapped her legs around his waist and leaned back in the water with her breasts just above the surface. She reached for his hands and put them on her breasts. Without thinking, he began to gently massage her nipples, which hardened almost immediately. A low moan came from Boots.

Through the tequila fog, Grant saw a light come on in the library. He unhooked her legs and turned in the pool, saying in a choked voice, "I've got to go."

As he moved away, she pulled him back to her by the waistband of his swim trunks and pressed herself against his back. When he didn't resist, she slipped his trunks down and began to massage his cock. Despite the three tequilas, it responded instantly.

Suddenly she was in front of him, pulling him by the hand up the steps and out of the pool. She led him quickly across the grass and into his room, both of them still streaming water from the pool. She pushed him down on the bed and climbed on top of him.

Grant awoke some time later, alone, in a tangle of damp sheets. He had a hint of a headache and was surrounded by the smell of a woman who was not there.

Chapter 32

The next morning, Boots arrived as Grant finished getting dressed. Her timing was impeccable. She walked in as he buttoned the last button on his shirt. His first thought was that there must be a surveillance camera in the room. His second thought was how stunning she looked in very short white shorts, a white scoop-neck peasant blouse, and strappy low-heeled sandals. His third thought caused his cock to grow firm.

"Come with me; breakfast is ready," she said with a wicked smile.

They walked along the veranda past the library and down three steps toward the pool. Grant kept his head still, but his eyes swept the deck for any sign of his swim trunks. Thank God they weren't floating in the water.

They walked along the deck toward a large cabana at the far end where a man and a woman were seated under an arbor covered with red bougainvilleas with their backs to them. As they approached the table, the man reached over and squeezed the woman's thigh.

As Grant and Boots rounded the table, she took his arm in a very possessive manner and said gaily, "Here we are. Hector, this is Grant Meredith."

Hector Sanchez stood and held out his hand. "Good morning, Mr. Meredith. I am pleased you could join us."

Grant took his hand reluctantly and looked down at the woman. It was as if his lungs had collapsed. He could not inhale or exhale. There sat Stephanie Chambers outfitted in a beautiful yellow sundress, with her hair drawn back into a ponytail showing off big gold hoop earrings. Her eyes widened, and her mouth opened as she looked from him to Boots and back again. Boots's hand slid down his arm, and she took hold of his hand before saying, "Grant, I am sure you remember Stephanie."

Grant looked at Boots whose ebony eyes were glowing with amusement. She had an impish smile on her face.

Hector looked from Grant to Stephanie and back and then smiled.

"Excuse me, Mr. Meredith," said Hector graciously. "I didn't make the connection at first. Please sit down and have some breakfast."

Beyond the perfunctory "good to see you again" and "how are you?" neither Stephanie nor Grant said very much during the meal. Hector conducted most of the conversation in a monologue about the history of the ranch. Whenever Grant looked at Stephanie, she averted her gaze. As he gradually regained his composure, it occurred to him that Stephanie seemed embarrassed.

Without warning, Hector changed the subject.

"Did you know, Mr. Meredith, that Thomas Jefferson once said, 'We are pointing the way to struggling nations who wish, like us, to emerge from their tyrannies'?"

"No, President Sanchez, I did not," Grant said, wondering where this was going.

"My reading of history tells me that the United States was founded on the concept that God, not the English or French, has given men—excuse me, ladies—certain natural rights which are to be enjoyed by all people regardless of their nationality, color, or history.

"The idea of natural rights, a product of the Age of Enlightenment, was not new, but the United States was the first country to base its government on those ideas.

"Given what Jefferson said, it seems to me that the Bush Doctrine is a simple extension of the principles upon which your country was founded." Hector gave him a probing look. "What do you think?"

Grant didn't know what to think. He was somewhere in Mexico, where he had been brought with a hood over his head. He had a hangover. He was sitting at a table next to a woman he knew only by reputation, who had sexually exhausted him last night. Across the table were the president of Mexico and the woman who had killed his brother; he had mixed emotions about her, to say the least. Hector's question was more suited to a graduate course in political philosophy than this motley gathering. Christ, Grant didn't know what to think.

"Mr. President, I think President Bush was simply articulating a willingness to help people who want to help themselves," Grant said without much conviction.

Hector cut a piece of melon and chewed it thoroughly while he studied Grant with a direct, unblinking gaze. Grant felt like a bug under a microscope.

Hector continued, "Tell me, Mr. Meredith, is there a consensus in the world that peace is better than war?"

This was easy. "Of course."

"Then please explain the American invasion of Iraq, the Russian invasion of Georgia, or the Israeli invasion of Lebanon. Each of these wars served as an instrument of foreign policy."

Grant's head was beginning to hurt. He felt like a bumbling college freshman transported into a graduate political science course. "Well, President Sanchez, I don't think I'm the one to answer that."

The corners of Hector's mouth turned up in what seemed to be a self-satisfied smile or even a smirk. "Tell me this, Mr. Meredith, is democracy always a better form of government than any other?"

A small light went on in the back of Grant's brain. Hector was trying to intellectually humiliate him. Why? Grant didn't even know the man. He had a flash of intuition; he was showing Stephanie that Grant was an intellectual lightweight. Rather than beat Grant up to prove he was the better man, he was trying to show that Grant was a moron. Grant was between the proverbial rock and hard place. He could not afford to irritate a man who could have him killed with a snap of his fingers; at the same time, he was unprepared for this type of discussion. He had to tread very lightly.

"We Americans certainly think so. This is a beautiful hacienda," Grant said, trying to change the subject.

"Thank you. Think of China. The government has pulled three hundred million Chinese out of poverty in a single generation, in a society where the government controls economic growth at the expense of political freedom. I suggest to you that political legitimacy is a function of performance, not just a process."

Grant was saved by Ramon Sanchez, who appeared at his side and said, "Mr. Meredith, I have made inquiries, and I am sorry to tell you that I could obtain no information concerning those who are terrorizing the United States.

"Margarita, if you will take Mr. Meredith to the helicopter immediately, they are ready to return him to Nogales."

Grant could only nod at Stephanie as he excused himself. Boots once again possessively took his arm as they left the table.

They were alone in the jeep for the short ride to the landing pad. When they got out, she put her hands on his cheeks and kissed him deeply. Then she pushed him gently toward the helicopter saying, "Come again, cowboy." Then she giggled at her own joke.

———————

As Grant and Boots disappeared from view, Hector turned to Stephanie with a smile tugging at the corners of his mouth and put his hand on hers. "Well … well, do you think Margarita has made a new conquest?"

Stephanie withdrew her hand and took a sip of water. The words rushed out as she stood up. "She can fuck whoever she wants. Excuse me; I have to go to the bathroom."

She felt his eyes on her as she strode purposefully to the cabana bathroom and disappeared inside.

She moistened a towel and pressed it to the back of her neck as she stood staring at herself in the mirror. She was still standing there when Boots came in looking like the proverbial cat that swallowed the canary.

"Now, that was what I call fun," she chuckled. "That poor guy doesn't know which end is up. I bet he finds a reason to come back very, very soon."

She looked at Stephanie, who was still staring at herself in the mirror. "Oh, come on, don't be jealous. You're still my number one girl," she laughed.

Stephanie turned and left without saying anything. As she walked slowly back to the hacienda, she was obsessed with an image of Grant on top of Boots, humping away; Boots was looking at Stephanie over his shoulder, laughing. Her vision clouded with tears, and she stumbled on the first step leading from the pool and almost fell. She rushed up the steps, pushing an astonished Hector out of the way, fled to her room, and flopped down on the bed, sobbing uncontrollably.

The BlackRock plane lifted off from the Tucson airport on the way to Durango. Grant was alone with his third Coors Light, staring out the window at nothing. *Stephanie ... Boots ... terrorists ... the*

Sanchez family ... My God, what a mess. He wanted to focus on what he could do to help stop the terrorist attacks, but his mind kept wandering back to Boots in the pool—her legs wrapped around his waist, floating on her back with the water lapping around her breasts, her hair fanning out around her head, her full lips parted. Grant thought about what they had done in bed, and he was as hard as a high school quarterback with the head cheerleader.

Then the image of Boots was replaced by Stephanie and her expression of stunned astonishment when she saw him standing there with Boots. He still could not get a handle on how he felt about Stephanie. He'd been sure he had put her out of his mind. She had murdered his brother and run off with a Mexican drug lord cum politician. Within a few weeks, Grant's love life—no, his sex life revolved around Cat Rollins. He was embarrassed that Stephanie must realize he had been with Boots. What did she think of him now? What did he think of himself?

Tommy met him at the airport. On the way back to the ranch, his ceaseless chatter about the terrorist attacks, that were being reported nonstop on television and radio, put a hold on Grant's pitiful attempt at self-analysis. By the time they reached the ranch, Grant had decided to call Homer Johnson and suggest that BlackRock volunteer to assist law enforcement wherever possible

Chapter 33

Ed Bailey sat staring at the computer screen on his desk. It was 3 a.m. in Washington and midnight on the West Coast. There had not been a terrorist incident for an hour.

His phone rang. He sighed and picked it up.

"Ed, this is Jorge Dias in LA. It may not be related to all of this terrorism, but the local cops just got a report that Savannah Summers's Bentley was found on Camden Drive in Beverly Hills. It looks like the car was forced off the road, and the driver's door was open. The cops are so busy here that there is no one to follow up on it. Should we do anything?"

Bailey's frustration boiled over. "Look, Jorge, it's three in the morning here. This country is under terrorist attack. Savannah Summers's whereabouts are certainly not a national security issue. Leave it to the locals. Hell, leave it to the paparazzi."

He stumbled across the room to his sofa and flopped down for a few minutes of rest.

The ringing telephone startled him from sleep. He looked at his watch. It was 5:30 a.m. He stumbled across the room, snatched up the phone, and punched the blinking light. "Bailey," he growled.

"Ed, this is Keith. You aren't going to believe this. The cops just found Adam Callous, the hedge fund guy, hanging from the statute of Andrew Jackson in Lafayette Park, right across from the White House. There was a piece of cardboard stuck to his chest with an ice pick. Written on the cardboard was an Internet address."

Bailey was instantly alert. "Get the Secret Service there immediately, and quarantine the area and anyone who has seen or heard about this. What is the address?"

Keith gave it to him, and Bailey hung up. He turned to his computer and tentatively typed in the address.

When Bailey saw the severed head of Savannah Summers being held aloft by a woman wearing a ski mask, he gagged. To the right of the picture was the following message:

> The United States was previously warned to withdraw all of its armed forces from foreign soil or continue to face the consequences. Your government has failed to agree to our requirements. Hundreds of you have died since the first request was ignored. If your government fails to honor our prior request within 24 hours, one of many nuclear weapons under our control will be detonated in your country, killing hundreds of thousands of you. If your government does not agree to pull its troops back another nuclear weapon will be detonated and so on until the troops come home

to you. While your government makes up its mind, the carnage will continue.

All of this can be avoided if you will simply bring your troops home to your own country and leave the rest of the world alone. If you refuse, your way of life is over.

The Rest of the World

Oh, my God, thought Bailey as he rushed to the War Room.

Chapter 34

Janet Sampson's second press conference was scheduled to take place in one hour. She sat alone in the Oval Office trying to digest what had happened in the Situation Room, more than ever the nerve center of the free world. As the reports had come in, the room had gotten quieter and quieter.

The latest terrorist demand had hit the airwaves before 6 a.m. She had been unable to shut down access to the Internet site, and in any event, it was too late. The reports had started coming in by 7 a.m.

Public schools and universities were closed.

Commercial airlines had shut down.

People were not showing up for work.

There were queues outside grocery stores and banks.

Long lines of cars were streaming out of major cities.

The stock exchanges were not going to open.

Private airports were chaotic with demands from owners to get their planes in the air.

Yacht harbors were emptying.

There were reports of sporadic looting.

Police were being inundated with major increases in criminal activity.

Bus, subway, and rail systems were grinding to a halt without employees on duty.

By 7:45, President Sampson had no choice. She ordered all but military airplanes to be grounded. All rail traffic was to be halted, and she closed the borders. No one was leaving the country, and no one was coming in.

By 8:30 demonstrators were outside the White House gates with hastily made signs, chanting, "Bring our troops home, *now*."

Her advisers, usually so confident, were of little help. The ones who wanted to call the terrorists' bluff and never give in also wanted to know when they would be moved to a secure facility. They were moving their families away from Washington. The ones who wanted to give in to the demand argued that they could always send the troops back after the crisis passed. The political advisers were busy polling but having a hard time because phone lines were jammed.

At 9:15 she turned on Fox News. The program was being broadcast from St. Louis. Sampson guessed that the Washington and New York studios were too understaffed to air a program. Apparently the talking heads were also on the run. However, the program switched to an interview being conducted with one of the demonstrators outside the White House.

The blond young female reporter was breathlessly questioning an elderly woman demonstrator with gray hair dressed in jeans and a white T-shirt.

"What brings you here today?" gasped the reporter.

"My son-in-law was killed in the explosion at the Mormon Tabernacle. My daughter is heading for the mountains with her children along with God knows how many others. Someone has to stop this madness. We don't need to be the world's policemen; just look at what it has gotten us. President Sampson is a woman; she must know there has been enough innocent death. For me, it is not about giving in to terrorists, it is about protecting our families. It's time to realize we cannot do it all."

President Sampson switched off the television.

At 9:30 a.m. she called in her press secretary and cancelled the news conference. Instead, she planned to address the nation from the White House before the Secret Service moved her to a new facility that would be secure from a nuclear bomb.

Sampson sat at her desk with her hands folded and stared at the vase of flowers on the corner of her desk—a feminine touch to a historically masculine room. The irony of a woman president making this decision was not lost on her. She bowed her head and prayed. When she raised her head, the first thought that came into her mind was what the Iranian mullah had said during an interview with Lisa O'Brien on PBS.

"Your leaders want to bring your freedom to Islamic society. We don't want freedom. The difference between Muslims and the West is that we are controlled by God's laws, which haven't changed for 1,400 years. Your laws change with your leaders."

That comment expressed the fundamental tension between the United States and Islam. Each side held itself to be morally superior to the other.

She had twenty hours left to decide, but in the meantime, what was she going to say to the American people?

She knew the Scripture of John 14:6 wherein Jesus said, "I am the way, the truth, and the life. No one comes to the Father except through Me."

Janet Sampson was a deeply religious person, although she was a doctor. She had seen too much that could not be explained. Her belief in God was unshakable. She opened the top right-hand drawer of her desk and removed a well-worn Bible. She turned without hesitation to Matthew 5:38 and 39: "You have heard that it was said, 'An eye for an eye, and a tooth for a tooth.' But I tell you, do not resist an evil person. If someone strikes you on the right cheek, turn to him the other also ..."

Was this a test of her faith?

Then she remembered Meredith's comment. Did this have anything at all to do with religion? Was she just assuming it was Muslim extremists? What if the impetus behind it all was political? Did that make a difference?

There was no practical way to retaliate or threaten Muslim extremists who were essentially stateless; however, if these terrorist activities were sponsored by a country, maybe there was a way to bring things to an end.

She picked up her phone and said, "Please get Mike O'Brien in here immediately."

Chapter 35

Mike O'Brien, husband of Lisa O'Brien, the PBS reporter, was President Sampson's adviser without a title. He was an iconoclastic former political science professor at Arizona State University who had been denied tenure after publishing a book entitled *American Exceptionalism and Manifest Destiny in the Twenty-First Century,* which argued that the United States should annex Mexico and Canada. Sampson had brought him into the White House to provoke unorthodox thought. It was his job to tell her the emperor had no clothes.

O'Brien stood well over six feet tall and spent an hour a day in the White House gym. He rode a Harley Davidson motorcycle to work and always dressed in monochromatic black. With spiky moussed black hair, heavy black-framed glasses, and cowboy boots, he cut quite a figure around the White House.

O'Brien entered the Oval Office with a mug of coffee. He crossed immediately to the sofa opposite the president's desk, settled in, pushed his glasses onto the top of his head, said, "You rang, Madame President?" and languidly took a sip of coffee.

Absolutely no one behaved this way around the president. Truth be told, she relished her time with O'Brien because he pulled her feet back to earth. Today he seemed perfectly at ease, while she and everyone else around her were on the edge of panic.

She rose from her desk chair and sat down across from O'Brien. "Mike, the intel people think the bomb threat is credible. Do I call the terrorists' bluff or give in?

"Hell, Janet, why don't you just find the bombs?" said O'Brien, as if haggling over a pizza topping.

"Be serious, Mike. We only have twenty hours, and I have to tell the people something this morning." She heaved a resigned sigh.

"I am serious. Jack Bauer did it on that TV program." O'Brien didn't bother to squelch his smile. "Seriously, think about it: all these other incidents, as bad as they are, are intended to occupy your resources so you can't find the bombs. You have to refocus on the bombs. Just tell people that you have decided to pull our troops back beginning in seventy-two hours, unless there are additional attacks inside the United States. The terrorism should stop, and you have some breathing room to find the bombs."

"What if we don't find the bombs?" asked President Sampson.

"The first question to answer is, are they bluffing? The second question is, what are the consequences of a wrong decision?

"If you call their bluff, and you are right, are you a hero? I don't think so. The country is in chaos without the bombs. If you are wrong, and the bombs go off, there will be more death, more chaos, and areas of the country made uninhabitable.

"Either way, it will pass, and the larger question is not the existence of the bombs but what is going to happen to the freedom we enjoy in this country. George Bush was right about one thing: fight the terrorists where they are, not here. Unfortunately, they are here now, and more are likely to come unless we root them out abroad. How are we going to deal with this? How much of our freedom are we going to give up to protect ourselves at home? Wiretap everyone? Warrantless searches? Random roadblocks? Secret police? Soldiers with machine guns on every corner? Army patrols on the Mexican and Canadian borders? How safe is safe enough?

"In my opinion, appeasement will not work. Bring the troops home, and we lose the ability to fight the terrorists effectively overseas. Next, they will demand that we give fifty percent of our agricultural production to the undeveloped world. Then we must give up the navy. There will be no end to the demands. The bombs, the attacks going on now—all that is tragic, devastating; but the primary job of government is to protect our citizens for the long run. We are at war, and there has never been a war without casualties."

O'Brien drained his coffee cup, stood, and said, "Janet, you were elected to make the hard decisions. Remember, George Santayana said, 'Those who do not remember the past are condemned to repeat it.'" With that, he was out the door.

President Janet Sampson went back to her desk and stared at nothing. She had no children, no siblings; her husband was deceased. She was without family, so when she died, it was the end of her bloodline. Why should she care about the future? She cared for the same reason she'd become a doctor. She wanted to help people; she wanted to make them better. The main reason she agreed to run for office was to do her part to provide people with opportunities to be all they could be.

She slammed her palms on the desk, stood up, and muttered, "I'll be damned before I allow this country to stand for safety before freedom," as she strode purposefully to the door.

"Nancy, get Secretary Thomson up here. He's in the Situation Room."

Chapter 36

Robert A. Thomson, her Secretary of State, was a career diplomat. A Princeton graduate, he personified Henry Kissinger's realpolitik philosophy of foreign affairs. He believed diplomacy must be based on purely practical rather than ideological notions. With Thomson, there was no room for moralizing in foreign affairs. This was in stark contrast to the foreign policy of the Bush administration which had been dominated by neoconservatives and given rise to the Bush Doctrine and the concept that "freedom for others means safety for ourselves."

Thomson entered the Oval Office five minutes later. He was seventy-five years old with a full head of long gray hair draping his ears and the back of his collar. Wearing a tailored gray pinstriped suit, blue striped shirt with a white collar and cuffs, sporting bright gold cufflinks, and a muted red tie, he was an elegant man.

"Madame President," he said as he stood before her desk waiting to be asked to sit.

"Mr. Secretary, please sit," said President Sampson, sitting behind her desk. "What is your assessment of the situation?"

"In my opinion," he said, crossing his legs and tugging at the crease in his trousers, "we are confronted with the inevitable consequences of the Bush Doctrine. It is inconceivable to think that the United States could pursue a foreign policy designed to change the form of governments throughout the world without drawing a response. If we propose to export democracy to other nations, should we not expect existing governments and people with vested interests in those forms of government to respond? What we have here is a response that, in my opinion, is not rooted in Islamic extremism but in political opposition to our frank, unilateral policy of disrupting foreign governments. I think the terrorists are the instrument of one or more nation's foreign policy."

"But, Mr. Secretary, don't all people want freedom?" queried President Sampson.

"It all depends on the question. If you ask anyone anywhere, 'Do you want to be free?' of course they will say yes because the alternative is being a prisoner. The problem is democracy, not freedom. In the Middle East they look at the situation and ask if it is approved by religion or not. In tribal cultures, unwritten tribal law is much more important than national law. We seem to be incapable of understanding foreign cultures. It should not be a surprise that not everyone thinks like Americans."

"All right, assuming your analysis is correct, how do we deal with today's problem?"

"Much of our foreign military deployment is a relic of World War II and the Cold War. It serves no useful purpose today. We have been unable to withdraw from those commitments because of the negative economic impact withdrawal would cause on the host countries. I think there is an opportunity here to rid ourselves of outdated foreign deployments. Use this crisis to bring our troops home and develop a military based upon technology and rapid response. Let our future use of force be determined by the United Nations."

President Sampson got up, turned away from Secretary Thomson, and walked to the large window where she gazed at the gardens for a few moments. He was partially right. Much of the current deployment outside the Middle East was a relic of the Cold War. Withdrawal from the Middle East, however, was a different matter, and certainly she was not prepared to give up sovereignty to the United Nations.

"Mr. Secretary, it seems to me you are suggesting that we give in to the demands. You put a nice spin on it, but aren't you recommending appeasement? Didn't World War II teach us that you cannot appease madmen? Appeasement just feeds their appetite."

"With due respect, Madame President, the situations are not comparable," said Secretary Thomson. "America has the empire, not Iran or North Korea or Syria. We are threatening their governments, not the other way around."

Turning to face him, she said, "Secretary Thomson, if you are correct and these terrorist attacks represent a response from those who do not want us exporting democracy, who or what country is behind it?"

Secretary Thomson thought for only a moment. "I could speculate, but I won't. The situation is much too serious for that. A response, if any, must be based upon actual facts. As I understand it, we know about a Sudanese terrorist and a Philippine terrorist, but not one confirmed Saudi terrorist. I suspect that as more of these terrorists are captured or killed, we will find they come from many countries. I believe religious fervor has been harnessed for political purposes."

President Sampson dropped into her chair, sighed, and shook her head. "You may be right. We have some reason to believe that a very high Saudi government official is involved."

Secretary Thomson laced his fingers in front of him and patiently replied, "Assuming that is true, are you positive he is carrying out government policy? I don't think you are. Perhaps he and his conspirators are actually seeking to have the United States depose the monarchy, so they can install themselves in some sort of faux democracy. Perhaps some other government, Iran for example, is trying to get the United States out of the Middle East in order to preserve its form of government and has set up Saudi Arabia to appear responsible if their plan does not work. The bottom line is that you are not in a position to retaliate. Compromise is the only way to try and stop the slaughter."

A few days ago, President Sampson would not have felt comfortable challenging Secretary Thomson, but it was not a few days ago.

"I wonder whether you are being too shortsighted," said President Sampson. "Regardless of whether a government is using terrorists or the terrorists are acting on their own, if we give in, the terrorists essentially have our number: just claim to have a bomb and make demands. Your solution has the short-term benefit of perhaps avoiding an immediate slaughter of Americans, but in the long run I think we will see the same scenario again and again."

"Something like that has never happened before; there is no reason to think it will happen again. Madame President, if I may be blunt?" He drove on without allowing her to reply, "The twenty-first century will not be an ideological rerun of the past hundred years. Modernization has not brought homogenization to the United States; we are a diverse nation that is home to many different cultures and identities. The 'be like us' era is simply over. In my opinion, it is time for the United States to join the community of nations as an equal partner and give up on the idea that we can control the world."

As if on some secret signal, they both stood.

"Thank you for your input, Mr. Secretary."

Chapter 37

Carlos, Hector, and Ramon Sanchez sat in the library of the hacienda. The meeting had been called to decide which of their competitors to extradite to the United States for trial. The terrorist threat to explode nuclear bombs in the United States had disrupted the meeting.

"I didn't like this from the beginning," said Ramon. "If those bombs go off, there is going to be hell to pay."

"Take it easy, Ramon," said Hector in a soothing voice. "The Americans will be totally focused on the Muslims; we don't have anything to worry about. If they come to us, I will make some arrests and send them some coyotes. We are completely insulated from blame."

"That may be so," said Ramon, "but that's not what's bothering me. Look, I don't like the American government either. I can't stand their sense of moral superiority, their conviction they know what is best for other peoples and nations, when all they know is what is best for themselves. Having said that, for me the issue is the hundreds of thousands of people, many of whom are innocent Mexicans that we helped enter the United States, who will die if those bombs are detonated. I am perfectly willing to kill to protect and further our family business, but these terrorist murders and now the bomb threat go too far."

"Look, Ramon, if these terrorists have their way, it will get the United States to stop meddling in other countries," said Hector dismissively.

"For all your political intuition, I think you may be wrong. If the Americans do withdraw within their borders, the government is going to have to show that it can protect its people at home. I think one of the first things they may do is station those returning troops along our border.

"They will believe, even without proof, that the terrorists and the bombs crossed our border. Thanks to Meredith, they know about us but tolerate us. I think the whole organization is in jeopardy."

Carlos spoke at last. "You both have made good points. However, it is all water under the bridge. We may want to consider some damage control if things get too close to our coyotes."

"But Father," said Ramon, "if a bomb goes off in San Diego, Phoenix, El Paso, or any other border town, the radioactive fallout could be carried into Mexico, perhaps even here."

Carlos considered for almost a minute as his sons watched him without moving.

"That is possible, yes, but not very likely. They will probably pick larger cities such as Los Angeles, Chicago, New York, Washington."

This time it was Hector who spoke. "We have family in Los Angeles; what about them?"

Carlos stood and said, "True, this may not have been my best idea, but there is nothing we can do about it now. Let's deal with things we can do something about."

Chapter 38

Sher Tabrizi sat in a straight-backed chair facing a half-moon table around which sat the ruling mullahs of Iran. He had told them of the chaos into which the United States had descended and that he hoped a decision on withdrawal from the Middle East would come shortly. Tabrizi never thought that the United States would actually withdraw to within its own borders; however, he did think it highly likely that it would withdraw from the Middle East. The price of staying was just too high for the Americans to pay.

He had been watching the young mullah on the far left during his report and could see that he was troubled by what he heard. Now the mullah asked, "I understand that there are multiple nationalities involved in the attack force, but if the plan does not work and the Saudis turn on us, what is to keep the United States from retaliating against us?"

Tabrizi had been waiting for someone to focus on the downside, and he was ready.

"I have arranged to destroy the Saudis' credibility with the Americans. I recruited two Saudi Wahhabi martyrs and had them implanted with the same device that was used in those going to the United States, utilizing the same surgical technique. I sent them to Saudi Arabia to bungle an attempt to blow up BlackRock barracks there. When they were caught as planned, they gave up the name of the Saudi doctor who did the implants. I am sure BlackRock will share this information with their government. We have information that BlackRock interrogated the Saudi doctor, who gave them the name of Ali Alwaleed. If the Americans need someone to blame, we have given them the Saudis.

"I have created a no-lose situation for us. The Americans may withdraw from the Middle East, or they may retaliate against the Saudis, which would exponentially increase our influence and move us closer to molding the Middle East in our image. Finally, if the Saudis try to claim Iran was involved, they will have no credibility."

There were nods of approval from all the mullahs. The oldest of them spoke. "Sher, we appreciate your efforts for the true faith. We simply cannot continue to have the Muslim world dominated by infidels. Their way of life corrupts the religion and morality of our people. We can no longer allow them to flout God's law."

Another spoke. "It is clear that the so-called Bush Doctrine is a return to the Crusades in another form. The only difference is that the current pretext is democracy instead of Christianity. We must combat the new Crusaders with something greater than the petty sovereignties into which we were divided by the colonial powers. We will combat them with Islam, which is greater than any nation, tribe, or ethnic group. From a stable base in the Middle East, true believers will dominate the world, and we will have a truly just society based upon *sharia*."

Chapter 39

Ali Alwaleed had barely entered the Crown Prince's opulent office when the verbal assault began.

"Please tell me, most trusted adviser, what happened at the BlackRock barracks?" said the Crown Prince.

"Honestly, sire, I have no information whatsoever about the attempt to bomb the barracks. The good and bad news is that the perpetrators are dead."

The Crown Prince pounded his desk and lunged to his feet. "You idiot, we brought BlackRock here to protect us. You have spies everywhere. How can you know nothing about this?

"If this is not resolved immediately, it will jeopardize our plan against the Americans. We will end up with the blame. They will bomb us in a heartbeat and use it as an excuse to take our oil."

Alwaleed stood mute.

"Well, you moron, what are you going to do about this?" fumed the Crown Prince.

"I will do everything I can to find out, sire," said Ali.

"You surely will. You will get to the bottom of it within twenty-four hours and report to me. Now get out of here," said the Crown Prince with a wave of his hand.

Ali left the office, clearly grasping the precariousness of his position. He had been working directly for the Crown Prince for seven years, and he had never been talked to with such disrespect. He understood the anger, but still, his pride was deeply wounded.

Six hours later, Alwaleed walked slowly around the perimeter of the windowless ten-by-ten concrete room buried deep within the Buraiman prison. In the corners of the ceiling were powerful floodlights which could fill the little room with blinding brightness or murky shadows as needed for interrogation. Suspended naked from the ceiling, arms stretched overhead with his feet just inches above a drain in the floor, was Dr. Ali Al-Fulani. He was beyond moaning. The doctor's back was crisscrossed with oozing cuts inflicted by the cat-o'-nine-tails held by the impassive guard. Blood ran down the back of his legs and dripped off his heels into the drain. There was a hose outlet on the wall with a hose curled neatly below it.

"Tell me again, Al-Fulani, every word you spoke to the Americans," said Alwaleed in a soft voice. A low rattling sound escaped from the doctor's lips. He wasn't dead, but he would be of little use for quite a while. Alwaleed left the room without a word to the guards.

The Americans knew about the head implants and would easily connect Al-Fulani's activities to the ongoing terrorist attacks in their country. Although Al-Fulani did not admit it, Alwaleed was certain that he had told the Americans that he had acted on Alwaleed's orders. It was only a matter of time until they came calling. The Iranians must have done this. The North Koreans could not have recruited Muslims to martyr themselves, and he did not think they had the medical ability to implant the devices. It had to be the Iranians. Tabrizi had undoubtedly hatched the plan to cover Iranian involvement and put the blame on the Saudis.

Ali needed a plan, and he needed it quick. He had to save himself and protect the Kingdom. At the very least he had to save himself. He could protect himself from the Crown Prince by arranging for him to have a fatal accident, but that would not help him with the Americans, and he might need support from the Crown Prince.

He could run but not for long, unless he headed for Pakistan's tribal areas. Live like a tribesman? No, that would not do.

He could approach the Americans and negotiate for a pardon if he gave up the plan. He did know the radio frequencies to detonate the head bombs in his agents, but he did not know where the nuclear bombs were or how they would be detonated. He could give up the North Koreans, but they would just deny involvement, and he had no proof. If the bombs went off, the best he could hope for was a life sentence in an American prison.

Maybe he could work with the Crown Prince by having the prince give him up to the Americans. He would say that the Iranians had bribed him to recruit the terrorists and have the implants inserted. Their goal was to have the Americans overthrow the Saudi monarchy so they could step into the void and control the oil. No, that wouldn't work; the Americans would never believe the Shiite Iranians could dominate Sunni Saudi Arabia.

Maybe he could say he was trying to use the Americans to topple the monarchy, and he and a few others would take over with Iranian help.

Whatever story he came up with would only work if he could count on the Americans not to torture him or use drugs in the interrogation process. Could he trust the Americans after what was happening to their country at his instigation, regardless of the reason? He would probably end up in a dark hole while he could be useful, and then his cremated remains would disappear.

Death. He could fake his own death and run. The only question was whether to involve the Crown Prince in the charade. The Crown Prince could claim that after investigating the matter, he had discovered a plot to bring down the monarchy and had immediately executed the doctor and Alwaleed along with other plotters. The Americans could believe what they wanted, but the Crown Prince would be safe. The only problem with this plan was that the Crown Prince would be safer if Alwaleed was really dead. He would surely not want to risk Alwaleed coming back to life and exposing the subterfuge.

Alwaleed thought some more. He could arrange for a Brazilian plastic surgeon to come to Dubai and alter his features. He already had hidden overseas bank accounts that he could access. The safest course would be to fake his own death, change his appearance, and run. The Crown Prince could pick up the pieces.

Alwaleed shook his head. He would continue to think about this.

Chapter 40

President Janet Sampson was putting the finishing touches on her speech when Nancy buzzed to inform her that former President Johnson was on the line.

"Hello, Homer. I don't mean to be rude, but please make this quick," said President Sampson.

"Madam President, I am calling to offer the assistance of BlackRock in any way possible. You know the company and what we can accomplish, so just give us the word."

"Thank you," said President Sampson. "As you know, we can use all the help we can get. Have your people contact DHS for an assignment. I do have a special idea for Grant Meredith's help. I think it a plausible theory that some or all of the terrorists and perhaps the bombs entered this county from Mexico. Meredith is familiar with the Sanchez family and could hit the ground running on this possibility. Let's have him investigate this Sanchez/border idea and see if it leads to any useful information."

She heard a change in Johnson's voice. "I'll get him on it immediately."

Two hours later President Sampson was behind her desk in the Oval Office, giving her televised address: "My fellow Americans,

I come before you with an indescribable sadness in my heart. My prayers and the prayers of the nation go out to all who have lost loved ones in these despicable terrorist attacks.

"Our nation is under attack by unknown forces that care nothing about innocent human life. Stateless forces that make it impossible for us to retaliate against another country to bring hostilities to an end. Random vicious attacks against our citizens are intolerable, but I cannot allow a nuclear explosion in our midst if I have the power to prevent it.

"I have received advice from my staff, the military, and members of Congress. It is fair to say that there was no unanimity of opinion as to the proper course of action. I will not discuss the various opinions and options that our country has for dealing with this situation. Most are obvious, and the news media, elected officials, and others have expressed and will continue to express opinions.

"In our system of government, under these unique circumstances, it falls to the president to make a decision, not offer an opinion.

"I must balance protecting those at home with protecting those abroad. A soldier chooses to put his or her life on the line to protect the country and the helpless. An innocent civilian does not. I believe that it is my job to protect the country and the innocent.

"For these reasons, I have ordered the Secretary of Defense to begin withdrawal of our armed forces from South Korea and Japan forthwith. I have also requested a plan outlining how to withdraw the rest of our forces from around the world as soon as possible. If there is one more terrorist attack in the United States, I will have the forces from South Korea and Japan redeployed throughout the Middle East and will exercise no mercy in finding those who sent terrorists to our country.

"Thank you, and good night."

She switched off the mike, stood, and thought: *Now I have some time to find those bombs.*

Later the president sat alone in her private room off the Oval Office watching a Fox News panel discuss her speech. Each member of the panel was in a different location.

A noted columnist, Susan Klinger, said, "President Sampson has made the worst blunder possible under the circumstances. She doesn't know whether there are bombs here. By giving in now, she opens the door to more of the same. The Congress should rise up and impeach her forthwith …"

She was interrupted by another panel member. "Susan, I live in New York but am at our summer home in Maine. Where are you?"

"Why … I am in Montana. Why do you ask?"

"Isn't it true you are there to protect your family and yourself from a possible nuclear explosion?"

"Well …"

"You have the option of getting out of harm's way, probably, but millions of Americans do not. You are willing to risk the lives of others but not your own and your family's. With nothing at risk, your opinion is worthless."

The panel moderator said, "Fox News has determined that 95 percent of the members of Congress are no longer in Washington. We report, you decide."

President Sampson turned off the television. It would all be more of the same.

Chapter 41

Ali Alwaleed listened to the President Sampson's speech on satellite television. Sampson was getting good advice from someone. If the attacks continued, they had no chance of achieving their objective; but stopping the attacks took the pressure off the Americans and gave them time to find the bombs. Given the Americans' eavesdropping capability, there was no safe way to communicate with Tabrizi or Ri. He did not believe for a minute that the Americans would pay any attention to warrant requirements in the current circumstances. He would have to make the decision himself.

Before sending his agents to America, Alwaleed had set up a special Web site named ChristiansRUS.org. He filled the site with Southern Baptist propaganda and linked to a multitude of fundamentalist Christian Web sites. In the top corner of the home page was a section for current events. This section changed every day and appeared innocuous to the casual observer. In fact, the material that appeared there contained coded messages for his agents. Today's message was to stop attacks until further notice, keep a low profile, and avoid raising suspicions.

After posting the message, Alwaleed tuned to Fox News, where the Freebird & Crowe program was on. Alan Freebird and Rush Crowe had a very successful liberal/conservative news program which was followed by millions of viewers. They were in the process of interviewing the junior senator from New York, Abigail Norton.

Rush Crowe was talking. "Here we are, Senator, the 'ticking time bomb' scenario for real. Given that the anti-torture legislation passed by Congress has no exception for this 'ticking time bomb' scenario, what options does the president have if we capture someone who may know where the bomb is located?"

Senator Norton shook her head sadly. "Well, Rush, as I have said, there should have been an exception in the statute giving the president lawful authority for torture in some cases; but the statute contains no exception."

"Excuse me, Senator, during your Columbia University debate in last year's senatorial race, the moderator asked you the following question: 'We know there is a bomb about to go off, and we have three days, and we know this guy knows where it is. Should there be a presidential exception to allow torture in that kind of situation?'

"You responded as follows: 'As a matter of policy it cannot be American policy, period.'"

"I said no such thing," she snapped.

Crowe then played a tape of the question and answer from the debate.

Alwaleed chuckled to himself as the senator jerked in her chair like she had been slapped. He turned to CNBC where Larry

Lancaster was interviewing the dean of the University of Virginia School of Law. The dean was speaking.

"I think the action, so to speak, is in the definition of torture. If one acts to inflict pain and death for no purpose other than the desire to inflict pain and death, that is surely torture.

"However, if one is inflicting physical duress on someone to gather intelligence, the object is not pain and death for its own sake but to produce extreme fear and anxiety, which tends to break down defenses. There is a clear difference."

"Really," said Lancaster, "are you saying that torture is defined by the intentions of the torturer, not what is done to the victim?"

"Yes, that makes as much sense as defining torture by the impact of the conduct on the prisoner's mental state," replied the Dean.

Alwaleed turned off the television and shook his head. He would never understand why, in the name of Allah, the Americans allowed lawyers to run everything. It was simple. If you needed information, and someone else had it, you got the information out of him. How you got it was beside the point.

Alwaleed sat at his desk thinking. He was in a delicate spot thanks to the Iranians. If he could kill Tabrizi, he would; since he couldn't, he had to deal with what he could control or try to control.

The Americans knew about him and would be coming for him. If one of the bombs went off, he was probably a dead man. He took a pad of paper and his Mont Blanc fountain pen and began a list under the heading *possibilities*:

1. The Crown Prince has me killed;

2. Run and hide;

3. Flee to a country with no extradition treaty with the US;

4. The US captures me overseas and I am designated an enemy combatant;

5. Give myself up in the US and take advantage of its court system;

6. Suicide.

It didn't take long for him to decide he wanted to stay alive and not live like a hunted animal, so he crossed off numbers 1, 2, 3, and 6.

If the US captured him overseas or the Crown Prince handed him over to the Americans, he would undoubtedly be labeled an enemy combatant and disappear for the rest of his life into some dark hole that would make Guantánamo look like a resort. Bottom line, he could not trust the Crown Prince to protect him. If the Americans got serious with Saudi Arabia, he would be killed or turned over to the Americans in a heartbeat.

He needed to stay in control of the situation. The best way to protect himself was to get to the US and the relative safety of the court system. After the infamous Al-Marri and Boumediene cases, the military could not remove him from the court system or imprison him indefinitely. In fact, he might even get out on bail pending trial.

To be sure of this, he had to get to the US safely. After some careful thought, he outlined a plan. His attorneys in London were international in scope and had offices in the US. They would arrange for a press conference in London. He would tell the world a story to protect himself and, at worst, get himself into the US court system.

After hearing his story, the conspiracy theorists would go wild with the news. He would have the lawyers work out arrangements for his secure transportation to the US. While he couldn't be certain, he was confident his plan had an excellent chance for success. After the press conference, the Americans could not make him disappear. He was confident his lawyers would keep him on the front page of *The New York Times* and the *Washington Post*. The free publicity they would get would be priceless for them. In the final analysis, he had the trump card; he knew how to deactivate the terrorists. Unfortunately, he had no idea where the bombs were, and giving up the North Koreans, even if he was believed, would not help him very much.

Alwaleed picked up his secure satellite phone and called London.

Chapter 42

Grant was sitting on the north deck of the ranch house staring at the dimming shades of gold and blue light playing across the Colorado Rockies as the sun sank in the western sky. Five buck deer crossed the pasture on the way to the river for their evening watering. Grant sipped his martini and thought how much more he could enjoy this scene if he was sharing it with someone else.

His thoughts shifted to Stephanie. What in God's name was she doing with Hector Sanchez? His family controlled the smuggling routes that supplied the US with 90 percent of its cocaine and marijuana. He was president of Mexico and the key to protecting the family. Grant thought he knew her, but maybe he didn't. Had she given up her personal integrity for money and glamour? The phone was ringing. Oh well, she wouldn't be the first or the last.

It was Homer Johnson. "Grant, I have been speaking with President Sampson, and she has asked that you attempt to contact the Sanchez family for help with the terrorist situation."

"Homer, I just came back from trying that on my own and got nowhere. They claim they know nothing. Besides, President Sampson said she would give in to the terrorist's demands, a mistake in my opinion, but there you are."

"I have no official knowledge of what is going on," said Homer, "but it would not surprise me if she is just stalling for time to find the bombs. Regardless, the terrorists and the bombs, if they exist, are still here, and we have to find them. If you ask them as an official representative of the United States government, you might get a different response."

"Okay, I'll give it a try. Maybe the bomb threat will give us some leverage."

"Get to the airport as soon as you can. A plane will be waiting to take you to Nogales. And good luck."

"Yes sir," said Grant.

He hastily packed an overnight bag. He opened the top drawer of his bedside table and picked up his Glock G31 pistol. He tested the action. Thought about where he was going and the risk he would be taking. He put the pistol back in the drawer and reluctantly closed it. An official representative of the president of the United States did not carry a firearm; besides, he would be searched and outnumbered, so a gun would be of little use.

At the Durango airport a private jet had been chartered to take him to the Nogales, Arizona, airport, where he would be on his own.

The Learjet covered the high desert of the Four Corners and then descended into the Valley of the Sun, bypassing Phoenix and crossing the barren desert toward Tucson. During this part of the flight, Grant thought about how to approach Ramon and the Sanchez family. Why should they help the US—particularly if they had helped the terrorists infiltrate the people and the bombs? Patriotism certainly wasn't the answer. Threats were not practical since the Sanchez family was the de facto government of Mexico, with Hector Sanchez as president. Grant had to show them it would be in their best interests to help the US find the terrorists and the bombs, if they could. He settled on an appeal to their self-interest. That meant money; serious money.

Grant called Homer Johnson and explained his thinking to him. Fifteen minutes later Johnson called back and said President Sampson had authorized up to one hundred million dollars to persuade the Sanchez family to cooperate.

As the Learjet streaked over the Arizona desert, Grant tilted the plush leather seat back, closed his eyes, and tried for a quick power nap before the plane landed in Nogales. There was the pool at the Sanchez hacienda shimmering in the sunlight. A naked female form swam underwater toward him. Boots emerged from the water and slowly climbed the pool steps toward him. As she reached the top step, Stephanie drifted into the scene and handed Boots a towel. Grant was rudely awakened when the plane hit the runway. There was no time to ruminate on his dream as he climbed into the unmarked car which took him to the border.

Chapter 43

Two and a half hours after leaving the ranch, Grant pushed through the turnstiles and entered Nogales, Mexico. The same two men were sitting in the doorway just as before. He approached them and said, "Tell Ramon Sanchez that I need to see him. I will be at the Casona del Patron." They said nothing, and Grant walked away.

The patio now had a familiar feel to it as he settled in with a Corona with lime under the big shade tree. He was only halfway through his beer when the man with the mechanical arm appeared and ushered him through the blanket-covered opening in the back wall. It was déjà vu all over again as Grant was frisked and pushed into the van and had a hood placed over his head. At least they didn't cuff him to the seat this time. The helicopter ride seemed shorter than before.

Grant was pulled roughly from the helicopter before the hood was jerked off his head. Instead of Boots, standing in front of him were two men in Mexican military uniforms. M16s slung on their shoulders, they were smoking cigarettes and looking bored. Behind them was a Gulfstream G550 jet with the Mexican flag emblazoned on the tail. As the jeep took Grant for the short ride to the hacienda, he wondered whether Hector was here and whether he had brought Stephanie.

The noise of the arriving helicopter caused Stephanie and Hector to look out the window of their bedroom suite. They watched Grant exit the helicopter and saw the hood jerked off his head.

"My dear, you will have to excuse me for a few minutes," said Hector. "It seems Mr. Meredith has returned."

Stephanie said nothing as Hector left the suite. What was going on? Was Grant a prisoner? She had to find out. She waited a full minute and then followed Hector and waited outside the interior library door which was slightly ajar.

Grant was ushered into the library. The sunlight was blinding outside, but it was dim in the library, where the only light came from a Tiffany desk lamp of butterfly-cut glass rich with blues, reds, and greens. The red eyes of the butterflies were otherworldly. The cool atmosphere of the library held the pungent aroma of expensive cigars.

Ramon was sitting at the desk. Hector, who had been sitting across from him, stood and moved around the desk and stood beside his brother. Ramon was wearing a crisp tan safari shirt. Hector was resplendent in a blue blazer with a gold crest on the pocket, starched white shirt without a tie, and gray slacks. Both seemed physically relaxed but had serious expressions as they nodded to acknowledge Grant's presence without saying anything.

Grant was suddenly uncomfortable as the reality of the situation settled upon him. He regretted not having the Glock. He was completely alone in a foreign country facing two of the most ruthless men in the world. If he disappeared, no one would even know he had gotten this far. All his government would know was that he had passed through the turnstiles into Mexico and had not returned. No one would know anything, and no one could do anything. These two men just looked at him with unblinking eyes and waited.

Grant began, "Gentlemen, I am here as the special envoy of President Sampson to ask for your assistance in tracking down the terrorists who are creating havoc in the United States and to locate the nuclear bombs which they intend to detonate if we do not meet their demands. We have reason to believe these people entered the US from Mexico and probably did so with your help. I would like to think you did not know what these people were going to do and that you are as anxious as we are to restore order north of the border."

Ramon looked up at Hector, who took his time inhaling and expelling cigar smoke. "We know nothing of these people. What makes you think they entered your country from Mexico?" said Hector.

"Because it's so easy," Grant said.

Hector's mouth twisted into a humorless smile as he said, "The US/Canadian border is 4,000 miles long, and there are hundreds of unmarked, unguarded, and unpatrolled roads crossing that border. I recently read your Government Accounting Office report that says security on your border with Canada has not increased too much since the French and Indian War. I believe your appearance here is further evidence of your government's racist attitude toward people of color and Mexicans in particular."

He was right about the Canadian border. Grant had read the report that GAO investigators had carried a red duffel bag across the border at multiple locations, simulating how radioactive material could be brought into the United States from Canada. The bottom line was a complete absence of security at multiple locations along the Canadian border.

"Why do you think my family has anything to do with such activities?" said Hector.

"Just playing the odds. To pull this off, the terrorists have to be very well funded. If they came in through Mexico, they would have used the best help money could buy, and that would be you. That is also why we think it is more probable they came in through Mexico. They needed experienced help to move that many people and the bombs. Canada has nothing comparable to your family." Grant didn't know that for sure, but he had to say something.

"Even if we could help you, why should we?" asked Ramon.

"Money," Grant said, "a lot of money."

"Is your request directed to the Mexican government?" asked Hector.

"Naturally," Grant said.

Hector was quiet for several moments before speaking. "The Mexican government is not interested in your money. We may be able to draw upon certain resources for information, but we require something other than money in return."

"What do you want?" Grant asked.

"I want your government to honor its promises. First, I want immediate full implementation of NAFTA, particularly the right of Mexican trucks to deliver cargo into the US. Put an end to the Teamsters lawsuit, and remind your politicians that all Mexico wants is your country to honor NAFTA. When you agreed to NAFTA, you agreed to let our trucks transport goods from Mexico into the US.

"Second, I want you to fast-track the NASCO superhighway project," said Hector. "Your federal government can do it without state approval. I want at least three lanes in each direction from Laredo to Kansas City within ten years, and I want the promise in writing. I want the US Treasury to deposit ten billion dollars in Banco de Mexico's branch in Mexico City as a non-interest-bearing certificate of deposit which will be released when the highway is completed. If it isn't, the money is forfeited. Oh, yes, this is nonnegotiable, and the money must be deposited before we do anything to help you."

Grant did not know how to react to these completely unexpected demands. Hector moved to a chair in the corner of the room and removed himself from the conversation. The silence was deafening. Grant was stunned both by the implied admission that they could and would help and the enormity of his demand.

Then Ramon spoke. "I, on the other hand, *am* interested in money."

Hector's demands had Grant off balance. He could only croak, "How much?"

Ramon looked at the tip of his cigar for a while before saying, "One hundred million to seek the information and another hundred million if the information we provide is useful. One hundred million must be deposited in accounts I will give you. The next hundred million will be deposited when and if I find out anything I deem useful. Upon receipt of the second deposit; I will give you the information."

Grant felt like he had been sucker punched. He really had no idea what to expect from the Sanchezes, but this one-two mauling was surely not it. He stammered, "How do I know we can trust you to do anything?,

Ramon smiled and said, "You don't, but you have no choice. You brought a satellite phone. I suggest you use it … now."

Ramon just sat there smoking his cigar and staring at Grant with those unblinking black eyes. He didn't offer Grant a seat, nor did he offer him any privacy. Grant really did have no choice, so he called Homer Johnson and explained the demands.

While Grant waited for him to call back, he took it upon himself to sit in the chair across the desk from Ramon, who remained still, content to smoke his cigar and stare at Grant. There was no anger in his eyes, nor was there any curiosity. He just stared. It was so uncomfortable that after a few moments of trying to stare back at him, Grant gave up and looked out the French doors at the pool.

Ramon's demand for money was straightforward; Hector's demands, by contrast, were completely unexpected. Grant was sure Homer Johnson could understand the demands in this context, but this was not the place, and there was no time for Grant's education. As he thought about it some more, he realized that there was a lot in those demands for the Sanchez family. The increased flow of Mexican trucks across the border would benefit their trucking company and increase their capacity for smuggling drugs and people into the US. The Border Patrol inspected less than 5 percent of the traffic crossing the border now. If the volume of truck traffic increased significantly, the percentage being inspected would drop precipitously. The reality was that virtually anything that benefited the Mexican economy benefited the Sanchez family.

It took less than ten minutes for the return call agreeing to the demands. Grant was told to surrender his phone to Ramon so there would be a secure means of communication between the Sanchezes and President Sampson's chief of staff.

The exterior library door opened. Boots walked in and said to Ramon, "You rang?"

Grant hadn't seen Ramon do anything.

"Yes, Margarita. Could you entertain Mr. Meredith while I make a few calls?"

"Certainly." She gave Grant a wicked smile. "We'll be by the pool."

Carlos Sanchez emerged from a corner of the library shrouded in shadows and watched Boots and Grant walk toward the pool.

"I am tired of this Grant Meredith," said Carlos. "The American government knows too much about us as it is, and that is his doing."

Ramon got up from the desk and joined his father by the French doors. "Father, I think we made a mistake by helping these terrorists."

"We didn't know they were terrorists," said Hector.

Ramon took a step toward Hector and said "Come on, brother, who did you think they were, Muslim missionaries?"

"Quiet, both of you," hissed Carlos. "Your demands were very creative. The only problem is that I have no idea how to help them, and even if I did, I am not sure I would."

"It would be very, very lucrative for us and good for Mexico, if we could find a way to help them," said Hector.

"If either of you come up with something, let me know," said Carlos. "In the meantime, I am going to arrange for Meredith to have an accident, a fatal one."

Hector and Ramon looked at one another with raised eyebrows but said nothing. Once Carlos Sanchez made up his mind, it did no good to disagree.

Stephanie rushed to the room she shared with Hector, closed the door, went into the bathroom, and locked the door. She stood at the sink and studied herself in the mirror. *What am I going to do?*

It had to come to this point sooner or later. She had run away from her life and from Grant and lost herself in Mexico. It was like a line from a bad county song. Well, if that was the case, she had reached the worm at the bottom of the bottle. Her father would have known exactly what to do, and she was his daughter after all.

Stephanie changed into sneakers, jeans, and a T-shirt. She pulled her hair back into a ponytail and secured it with a rubber band. She put her passport, driver's license, and a credit card in her back pocket. Finally she looked at herself in the bathroom mirror and hummed a verse from *Oklahoma*. "Oh what a beautiful morning …"

Boots took Grant's arm and held it against her breast as they walked to the far end of the pool and the inviting shade of the bougainvillea arbor. Grant wondered if she used this technique with anyone else, or everyone else. When they sat across from each other, Boots' very short, tight white skirt exposed almost all of her legs. As she languidly crossed them, he could see she was without panties. Boots smiled slowly and leaned forward placing her forearms on her knee. Her low-cut peasant blouse gaped downward, exposing her braless breasts. This time Grant was sober and was here as a representative of the president of the United States. Sex was not on his agenda.

"I knew you would be coming back to see me," she said coyly.

When Grant offered no reply, she said, "To tell you the truth, I think Hector's Stephanie has a thing for you, Mr. Meredith."

Grant kept silent.

"Perhaps you would like something to drink," she said as she bounced out of her chair and over to the wet bar where she bent over to pick up a towel off the tile deck.

Chapter 44

The telephone on the poolside bar rang. Boots picked it up and listened for almost a full minute. She sighed, turned toward Grant and shrugged.

"Grant, this has been such fun, but as they say, all good things …"

Grant pushed himself to his feet and saw two large men hurrying along the side of the pool toward them. In a blur, they grabbed him and dragged him behind the pool house. One of the men pulled open two doors to reveal a stairway descending to another door. Grant was pulled down the stairs and into the basement and could see that it had no other entry. Boots followed them inside.

The men pinned Grant to the floor. He was helpless. Boots stood directly over him with her legs spread. He ignored the softness at the top of her legs and looked into her eyes—the flat black Sanchez eyes, now utterly blank and emotionless.

"Grant, Grant, Grant," she said as if to a small child, "don't bother to struggle; it will accomplish nothing. In a few moments Dr. Madrid will be here, and it will be over peacefully."

"What in God's name do you think you are doing? I am a special envoy from the president of the United States. You can't do this," Grant said as forcefully as he could.

"Poor Grant," she said with a slow shake of her head. "Dr. Madrid will inject you with the HIV virus, after which you will be held for a short time. But do not worry, he will then administer an overdose of cocaine which will bring you to a tranquil end."

"It will never work. The autopsy will show what you did to me," Grant shouted again.

"We are not such fools," she said, staring down at him. "Dr. Madrid will do the autopsy with all of the proper tests, and then, through a clerical error, your body will be cremated. Naturally the morgue attendant will be punished for his stupidity. All your government will have is the bona fide autopsy report. Good-bye, Grant." She turned and left the cellar.

Grant struggled to get free, and one of the goons grabbed his hair and slammed his head into the concrete floor.

The next thing Grant heard was the noise of human conversation, as light began to filter through his eyelids. He barely opened his eyes and saw a small man in an ill-fitting dark brown suit bending over him with a syringe in his hand.

"Hold him still," said the small man.

The door opened, and all three men looked in that direction. In one continuous motion Grant jerked his right arm free and slammed his fist into the nose of the man holding his left arm, rolled across him, and jumped to his feet. As the man struggled to his feet, Grant swung his right leg up and into his groin with all the power he had. The man actually came off the ground and fell forward with his face smacking into the concrete floor.

Grant spun toward the other goon and saw him flat on his back with an obviously broken neck. The doctor was slumped against the wall with eyes gaping wide, staring dumbfounded at Stephanie and Grant from behind thick glasses.

"Follow me now. We can talk later," she said.

They raced up the steps and emerged poolside. Standing there with a smile on her face was Boots. Her left foot was slightly forward, she was balanced on the balls of her feet. Her right arm was at her side with her hand pointing straight down, index finger extended. Grant could see nothing in her hand, but the stance was familiar, as was the position of her arm and hand. A combat knife-fighting position.

"Well, well, girlfriend, now is the time to choose. You have so much to live for, including me, but if you wish to die for this man, well, so be it."

"Stephanie, she's got a knife in her right hand," Grant said as he moved to his left, away from Stephanie.

As Boots took a step toward Stephanie, Grant launched himself at her in a classic open-field tackle. His shoulder hit her in mid-thigh and propelled them both into the pool. They came to the surface at the edge of the pool. As Grant's head broke water, he was two feet in front of Boots, whose right arm was in the air above him. As the arm started down, Stephanie's denim-clad leg flashed into sight and sent the knife flying. Grant swung at Boots and caught her on the jaw. She slumped into the water.

"Come on, Grant, we've got to get out of here." Stephanie's voice was a hoarse whisper.

Grant pulled himself from the water and started after her. Then he stopped, turned, and looked at Boots floating facedown in the water. He grabbed a handful of hair, pulled her halfway out of the pool, and left her prone on the deck, legs still in the water.

Stephanie grabbed him by the arm. "Move."

They ran toward the back stucco wall, eight feet high. When they got there, Stephanie clasped her hands together and bent her knees. "Up you go, cowboy."

With a boost from her, Grant grabbed the top of the wall and hauled himself onto it. He reached down, and Stephanie jumped, grabbing his hand. Grant pulled her up, and they dropped to the other side of the wall. It was less than a quarter mile to the helicopter and Learjet.

Grant could hear shouting on the other side of the wall as they took off at a sprint toward the airstrip. As they ran, Stephanie shouted, "I hope you can still fly a helicopter!"

Fortunately, no one was around, and the helicopter started easily. As Grant banked away from the ranch to the north, he saw one of the soldiers with his rifle to his shoulder. He banked the helicopter sharply to the right. The noise drowned out any gunshot noise. The side window shattered, and Grant flinched. He turned to Stephanie, who was wiping blood off her cheek.

"I'm all right!" she shouted above the roar. "Get us out of here."

The last thing Grant saw was a man standing in the shadows of the veranda watching the helicopter head north. He didn't think he was through with the Sanchez family.

Chapter 45

Ali Alwaleed strode confidently to the podium in the London Press Club. His London solicitor had arranged this venue for his press conference. Every major news outlet was present. Once the word got out that a Saudi official was going to make a major disclosure pertaining to the terrorist attacks in the United States, so many wanted to attend that the Press Club had arranged for a live closed-circuit feed to another room where the second tier organizations were placed. There were so many networks that wanted to broadcast the press conference that CBC, CNN, Fox, ABC, NBC, and CBS had to settle for a pool broadcast of the event.

Alwaleed left his traditional garb in his plane and dressed in a Savile Row blue pinstriped suit, blue Turnbull and Asser shirt, and red, white, and blue tie. He looked exactly like one would expect a diplomat to look. He put on gold-rimmed reading glasses and began to speak from his prepared text.

"Let me introduce myself. I am Ali Alwaleed, and until today I have served the Crown Prince of Saudi Arabia. Today I come forward to serve the United States of America. In the last few months of the Bush administration, I was approached by representatives of the Iranian government to work with them to launch terrorist attacks within the United States. I immediately reported this contact to the Crown Prince, who instructed me to contact President Bush. Shortly thereafter, I met with President Bush and Vice President Cheney and gave them a full report. They asked me to go along with the plot and provide them with intelligence as the plan developed. I did so.

"I understood that President Sampson was informed of my activities and approved of my continued participation.

"Approximately thirty days ago, my Iranian counterpart ceased communicating with me, and the current attacks were launched without my knowledge, so I was unable to warn Washington.

"I have valuable information concerning the terrorists which I intend to personally deliver to President Sampson. When I leave here, I will fly directly to Andrews Air Force Base to deliver my report. I have made this public announcement because I have been advised that this is the best way to assure the safety of myself and my family. The publicity ought to bring such notoriety to myself that assassination is not a realistic option; in addition, I hope to avoid being made to disappear into some gulag such as Guantánamo.

"I am fully confident that I will be treated fairly by the United States government, since I trust the press corps to follow my journey and to watch out for me and my family.

"I intend to hold another press conference upon my arrival at Andrews Air Force Base so that you may monitor my progress. I am unable to respond to questions at this time. Thank you."

The room erupted into a thunderstorm of noise. The mass of reporters surged toward the podium shouting questions. British police moved in to keep them at bay while Ali strode purposefully out of the room through a door behind the podium.

At the rear of the room stood a television reporter for CNN news facing his cameraman and shouting to be heard above the din.

"This is stunning news. According to Alwaleed, the Bush and Sampson administrations knew about the terrorist plot and failed to stop it. The political fallout from this disclosure is incalculable. Many in Congress and elsewhere are already saying the administration did not do enough to protect the country from internal terrorist attacks. By focusing their efforts overseas, they left the country vulnerable. This disclosure in the midst of the chaotic situation in the country ... Well, Jane, frankly I just don't know ... I am without words, so I'll send it back to you."

Jane Walsh, the CNN anchor said, "Now we have instant analysis from retired general Evan Wayne, our national security expert. What do you make of this new disclosure, General?"

"Chaos, Jane, absolute chaos. It is obvious both administrations share the blame for this turn of events. If they knew the attacks were in the planning stage and failed to take preemptive action, no one will listen to any excuses. On the other hand, if they were not certain, you can understand that after the WMD fiasco in Iraq, they would not want to rush into anything. That said, I do not believe that anyone will be interested in excuses. The most fundamental role of government, the main reason it exists, is to protect the country, and the government has failed miserably."

"Thank you, General. We will be following these developments closely. Now to John Rider in Salt Lake City with the latest on the bombing of the Mormon Tabernacle."

Chapter 46

Five and a half hours later, Alwaleed emerged from his private jet at Andrews Air Force Base. Immediately behind him was a tall gray-haired man with wild bushy eyebrows that met across the bridge of his nose. To the middle-aged woman watching through a tinted window, he looked like he shared Alwaleed's tailor.

Priscilla Osborn was waiting for them in a black-glassed building next to the main terminal. For her part, she wore a black pinstriped pants suit. She nervously touched her severe helmet of gray hair.

At the bottom of the ramp were two military policemen who drove Alwaleed and the tall man toward her. As they entered the building, she walked briskly up to them. She didn't offer her hand.

"Good morning, Mr. Alwaleed, I am Priscilla Osborn, the assistant director of the National Counterterrorism Center, Department of Homeland Security. I have been sent by President Sampson to speak with you. Who is this man?" she said, pointing at Alwaleed's companion.

The man extended his hand, which she ignored, and said with a proper British accent, "Good morning, Ms. Osborn, I

216

am J. Reginald Allen III from the law firm of Jekel, Howard & Thomson. I represent Mr. Alwaleed."

Osborn felt as if she had bitten into a lemon. "Are you licensed to practice law in the United States?"

Allen smiled and said, "Oh yes, quite so. You see, my firm has offices on K Street in Washington and on Park Avenue in New York. We have over one thousand lawyers around the world. You may be assured that I am properly licensed and completely familiar with the legal questions at issue."

"Very well," said Osborn. "It was nice of you to come, but we are going to question Mr. Alwaleed alone. National security and so forth, and you do not have the necessary clearances."

"If I may be direct, Ms. Osborn, you may not question Mr. Alwaleed outside my presence," said Allen. "Period; end of discussion."

"If I may be direct, Mr. Allen, I will have Mr. Alwaleed declared an enemy combatant, and you will never see him again," said Osborn in an easy tone. She was used to being obeyed.

Allen sighed. "You disappoint me, Assistant Director Osborn. We are not engaged in child's play. At this moment, one of my partners is sitting in the chambers of Judge John Clancy of the United States District Court for Washington DC with an emergency habeas corpus petition. I am sure you know of Judge Clancy. He is the one who released Sheikh Abdel-Rahman when the FBI would not identify its confidential informants. The young man from the Justice Department, who is representing you before Judge Clancy, is in over his head at this point.

"Mr. Alwaleed is ready to cooperate with you as soon as you agree to his preconditions. With all due respect, I humbly suggest you have no more time to waste."

Osborn bit back her anger. *Remember, you're not a bureaucrat but a professional intelligence officer.* "Very well. Come with me."

They took an elevator that went down for almost a minute. About the length of time it used to take to ascend the World Trade Center towers. Osborn led them down a short hallway and into a small conference room with a one-way mirror in a wall, cameras in the corners, and a recording device built into the small table. Osborn sat with her back to the mirror, with Alwaleed and Allen facing it.

Allen settled himself in his wooden chair, and looked around the room, and smiled. "This looks like a set from *Law and Order.*"

Osborn had a blank legal pad in front of her with reading glasses and a felt-tipped pen neatly arranged on top of the pad. She ignored Allen, put her elbows on the table, folded her hands in front of her, and said, "Alwaleed, you are a liar."

Alwaleed jerked in his chair, clearly startled at this frontal attack. Allen, on the other hand, did not move or change expression. He acted as if she had not said anything. "Mr. Alwaleed can assist you in terminating the terrorists that are terrorizing the United States. Unfortunately, he cannot help you locate the bombs. In exchange for his cooperation he requires an immediate full pardon from President Sampson, assistance in creating new identities for him and his family, round-the-clock security until he decides it is time to assume his new identity, and unfettered access to his bank accounts. Under the circumstances, these requests are quite reasonable."

"I must be getting senile, Mr. Allen. I thought I heard you demand a full pardon *before* your client says anything. We don't work that way. I want to hear what he has to say. Then we will decide if his information warrants a pardon. We all know he is lying about working with the Bush Administration and President Sampson getting information from him. My guess is that he is lying about Iranian involvement and that everything else he plans to say is a lie also."

Allen's tone was firm but without a trace of anger when he said, "Listen to me very carefully, Assistant Director. Mr. Alwaleed can show you how to eliminate all of these terrorists simultaneously. You know that these people have explosive implants in their heads which can be activated by secret radio frequencies. Using such a signal to terminate the terrorists will save untold innocent lives and is indisputably worth a pardon."

With her right elbow on the table, Osborn leaned forward slightly, pointed at Allen, and said, "My people can get the same information from him in very short order with or without his cooperation, so I do not believe that we need to be talking about a pardon. If you are right, perhaps something less than the death penalty. I would recommend life imprisonment, without possibility of parole."

Allen raised both hands off the table, smiled, and said, enunciating precisely, "Why, Assistant Director Osborn, I do believe you are threatening to torture Mr. Alwaleed. Your threat has been recorded by your system, and by me," he said as he pulled a fountain pen from the breast pocket of his suit coat. "Handy little recorder, this; it also takes video. Absolutely amazing; you can buy one anywhere.

"If you remove Mr. Alwaleed from my presence for any reason whatsoever, I shall walk directly from here to the press mob just outside the gates, tell them you are in the process of torturing Mr. Alwaleed, and demand his immediate release. This press announcement will be carried on national television and will be seen in Judge Clancy's chambers."

Osborn allowed herself a thin smile. "I will simply hold you as a conspirator with an enemy combatant. I am sure we can sort out your status in a few years."

"Your threats are becoming tiresome, Assistant Director Osborn. We have one of my partners with the CNN correspondent outside. If I have not communicated with him" —he looked at his wristwatch—"in ten minutes, he will announce to the world that you are, despite Mr. Alwaleed's cooperation, torturing him and holding me incommunicado. My partner in Judge Clancy's chambers will request immediate habeas corpus release of both of us.

"Oh yes, they will both say that Mr. Alwaleed is offering up the terrorists in exchange for a pardon, and you are refusing. Instead you are relying on torture to get information he would give you willingly.

"Further complicating things is the fact that the terrorists, who are presently standing down, are on martyr missions. Once they hear that you have Alwaleed and he will give them up, you can be sure they will go out in a blaze of glory, killing unknown numbers of innocent civilians. You simply cannot allow that to happen.

"Mr. Alwaleed's requests are reasonable and fair. He does not ask you for money, only access to his own. He is willing to stop the carnage. He does not ask you to forgive those who plotted these attacks, only that he be left alone when this is over. Frankly, I am amazed that you are not jumping at the chance to eliminate one hundred terrorists inside the United States who are going to kill many, many more innocent civilians if you do not eliminate them first."

Osborn moved her hands in front of her as if to clear the air. "Where are the bombs?"

"As I told you, and as he himself announced in London, my client does not know," said Allen pleasantly.

"What can he tell me about the bombs?" asked Osborn.

"Nothing, I am sorry to say. He was not involved with the bombs. In fact, that part of the plan was hidden from him, and he is as surprised and upset as you are that the United States faces such catastrophic loss of life."

"I don't believe him," said Osborn, pointing at Alwaleed but controlling the tone of her voice. Osborn knew well enough that in this situation, anger would get her nowhere.

Assistant NCTC Director Priscilla Osborn sat silently weighing her options. She looked at her watch and began doodling on her pad. After almost a minute, she decided that it wasn't her decision.

She stood and said, "Excuse me while I consult with my superiors."

As she was leaving the room, she glanced in the mirror and saw Alwaleed and Allen exchange a furtive smile.

Chapter 47

Janet Sampson put Assistant Director Osborn on the speaker, and they listened to her report. When she finished, President Sampson said, "I'll call you back shortly." She punched the intercom button and directed her secretary to get the attorney general on the line.

Seated in the Oval Office with President Sampson were Howard Meyers, director of the FBI, and Omar Watson, secretary of Homeland Security. She pushed the speaker button on her phone, and they were joined by Attorney General Christine A. Simmons.

Without any preamble, President Sampson said, "Alwaleed says he can give us the radio frequencies which will detonate the explosive devices implanted in the terrorists. He wants a presidential pardon, a new identity, and access to his bank accounts. He claims he knows nothing about the bombs."

There was complete silence until she continued, "Chris, can we do it legally?"

"Yes, Madame President, you can. Article II Section 2 of the Constitution gives you the power to grant pardons for offenses against the United States. There are no standards, and the only limitation is that you cannot pardon those who have been impeached. Title 28 of the Code of Federal Regulations sets forth the procedure for applying for a pardon through the Justice Department's Office of Pardon Attorney. However, that procedure does not have to be followed. President Ford pardoned President Nixon, and President Clinton pardoned Marc Rich, without following standard procedure."

President Sampson looked at Watson and asked, "Omar, should we do it?"

Without hesitation, Watson said, "Give him the pardon, give him a deed to the White House; promise him anything to stop the terrorists. Then give him a one-way ticket to Gitmo."

The president turned back to the attorney general. "Chris, if I grant him the pardon, can we ignore it after we get the information?"

"There are serious implications if we ignore the pardon. First, he has top-flight lawyers, and they will be in court with a habeas corpus petition seeking to enforce the pardon. If the court follows the law, he will be released. If the court does not follow the law, it raises a serious question about the future of our country. Do we have the rule of law in the United States, or do we have it only when it is convenient? Put another way, do the needs of national security, as determined solely by the president, trump the law of the land? If so, what neutral principle limits the president's power to ignore the law?

"Second, you will set a precedent that an official act of the president of the United States cannot be relied upon."

Watson interrupted. "This is not the time for philosophical discussions about the rule of law; we can save no telling how many lives if we kill these terrorists. My God, there are a hundred of them running loose; how many more innocent people will they kill? We can get the information to kill them and then decide what to do with this raghead."

Now the attorney general cut in: "Excuse me, Secretary Watson, the question is not whether we should get the information. The question is whether the president can grant a pardon and then ignore it. This is precisely the time to follow the law. If you choose to grant the pardon, it must be honored. This is not some third-world country where lies to the infidels can be justified in furtherance of religious objectives. This is the United States of America. If you grant the pardon and fail to honor it, I will have to resign and make my case to the American people."

The president turned to Meyers. "Howard, what do you think?"

"While I am obviously concerned about the individual terrorists, I am more concerned about the bombs. It is hard for me to believe he knows about one and not the other. If I was sure he didn't know about the bombs, I would reluctantly go for the pardon. Even if he was sentenced to death, it would take a quarter century, if ever, before he was executed. To paraphrase the criminal law cant, it is better to let him go than have hundreds more of our innocent citizens murdered. Having said that, if I had to guess, and that is just what I am doing, I would guess he knows about the bombs, and we should squeeze him a little and see what he knows. The only thing we know for sure is that he is a diabolically clever liar. We found out about him by a stroke of luck, and look at the position he has put us in."

The attorney general asked, "Howard, what do you mean by 'squeeze him a little'? Surely you are not suggesting torture. We can't do that; this is the United States of America!"

Watson spoke up. "I think Howard is right, but there is no time for torture, so we don't have to debate the issue. For all we know, they could be lying about the bombs. We have no proof they are here; it might be nothing more than a scare tactic. We need to stop what we can stop right now. Maybe there are no bombs; perhaps he will cooperate on the bombs after he gets the pardon."

"In your dreams," snorted Meyers.

President Sampson pounded her desk and said, "All right, calm down, everyone.

"All of you have made excellent points. There is no more time to reach a consensus. Someone has to make a decision, and that is my job. I am going to grant him a pardon based upon what he has told us and will tell us. Madame Attorney General, draft the pardon immediately, with language that gives me an out if we learn that he knew something about the bombs."

Less than an hour later, J. Reginald Allen III sat at the wooden table far underground at Andrews Air Force Base and calmly read the proposed pardon. After less than a minute, he lifted his head and said to Assistant Director Osborn, "This is unacceptable. Mr. Alwaleed is to receive a full and complete pardon for any actions surrounding the terrorist attacks, including the bomb plot. This document is cleverly drafted to create an exception for the bomb plot if it is determined he knows something about it and fails to disclose that knowledge. You get to determine whether the exception applies. This document is unacceptable."

"What do you want?" asked Osborn.

"Exactly what we requested and you agreed to; nothing more, and nothing less. This is no time to be clever. Use plain, everyday English, as difficult as that may be for you American attorneys."

Osborn left the room.

She called the Oval Office and was put on the speakerphone. "Alwaleed's lawyer says no deal, the way the pardon is presently drafted. He says the pardon must include the bombs. He says his client is justifiably afraid that we will fabricate evidence about his participation in the bomb plot to get around the pardon."

President Sampson sighed and said, "Tell them we'll include the bomb plot."

Chapter 48

Ramon couldn't sit still. He was pacing the hacienda library like a lion waiting for dinner. Hector was just finishing a telephone call while sitting at the desk. Carlos had gone to Ciudad Juárez on business, and Boots was in the gym.

"Calm down, brother," said Hector, "you're making me nervous."

"Hector, I am happy that Meredith escaped. Killing an official US representative, no matter how well we disguised it, would do much more than irritate the Americans. The fallout would be unpredictable. There is a place for vengeance, but this was not the time or the place. Sometimes father is too impulsive."

"You may be right about that, but losing Stephanie pisses me off," said Hector. "I enjoyed her company, and she was a great lay."

Although Ramon didn't say it, he was especially glad that Stephanie was gone. He had never trusted her, thinking she was either a mole or unstable. It didn't matter which: he considered her a danger to the family.

"Knowing you, you already have her replacement in the wings," said Ramon. "I just hope she doesn't know anything useful about our business."

"Don't worry, I don't share secrets with arm candy," said Hector.

"I am also worried about father's decision to help the terrorists get into the United States," Ramon said. "It was a serious mistake. He was blinded by the money, as he often is. Sometimes he just doesn't understand the long-term consequences of his actions. He didn't fully appreciate the potential consequences of nuclear explosions in the United States."

"Well, you didn't stand up to him, did you?"

"No we didn't, Mr. President, but we have got to do something to fix the mess. The Americans are guessing now, but sooner or later, they will identify the terrorists and determine that they entered the country illegally. One of them will surely talk, and the Americans will know they came in from Mexico. That would be the last straw. They will retaliate by taking control of the border."

"I don't think so," said Hector. "The administration and anyone in Congress with half a brain knows that the people we send there make their economy work. Who else will pick the crops, bus the tables, wash the dishes, clean the rooms, and care for their children? One thing for certain, it won't be the Americans themselves."

"Hector, you're living in the past. They have the money, the technology, and the manpower to close the border. Until now they lacked the political will. These attacks would weight the scales in favor of security and against economics and trade. A secure border will financially cripple our business."

"Politics is my business, and I know they will never accept the consequences to their economy of a secure border. Don't worry about it. I've got to get back to Mexico City. I'll talk to you later." With that, Hector headed for the door.

Ramon had been working to develop an infrastructure in Canada to smuggle drugs across that border. Getting across the border was the easy part; the logistics of moving the drugs into Canada was still several years away. He needed more time.

The blowback from this terrorist mess could not have come at a worse time. There was an uprising in Tijuana and Ciudad Juárez which was spreading to Nogales. Several groups of drug couriers had decided they could stand on their own and did not need to pay tribute to the Sanchez family. It was a nasty business, but they could not tolerate dissent. Carlos had ordered the extermination of anyone involved in the uprising. The death toll after two years of virtual warfare was more than 11,000—four times what the Americans had lost in Iraq after five years of warfare. It had almost spun out of control before Hector sent in the army.

There was nothing Ramon could do about the terrorists already in the United States, but he had an idea about the bombs. For the last several years, on his orders, Jamie Ruiz had been developing a loose network of Mexicans who they had helped enter the United States. The business purpose had been twofold. First, they cultivated a relationship with those who moved back and forth across the border and those who might bring family members across the border in the future. Second, Mexicans wired vast sums of money from the United States to their families in Mexico. The Sanchez family wanted those funds to go into their banks and have the transfers cashed by their facilities.

He called Jamie Ruiz. "Jamie, what is the status of our MexAm network?"

"The network has been computerized," Jamie reported, "and we have contact information for over three million people broken down by state, county, and city.

"Within a few months, certainly less than a year, we will be ready to market goods and services to our members working all across the United States in hotels, restaurants, construction, agriculture, and factories."

"What about the enforcer network?" asked Ramon.

Ramon utilized the Zetas to enforce a relationship with Hispanic gangs in the United States including the Border Brothers, La Gran Raza, and Barrio Azteca. The Zetas, who had no direct presence in the United States, worked with the notorious MS-13 gang which had originated in El Salvador but now included many Mexican illegals to act as *sicarios* or executioners for the Sanchez family.

"As you can imagine, not very many US gang members have computers or BlackBerries, but the key people do, and they can contact the others."

"What about that telephone tree you were talking about earlier this year?" asked Ramon.

One of Ruiz's people had developed a telephone tree to contact the entire network. They would initiate one hundred calls to members of the network, who would in turn call others and, so on.

"We haven't used it yet," answered Jamie, "but I have been planning a test run to find and eliminate any bugs in the idea."

"Okay, I have the trial run for you. I want you to utilize the telephone tree and ask the members if they have seen or heard anything or anyone that might have something to do with the terrorist bombs that are in the United States. I want this done as soon as possible, and I want whatever information there is within twenty-four hours. Is that clear?"

"Yes, perfectly clear. I'll get started now," said Ruiz.

Ramon knew any information would be passed back up the telephone tree and filtered at each level. It was a long shot, but there was no telling what over three million pairs of eyes might have seen. He was particularly interested in the hospitality industry reports.

Chapter 49

Grant landed the helicopter in a far corner of the airport in Nogales, Arizona. When he cut the engine, he could see three Border Patrol cars speeding toward him with lights flashing and sirens at full cry.

He put his arm around Stephanie and said, "Well, Ms. Chambers, welcome home."

An hour later, they were in a windowless conference room at the Tucson FBI office with John Alvarez, Assistant Director of DHS for the Southwest Region.

"I have filed your report with Washington, and Secretary Watson asked me to convey his thanks for your efforts. Now tell me, Mr. Meredith, what am I to do with that helicopter—which, by the way, belongs to the Mexican government?" said Alvarez with a chuckle.

Grant looked at Stephanie and said, "Well, we need a ride back to Colorado."

Alvarez shook his head. "Sorry, Mr. Meredith, you are on your own now. I can have a car take you to the airport, if you wish."

Now that the adrenaline had worn off, Grant was exhausted. "Stephanie, what do you want to do?"

She said, "Mr. Alvarez, can you give us a moment alone, please."

When Alvarez had left the room, she turned to Grant and said, "To be honest, I don't know what I want to do. I have the clothes on my back, a credit card with a three-thousand-dollar limit but no money, no home, no job, and no prospects. I don't think there is much of a market for assassins, and frankly I'm tired of the mistress role. So I guess you could say I'm at loose ends."

Stephanie said this in an emotionless monotone. It was clear she was not looking for sympathy; just stating the facts. Grant reached for her hand, but she pulled it away.

"Look, Grant, I need time to sort things out and get my feet back on the ground. I—"

"Say no more. Come with me to the ranch. You can stay in the guest cabin while you sort things out. You saved my life; I'll take care of you."

She reached over and squeezed his hand. "I appreciate the offer, but I have no intention of being kept by another man. Nothing personal; I'm just not going there again. I can take care of myself, and I intend to do so."

"Okay, I understand, but you need a place to get your feet on the ground. Just come to the ranch, no strings and no obligations, and give yourself time to think things through without any pressure."

She sighed and said, "Thanks, Grant, I appreciate that. I will come with you, but I won't stay long."

He hadn't given any thought to what saving him had cost Stephanie. In his opinion she was better off not being with a criminal, even if he was the president of Mexico. However, he was not in her position. A few hours ago she had it all; money, mansions, clothes, bodyguards, and limousines. Now look where she was: basically destitute. He thought she was a strong person, but he wasn't sure she could make a new life for herself without some help.

Chapter 50

President Sampson and her advisers had not left the Situation Room. It was a little after three in the afternoon when Howard Meyers brought up the obvious question.

"Once we have the frequencies, when do we use them? Some of these people could be driving around in cars and cause fatal accidents. It's rush hour here, and it will be rolling across the country. It will be almost twelve hours before most of the cars are off the roads in LA. Anything could happen."

No one said anything. Except for Meyers and President Sampson, all eyes were on the table. The wrong decision could end political careers.

Sampson slowly drummed her fingers on the table. Still no one looked at her but Meyers. Sampson stood and began pacing around the table with her hands behind her back. She circled the table twice and then stopped to place her hands on the back of her chair.

"Well, your silence confirms that we are in a situation where there is no right answer. If I—notice I did not say *we*—act now, there may be innocent people killed. If we wait, the information may go stale, or even more innocent people could die. We all know we should shift our energies to the bombs, which threaten the largest loss of life. If I act now, it may provoke the bombers either to act immediately or to do something stupid which would allow us to find them."

Attorney General Simmons, who had come to the Situation Room while the pardon was being drafted, spoke in a hesitant voice. "President Sampson, I think you should consider putting out a public announcement that you have the frequency for each of the terrorists, and they should surrender or face the consequences. You could also announce that all motor traffic should come to a halt at a specific time. I believe that is the humane thing to do. We are not murderers. This is about who we are as a people. We must set an example for the world and for future generations."

Omar Watson looked at Simmons like she had developed a deadly communicable disease. "Have you lost your mind? One or two may try to save themselves, but these people came here on martyr missions. You make that announcement, and ninety of them will run out and start killing people. How many would they kill before you knew whether anyone would even accept your offer and surrender? I am quite confident that you and your family are safe. What gives you the right to risk the lives of other innocent people in the interests of being 'humane'? You are a sanctimonious idiot."

Simmons's face turned beet red. She hit the table and started to stand. Howard Meyers put his hand on her arm.

Sampson held up her arms. "Enough, all of you." She stood perfectly still for a moment and then moved her chair out of the way and punched the intercom button on the tabletop phone. "Kill them," she said.

Two hours later, there were no reports of major traffic accidents that could have been caused by a terrorist behind the wheel. During the same period of time, one hundred Americans had died tobacco-related deaths.

Four hours later twenty-three of the terrorists had been found leaking blood from eyes, ears, and nose. Identification was under way. It wouldn't be long before all of them were found. The issue would be identifying them.

Chapter 51

Ramon slowly closed his cell phone. His telephone tree had borne fruit.

There was a report from an undocumented hotel worker in Kansas City that an imam from Detroit had checked into the Marriott in North Kansas City two days ago, had not left his room, had not ordered room service, and had kept cleaning people out. There was nothing suspicious about his luggage, but it was strange and certainly worth checking out.

Another undocumented room service waiter at Los Angeles' Bonaventure Hotel had reported that an imam from Phoenix had checked into the hotel three days ago and had not left his room. LA would certainly be a good target, and the other information fit.

This was precisely what Ramon had feared from the beginning. A bomb in a heavily Mexican community like Los Angeles would be devastating. With the offshore breeze protecting the enclaves of Beverly Hills, Bel Air, Santa Monica, and everything west of the 405 Freeway, the brunt of the bomb's devastation would fall east of downtown in the heavily Latino, black, and Asian communities.

Until now, he had not been sure what he would do if he got any information; now he was sure. He would not stand by and let some lunatic fringe terrorists kill that many Mexicans. As far as he was concerned, the Sanchez family stood for law and order, even if it was a law dictated, interpreted, and enforced by them. If you obeyed their rules, the family would protect you.

He sat at his computer and sent an encrypted text message to the e-mail address Meredith had left for them to use. The message said:

"Send the final one hundred million to the account you were given. I may have the answers you were looking for."

He had confirmation of the wire transfer less than four minutes later. He sent another message:

"Try Bonaventure Hotel in downtown Los Angeles. Imam from Phoenix checked in three days ago. Try Marriott in North Kansas City. Imam from Detroit checked in two days ago."

Ramon lit a cigar and examined the glowing tip. A smile tugged gently at the corners of his mouth. He did not know if these were the people the Americans were looking for, but if he hadn't used illegal aliens to racially profile apparent Muslims, they would not have found these imams. It was amusing that the Americans were so absorbed in their self-anointed moral superiority that they probably were not racially profiling in their search for the bombs.

Grant and Stephanie were unaware of events when the telephone rang. It was President Janet Sampson. Grant punched the speaker button so Stephanie could hear.

"Mr. Meredith, on behalf of the United States of America, I want to thank you for your efforts with the Sanchezes. Thanks to information they provided, we have taken possession of the bombs and the men who had them. I cannot put into words what you have done for your country. Unfortunately, this is an operation whose details must remain classified for many years. If I could, I would sing your praises on Broadway."

"Madame President, I didn't do anything for glory. I just did what I could to help. It is no more than any American would have done, given the opportunity."

"Mr. Meredith, you are too modest. When you are available, I would be pleased to have you to the White House for a small private dinner."

"I would be honored."

"My social secretary will be in touch. Be safe, Mr. Meredith," said the president, ending the conversation.

He turned to Stephanie and said, "This nightmare is over."

"For now," said Stephanie.

Chapter 52

Two days later Stephanie and Grant took an all-day trail ride in the Weimenuche Wilderness. Later they unpacked the trailer, curried the horses, and put them in the corral. Now they were sitting on a bench outside the barn enjoying a beautiful sunset and a cold beer.

Stephanie took a deep breath and, without looking at him, said. "Grant, I have been talking to some people in New York about getting back into public relations. I've got a few appointments lined up for next week; I'll be leaving Sunday morning."

Grant felt like he had been slapped. He spun around to face her, but she kept her eyes fixed on the brilliant red-gold western horizon. Her facial muscles were rigid, and her teeth appeared to be clenched. He opened his mouth, but before he could say anything she abruptly stood and walked over to the corral fence. Other than today's ride, he had left her to her thoughts for the last few days, and now he was kicking himself. If she got caught up in the New York single professional lifestyle, he would lose her. He had been working on an idea, and maybe it wasn't too late. She didn't sound or look excited about going back to New York but seemed resigned, as if it was the only choice she thought she had.

Grant walked over to her and put his forearms on the top fence rail alongside hers. "Look, Stephanie, you have to do what is best for your future; I understand and agree with that. But I have been working on something; I don't have all the details yet, but I want … no, BlackRock wants you to join the company."

Stephanie turned toward him, stepped back, and said, "What in God's name are you talking about?" Her eyes were moist, and she was almost yelling. "I won't take your charity; how little you must think of me. I told you I will not be a kept woman again. What part of that do you not understand?" She turned and started to walk away.

Grant grabbed her arm to stop her. She jerked her arm free and kept walking.

"Listen to me, Stephanie, please. It isn't charity; BlackRock is in the process of expanding our bodyguard services worldwide. We have set up a new company, GreyRock, Limited, that will be based in London and provide bodyguard and personal security services. We need instructors. You would be a perfect instructor for the program. The potential for assassination is real for these clients. Who better to teach our people what to look for than you? It's a real job; BlackRock needs you. Why go back to that big city mill and get ground up?"

She stopped walking and turned to face him. The look on her face showed interest, and for a moment he thought he had her. Then the light went out of her eyes, and she started to turn away.

Grant wasn't prepared to present this idea to her yet, but here he was: it had to be now, or he would lose her. He was desperate. This was his last best chance. The words came tumbling out without being filtered by his brain. "You can make a contribution to saving lives by joining BlackRock. You will be fighting terrorism by equipping others to prevent it. Isn't that what you wanted? Isn't that what you said? Please, Steph, at least think about it."

She turned back toward him and looked into his eyes for a long moment. Then she said, "All right Grant, I owe you that much. I'll think about it."

Chapter 53

The United States attorney for the Northern District of California, Constance Fitzgerald, approached a lectern with a Justice Department seal on the front and an American flag on the wall behind it. She was dressed today in a navy blue pantsuit.

Fitzgerald was an up-and-coming star in the Democratic Party who many thought was prepping herself to run for governor of California. She was smart, a Berkeley and Stanford law grad, tall and attractive, but built like an NFL tight end; articulate, but completely without a sense of humor. Her name was Ms. Fitzgerald or Constance; woe unto anyone who called her Connie. *Connie* was for girls, and Constance Fitzgerald was a woman, a strong woman. The few who knew her well and liked her acknowledged that she was without compassion for anyone she considered to have run afoul of the law. Those who did not like her said that affirmative action together with the Peter Principle had allowed her to achieve a position for which her temperament made her uniquely unqualified.

Grant watched the television with interest as Fitzgerald cleared her throat and began to speak without notes. "I am here today to announce that the Federal Grand Jury has issued a three-count indictment against Grant Meredith of Durango, Colorado, and Paul Brandt of San Diego, California, for violation of 18 USC 2340, Section 1003 of the Detainee Treatment Act of 2005 and the UN Convention against Torture ratified by the United States in 1994.

"The indictment charges that both Meredith and Brandt are citizens of the United States in the employ of BlackRock, USA, which was engaged to provide security services in the Kingdom of Saudi Arabia, and they did knowingly conspire with others to commit acts, under the color of law, with the specific intent to inflict severe mental suffering upon a person within their custody and physical control.

"The second count of the indictment alleges that the conspirators committed acts of torture by abducting the victim, holding him against his will, striking him, and threatening to maim his child, which resulted in severe mental suffering to the victim.

"The third count of the indictment alleges that Brandt did knowingly carry a firearm during and in relation to a crime of violence, for which he may be prosecuted in the United States under Title 18 United States Code 924(c)(2)(A).

"This marks the second time the Department of Justice has charged defendants with the crime of torture. This case will send a clear message that the United States will not be a safe haven for human rights violators. Crimes such as these will not go unpunished. This case is a further demonstration of our tireless efforts to ensure that justice is served.

"I have time for a few questions."

The Fox News correspondent asked, "What specifically did these men do that violated the laws you cited?"

Fitzgerald looked directly into the camera and said, "On orders from Meredith, Brandt and others seized Dr. Ali Al-Fulani in the parking garage of his apartment building in Riyadh, Saudi Arabia, pulled him into a van with a hood over his head, struck him twice, and told the doctor that if he did not tell them about the explosive head charges he had planted in one hundred men, they would maim his baby. Doctor Al-Fulani provided them with the information they requested, and he was released. He was held against his will for five minutes."

The CNN reporter asked, "How did this doctor get to you?"

"Part of that is classified; however, I can tell you that in light of the terrorist incidents in this country, the Kingdom of Saudi Arabia is cooperating fully with our investigation into all, and I mean all, of the events leading up to those incidents."

A reporter from ABC asked, "How can what they did be considered torture?"

Fitzgerald said, "The statutes prohibit cruel, inhumane, or degrading treatment. Section 2340 defines torture, in relevant part, as an act intended to inflict severe mental suffering, which is itself defined as prolonged mental harm. Dr. Al-Fulani, who has been granted blanket immunity for his activities relating to the recent terrorist attacks, testified that he suffered and continues to suffer nightmares about his child being maimed and disfigured. His psychiatrist has testified that he is on medication and will require years of therapy to come to grips with what was done to him."

"Wait a minute," shouted the Fox News correspondent. "Are you telling us that under these statutes, torture is defined by the reaction of the victim, not what was done to him?"

"Yes," said Fitzgerald.

"Who decides if the victim is experiencing severe mental suffering?" asked a reporter from the *San Francisco Examiner.*

"A judge and jury," said Fitzgerald.

"Are you telling us that our agents will not know ahead of time if their activities constitute torture?" asked a *New York Times* reporter.

Fitzgerald held up her hand and, once again, looked directly into the camera. "I don't write the laws; it is my job to enforce them, and I intend to do just that. Thank you." She turned and strode from the podium, ignoring several shouted questions.

The phone rang, and Grant snatched it up.

"Do you know what this means?" said Homer Johnson.

Grant looked down as if the answer might be on the floor. "How bad is it?" he asked.

"Bad. You are now a political football. The case is all about politics, and you are in the middle. The Democrats cannot let President Sampson become a hero. They can't deny what happened, but they can challenge her methods. They want to change the dialogue from her success to her running roughshod over the law. Since they can't attack her directly just yet, they are going to use you, Brandt, and BlackRock to make a case against her.

"Understand this, Grant: the left is going all out to destroy you. Don't kid yourself; if you lose, there will be an outcry to put you in jail for a long time. You need to keep your mouth shut and get a good … no, the best lawyer you can find. I suggest you start with John Coroner in San Francisco. He is a friend of mine and one of the best criminal lawyers in the country. BlackRock will pick up the legal bills. You will also need a public relations person to deal with the press. BlackRock will cover that also.

"One last thing: as a former lawyer, let me advise you not to talk to Brandt. Anything you say will be subject to discovery. The only way you can talk to him is in a joint meeting with counsel."

Grant rang off, walked out on the porch, and sat in a rocker. The world looked the same as it had ten minutes ago, not at all as if it had come crashing down on him.

Stephanie came running across the lawn. When she saw him, she slowed to a walk and took several deep breaths, visibly collecting herself.

"Grant, you are not going to believe what I just saw on television," she said.

"I saw it. I just came out here to clear my head before the telephone starts ringing off the hook," said Grant.

She pulled a small table around in front of him and sat down. The words rushed out of her. "Grant, this is unbelievable. You are a hero. You found out about the implants, and you found out where the bombs were. I know all this is classified, but you should be getting the Medal of Freedom, not getting indicted."

Grant got up, walked to the porch railing, and turned to face her. "I don't know what to think. I have no experience with the criminal justice system, but I'm scared. OJ goes free; Martha Stewart goes to jail, not for the crime being investigated but for lying to the investigators. Scooter Libby is convicted because his memory differed from a reporter's. It is just crazy."

The phone rang. "Stephanie, could you please answer it? It's probably some reporter. Just say we have no comment at this time."

A moment later Stephanie came back with the phone in her hand; "Grant, it's John Coroner, an attorney. He said Homer Johnson asked him to call."

Ten minutes later Grant had an attorney. "That wasn't so bad. All calls should be referred to him until he lines up some PR people," he said to Stephanie, who had been quietly waiting and watching him.

She walked over and put her hands on his shoulders. "Grant, my old firm would be perfect for the job. They have a lot of experience with white collar criminal cases, and I could keep an eye on them."

Given her background, it was patently obvious that she could not be his PR person, but he thought it would be a good idea to have someone holding the PR people accountable. The only problem was that it put would put her in New York and San Francisco a lot; but then he would surely be in San Francisco a lot himself.

"What about your interviews?" he asked.

"They can wait."

He thought this would probably kill his idea for her to be a BlackRock instructor, for the time being at least, but at least they would be seeing a lot of each other.

Chapter 54

Grant was sitting at his desk in the library with the *Wall Street Journal* open in front of him. He couldn't believe what he was reading. The bold headline screamed, *"BlackRock Assailed on Tax Policy."*

According to the article, Representative Barney Wyman was looking at BlackRock's classification of its security guards as independent contractors for whom the company did not withhold taxes, rather than employees for whom there must be withholding. Wyman, a New Jersey Democrat, had written to the company that "BlackRock may have avoided paying millions of dollars in Social Security, Medicare, unemployment, and related taxes for which it is legally responsible."

The article went on to say that Wyman's staff estimated that BlackRock owed as much as $50 million in unpaid taxes for its State Department security personnel.

This was a serious matter because BlackRock's business model revolved around the classification of guards as freelance contractors and not employees. These people liked to come and go between assignments, which BlackRock policies made easy. If the company had to pay additional taxes, something would have to give: either bids would be higher, impacting on the amount of work, or the security personnel would be paid less. However one chose to look at it, this was not good for the company.

Grant supposed he was naïve; one would think that since he and BlackRock were the primary reason the country had been saved from the terrorist onslaught, they deserved a ticker-tape parade through Times Square. Instead, they were being attacked by the Democrats as part of a plan to put President Sampson on the defensive, rather than allow her to get credit for a job well done.

Grant thanked God for BlackRock's ownership structure, which gave it plenty of political clout to deal with this onslaught. He needed all his own energy to defend himself.

Never having been wrongly accused of a crime, Grant was having difficulty coping with what it was doing to him. First there was the disbelief; there must be some mistake. Next he thought if he could just talk to them quietly and in a reasonable manner, they would realize that they misunderstood what happened. But he had enough brains to talk to his lawyer.

In his case, he realized as the gray light of a winter dawn set in, that no matter what the prosecutor said, it was a political prosecution. Things could have been ignored in the exercise of prosecutorial discretion. They didn't have to prosecute every crime; but not only was this not ignored, the prosecutor intended to make a cause célèbre out of it, furthering the political goals of the Democratic Party and her own political ambitions

What kept Grant tossing and turning for hours at night was the inescapable reality that he and Brandt had done what they were charged with doing, and it might be a crime, even though it had saved the country from disaster.

He wasn't sleeping much.

Chapter 55

Grant walked into the lobby of the high-rise office building at One Market Street in San Francisco. He was scheduled to meet in twenty minutes with John Coroner, his attorney, in his twentieth-floor office. With time to kill, Grant got a coffee from the Starbucks kiosk and took a seat next to the fountain in the atrium.

John Coroner, 62, was a trial lawyer. He did criminal trials and civil trials alike; it didn't matter to him. The courtroom was his home away from home. Litigators sat around big tables, pushed paper, and settled cases. Coroner went to court. A former Marine, he had been badly wounded in Vietnam. When asked about pressure in high-profile trials, he said that after combat, trial pressure was trivial.

Maybe to him as the attorney, but Grant was the defendant facing a decade or more in prison. He couldn't pick up a newspaper without seeing himself described as a torturer; sometimes it was not preceded with the word *alleged*. Opinion pieces in *The New York Times* and *Washington Post* were calling for congressional investigations of him, BlackRock, and Brandt. His picture was in the newspapers and on the Internet. When strangers recognized him, they reacted as if he was some kind of monster.

Grant felt that he could handle the notoriety. After all, he had no choice. What drove him up the wall was the subjective nature of the crime he was charged with. Some things are pretty straightforward. If you pull out a guy's fingernails with pliers, all could agree that was torture. Electroshock to the genitals: torture. Right or wrong, necessary or not—in any context, these were torture.

But threatening a guy is torture? He could go to jail because he'd conspired to threaten a guy who had information necessary to protect the lives of his employees. This was Alice in Wonderland stuff. Dealing with this absurdity was pressure. For the first time in his life, he was considering taking sleeping pills.

This was his first face-to-face meeting with Coroner, and he was nervous. He knew Coroner had talked to Constance Fitzgerald, but he didn't know the outcome.

Grant stepped off the elevator into an ultramodern reception area: all chrome, glass, and black leather. The paintings were contemporary, bright, and full of color. The view of the Bay Bridge was spectacular. Seated at a chrome and glass reception desk was an elegant black woman of about forty dressed in a flattering St. Johns navy suit. She stood, gave him a smile that should have her on magazine covers, and said, "Hello, Mr. Meredith, we have been expecting you. Come with me to John's office."

As one would expect, Coroner had a corner office with views to the east and north. It was furnished in standard senior partner style with a big polished desk and high-backed leather chair. In front of the desk were two guest chairs. Off to the right was a five-foot diameter round conference table with four chairs.

Coroner stood when they came into his office and walked around his desk. He had a full head of neatly trimmed gray hair and was dressed in Wrangler jeans, cowboy boots, a blue work shirt, and an open brown leather vest. A lightweight leather sport coat was draped over one of the guest chairs. His hazel eyes looked directly into Grant's. His handshake was firm. Grant was surprised that his hands were callused, not soft like an office worker's. What got Grant's attention was the man's smile and the way the skin crinkled around his eyes. This was a man who laughed a lot. Grant's first impression was *What's not to like?*

"Mr. Meredith, may I bring you some coffee?" asked the receptionist.

"Yes, that would be great; black, please," Grant said.

"Sweetheart, would you get me a diet soda please?" said Coroner.

Grant tilted his head and gave Coroner an inquisitive look as the receptionist left.

Coroner laughed and put his arm around him, guiding him toward the conference table. "Don't worry, Audrey is my wife. We have a strict office policy against sexual harassment."

Grant and Coroner spent a few minutes exchanging pleasantries and shared military experiences. Nothing specific, just to let each other know they were on the same page.

Coroner said, "Before we get started, Grant, I want to tell you how grateful I am for what you did to stop the terrorists. You saved thousands from death and thousands more from tragedy. Thank you."

This came as a complete surprise, out of left field. After all Grant had been through, all the pressure of the indictment and vicious publicity, this was the first time someone other than the president had personally thanked him. His eyes started to moisten. It took all of his self-control to suck it up and croak, "Thank you, John. I appreciate that, especially coming from you. Where do we stand?"

Coroner sat back in his chair and said, "There are three elements to the crime of torture as defined by statute.

"First, you must have acted under color of law. Since BlackRock was in the employ of the Saudi government, you and Brandt were agents of the government and your activities satisfy the under-color-of-law requirement. Same thing for the former Liberian president's son who was convicted here for torture in Liberia."

Grant interrupted. "What was his sentence?"

"Ninety-seven years."

Grant had difficulty drawing a breath. "What did he do?"

"Oh, he was a bad guy, burning people, things we don't want to talk about. There is really no comparison with your situation."

Really, thought Grant, maybe he would only get twenty years. It was hard for him to follow what Coroner was now saying.

"Second, you must have intended to inflict severe mental suffering. You surely intended to make that man fear you would maim his child. That was the whole point. The statute defines severe mental suffering as prolonged mental harm resulting from the threat that another person will imminently be subjected to death, severe physical pain, or suffering. Brandt threatened to maim the doctor's baby. If this caused the doctor prolonged mental harm, the second prong of the statute is satisfied. Plenty of psychiatrists would testify that he has suffered mentally and will do so for a long time.

"Third, the victim must be in your custody and control, which he clearly was.

"Making your situation even worse is the fact that you are not in the military, so you are not subject to the Detainee Treatment Act of 2005. At least soldiers have some wiggle room that the act must 'shock the conscience.' That gives a judge or jury some ability to look at the context in which the activity took place.

"The way out of this at trial is to get the jury to buy the argument that the doctor's mental harm is something different than that contemplated by the statute. The problem with the argument is that the judge may decide before trial, as a matter of law, that his reaction, if believed, does constitute prolonged mental harm under the statute. The case has been assigned to Judge Arlen Feinstein, who is famously liberal, even for San Francisco. He will probably rule against you.

"We can also argue that the definition of torture in the statute is too vague for criminal prosecution and is unconstitutional. A person has a right to know what conduct constitutes a crime. Congress has deliberately failed to define torture in specifics. Having a court define torture after the fact applies the law ex post facto and is also unconstitutional. However, those arguments failed in the Liberian president's son's case. It is doubtful that Feinstein will reach a different result.

"I spoke to the US attorney, and she is adamant about this prosecution. She told me off the record that the Justice

Department wants to use this case to start developing a body of case law defining torture under the statute. She denied there is anything political about your case, but she ignores the fact that the definition of torture is political.

"Frankly, Grant, torture is like obscenity. Justice Potter Stewart famously said about obscenity in 1964 that he could not define it, but he knew it when he saw it."

Grant just sat there. He wanted to say something, but he couldn't; he was unable to construct a coherent thought.

Coroner shifted uneasily in his chair and looked out the window for a moment. Something bad was coming.

"Grant, I got a call from the Justice Department Office of International Affairs earlier this morning," he said in a soft voice. "It seems the Mexican government has filed papers seeking to extradite you and Stephanie Chambers to Mexico for stealing a government helicopter. They have also asked for your provisional arrest during the pendency of the extradition proceedings."

Grant clubbed the table with his fist and stood up, knocking his chair over backwards. The words exploded out of him. "What in the goddamn hell is going on? Those people were going to kill me. We took the helicopter to escape. Why am I being persecuted, why? Tell me why."

Coroner sat very still, looked at Grant, and shook his head. "Grant, if you blow up like that in court, you are going to do irreparable damage to your case and our relationship with the judge. Sit down, there is more.

"Since there is a case pending against you here, Justice forwarded the request to Fitzgerald. This is bad, not only because of Fitzgerald but because the OIA has made a preliminary finding that the request for extradition is legally sufficient under the treaty with Mexico. It is not a decision on the facts or the merits of the case against you, but just a finding that preliminary legal requirements have been met."

Grant could feel his body temperature rise. His face felt hot, and his heart threatened to pound out of his chest. He opened his mouth to scream or speak, he hadn't decided which, when Coroner held up his hand.

"Wait, please, there is more. Fitzgerald has obtained a warrant for your arrest. You must turn yourself in today. There will be a hearing before a federal magistrate tomorrow afternoon to set bail. Be sure that Fitzgerald will oppose bail. The magistrate will grant bail, or you will go to jail pending a 3184 hearing before a judge to determine if you are extraditable. Again, the merits are not at issue. The judge is limited to determining if you are extraditable. If the judge finds against you, he enters an order of extradition and forwards it to the Secretary of State, who makes the final decision whether to surrender you to Mexico."

"Whoa, whoa," Grant said, "go through this again, slowly."

He did, and it did not sound any better. All Grant could conclude was that he was in a god-awful mess.

He left Coroner's office in a fog. They had spent an hour going over his options, and nothing looked good.

Brandt and he were being criminally prosecuted for torture, a crime for which there was no meaningful definition. The prosecutor admitted that his case was being used to give substance to the statute. Congress should have done that.

BlackRock was being harassed by Democrats in Congress over the tax status of its security personnel. This came out of the blue. BlackRock had opinions from top tax attorneys that their classification of the guards as independent contractors was proper. BlackRock was being portrayed as an adjunct of the Sampson administration that was cheating the government with its tacit approval.

Now the Sanchez family piled on. Ramon had helped find the bombs. Had it not been for him … Grant couldn't even think about what might have happened. Obviously, he had not acted with the milk of human kindness; for whatever reason, it served his purposes to find the bombs. But now this whole extradition was vintage Ramon. Grant remembered the time in his Phoenix office when Ramon told him power came from manipulating the system to get the result you wanted. The Sanchez family wanted Stephanie and him. What better way than to have the government hand the two of them over?

Grant couldn't help but think that, if his own government had not started this torture prosecution, Ramon would never have thought of going after extradition.

Chapter 56

A full-mooned darkness had settled over Washington DC. Almost all but the night staff had finally called it a day after fourteen hours which had started as usual at 6 a.m. President Sampson, dressed in blue jeans and a blue and gold Huskies sweatshirt, sat in front of the fireplace in her private study in the White House living quarters sipping a cup of tea. Mike O'Brien sat across from her. O'Brien, as always, was dressed in black: jeans, boots, polo shirt, leather sport coat, and no tie. He held a glass of his trademark single-malt scotch.

"Mike, you seem to be nursing that drink. Off your feed?" asked the president, reaching for a levity she did not feel.

"Perceptive as always, aren't you, Janet? Tell you the truth, I began to limit myself to two drinks a day when this terrorist business started, and I like the way I feel in the morning. I've had my two for the day, but I didn't want to refuse your hospitality."

"Since we're telling the truth, I asked you here at this hour, knowing Lisa would understand, to simply vent. I don't have a husband, and my chief of staff will probably write a book about me when he leaves. He doesn't need any more material.

"Mike, I may be the most powerful person in the world, but I have learned one thing since I took office. I cannot control those who work for me. There are times I want to pound the table, scream at people, and fire whole departments. I do everything I can to make my policies and priorities clear. I appoint people to Cabinet positions, and they understand what I want. They hire their key people, who are supposed to ride herd on things, but the permanent bureaucracy just goes about their business as if I and my policies don't exist.

"Mike, some of these senior bureaucrats actively work against my objectives and policies with impunity. If I manage to have one fired, Congress will go ballistic, yammering about independence within the executive branch. I know that is BS, and so do they, but look what they did to Bush for firing some US attorneys who weren't with the administration program. The Democrats kept that non-scandal on the front pages for over a year.

"In rare lucid moments I think that politicians come and go, making a lot of noise, but the government is run by the civil service and by congressional staff bureaucrats. It flat doesn't matter what the administration policy is; they just do what they want because they will be here long after we're gone. State is the worst. Did you ever read that book by Michael Bolton?"

Sampson put down her tea, reached toward O'Brien, and said, "I need the scotch you aren't drinking; hand it over."

Wordlessly, he handed her his scotch. She relied on him to know when to speak up and when it was time to listen.

"This mess with Grant Meredith is a perfect example," she said, taking a pull of scotch and making a face as it burned her throat.

"State and Justice together have put me in an impossible position. First that bitch in San Francisco indicts a national freaking hero for torturing a Saudi terrorist, the very act that saved God only knows how many American lives. Even she wouldn't have done that without clearing it with Simmons. I didn't even get a heads-up from Justice that they were investigating Meredith, much less that they were going to indict him. I have no idea how they found out what happened in Saudi Arabia.

"Next the State Department screws me." President Sampson stopped for another sample of the scotch. It didn't burn quite so much this time. "The Mexican government's extradition request for Meredith went to them first. State could have sent it back for insufficiency or something; but no, they forward it to Justice without even telling me. I don't even know if the Secretary of State was informed. Justice then sends it to San Francisco, again without telling me. What am I, a potted plant?

"Now, if I start trying to find out how *my* administration indicted a true American hero, these clowns will be all over me for interfering with the impartial administration of justice or some other BS. It is *my* administration; I am supposed to be in charge. *I* am surely responsible when things go wrong.

"Mike ... my administration has been hijacked by the permanent bureaucracy and the Democratic Party. I can keep silent and let Meredith dangle in the wind; wait and see how the trial comes out. We can't extradite him before we try him. I could pardon him if he is convicted or pull a Bush-like weasel act and merely commute any sentence or fine he might receive. That would be so great. Meredith tagged as a torturer, not a hero.

"If I tell State to deny the extradition request, there I go again, interfering with the impartial administration of justice. Hell, they might even start talking about impeachment."

President Sampson finished off the scotch. She got up and poured herself a refill from the sideboard. When she sat back down, O'Brien cleared his throat.

"Janet, it is only your administration if you act like it. The genius of our country is divided government. Three equal branches, executive, legislative, and judicial, were meant to disagree and fight with one another. How else was the power of the federal government going to be kept in check?

"The constitution does not say that the judiciary has the power to determine the constitutionality of laws passed by the legislature and signed by the president, from which there is no appeal. That power was taken for itself by the court in *Marbury v. Madison* in 1803, and the other two branches let them get away with it. This kind of stuff has been going on ever since, each branch trying to improve its position.

"Janet, it was Harry Truman who coined the phrase, 'I'll stand by you, but if you can't take the heat, get out of the kitchen.' He was talking to his staff about criticism of political appointments, but it applies to the Meredith situation.

"Congress will be on you for this or for something else all the time. Yes, you saved the country from the terrorists, but that was yesterday. Today is a new day, and they are still out to get you, to bend you to their will and render you impotent for the rest of your term.

"You have to fight back," said O'Brien, "for yourself and the power of the presidency. That's the bottom line."

"All right, Mike; what should I do?" asked the president.

O'Brien smiled and said, "What do you think you should do?"

Sampson looked at him through narrowed eyes and then chuckled. "Always the law professor; I hate the Socratic method. Sometimes I just want someone to tell me what to do."

She stood and said, "Let me think about it. We both need some sleep."

Chapter 57

The next morning Attorney General Christine Simmons was ushered into the Oval Office. President Sampson, seated behind her desk, did not get up to greet her and did not ask her to sit.

"Tell me, Ms. Simmons, how is it that Grant Meredith has been indicted by my Justice Department without my knowledge?" she asked in a flat voice.

Simmons took an involuntary step backward and then started to sit in one of the guest chairs in front of the desk.

"I didn't invite you here to chat, and I didn't invite you sit down and make yourself comfortable while you try to bullshit me," said the president in the same emotionless voice.

Simmons jumped upright as if she had sat on a thorn.

"There was nothing I could do, Janet …"

"*Madame President* will be fine, Ms. Simmons."

"Yes, Madame President, as I was saying, there was nothing I could do. Congress wants the US attorneys to be independent from political influence, and when Fitzgerald told me she had evidence that Meredith and Brandt had tortured that Saudi, well, I couldn't interfere with her decision to prosecute. I knew she would blow the whistle to Congress if I tried to overrule her, and we would be in big trouble. I don't want to end up like Alberto Gonzales. I was going to tell you, but she made the announcement an hour after she ran it by me. There was nothing I could do." Simmons turned her palms up in a gesture of helplessness.

President Sampson sat perfectly still for almost a full minute just staring at her, while Simmons shifted uncomfortably on her feet.

At last the president began slowly speaking. "This may come as a shock to you, Ms. Simmons, but I am the president of the United States. I head the executive branch of the federal government. You and the US attorneys were appointed by me. You serve at my pleasure and are to carry out the priorities I set for this country. If you and the US attorneys are unwilling to do that, you, or they, or all of you can resign. You can even resign in protest. I want you to think about Elliot Richardson and William Ruckelshaus in the Nixon Administration.

"You have allowed a single US attorney, without any supervision, without any input from you or me, to indict an American hero for saving this country from a terrorist disaster. US attorneys are not free agents running around setting their own priorities and doing whatever seems like a good idea at the time or what is in their best political or personal interest. You have allowed me, this administration, Messrs. Meredith and Brandt, and their company, which this country needs very badly, to be humiliated.

"I have made arrangements," said President Sampson in the same blank voice, "for you to use an office across from my chief of staff to write your letter of resignation. Please do not leave the building until I have acted upon it."

Chapter 58

President Sampson's secretary ushered in her next appointment, Secretary of State Robert A. Thomson. She didn't get up but gestured Thomson to a chair in front of her desk. Maybe it was his age, maybe it was that he was male; but she felt a twinge of pity for him.

Without any exchange of pleasantries, she began. "Secretary Thomson, will you please tell me why the State Department is processing a request from the Mexican government to extradite Grant Meredith?"

Thomson took a moment to tug the crease in his trousers before he said, "I was in London until yesterday, so I did not learn about it until I returned. The request was apparently handled in a routine manner. All the paperwork was in order."

"Does anyone at the State Department know who Grant Meredith is?" asked the president in the same tone she had used with Simmons.

"Yes, Madame President, but the decision was that they did not want to harm relations with Mexico or violate the treaty with Mexico or endanger our extradition requests with other countries. You see, we have to keep the big picture in mind—"

President Sampson held up a hand. "Stop right there; don't say another word. Am I correct that this decision was made without consulting you?"

Thomson broke eye contact with the President briefly and looked down. If he had expected some dismay from the president, he must have felt sure he could demonstrate that the decision had served the greater good. Now, clearly, he wasn't so sure of himself.

"Yes, Madame President, that is correct. However, I must support the decision." Thomson raised his head so that he seemed to be looking down his nose at the president.

Her eyes bored into Thomson's, and she continued in her affectless tone, "Why?"

Thomson again broke eye contact and looked at the flag flanking her left shoulder. "I realize that Meredith is something of a hero, but the diplomatic posture of this country must be to honor valid requests for extradition made in conformity with our treaty obligations. While this may be inconvenient for Meredith, there is more at stake here than a single individual. In its largest sense, this is about world order, about peaceful relations between countries, and about respect for other sovereign nations. You see, Madame President—"

President Sampson interrupted him again. " Kindly don't begin to lecture me. Mr. Secretary, given who Mr. Meredith is, if you had been advised of this request, would you have consulted with me before allowing the State Department to pass it on to the Justice Department?"

Here Thomson did not look away and did not hesitate. "Absolutely not, Madame President. The paperwork was in order, which was all that State reviewed. It was up to Justice to get a judge to rule there was an extraditable offense. The matter would then come back to State, and we have discretion on what action to take. I might have discussed it with you then. At that point, however, all the formalities would have been satisfied, and our treaty obligations would require extradition of Mr. Meredith to the Mexican authorities." Thomson concluded in a confident tone, again lifting his chin imperiously.

Sampson sat and stared at him without speaking. After almost a minute of silence, Thomson began to stand and said, "If that will be all, Madame President—"

"Sit," said the president. "Would it interest you to know that Meredith was in Mexico at my request to try and get information from the Sanchez family about the terrorists who were attacking this country? Not President Sanchez, but his father and brother who run the largest drug and human smuggling operation in Mexico. Would it interest you to know that they tried to kill Meredith and that he escaped in the government helicopter that just happened to be at their ranch? Would it interest you to know that the helicopter was returned and no protest was made until the US attorney indicted Meredith?"

Now Thomson could not meet the president's eyes. His shoulders slumped, and he studied the thin layer of dust on his highly polished black wingtip shoes. President Sampson said nothing; she just sat and watched him. He moved his hands into his lap. His knuckles showed white. He took a deep breath before speaking.

"Madame President, my resignation will be on your desk in the morning."

"I want it accompanied by the resignation of whoever in the State Department processed this as a routine matter, and I want both resignations to contain an apology to Mr. Meredith and the American people. But before you submit your resignation, I want you to recall the extradition request from the Justice Department and send it back to Mexico, saying it is without justification in whatever diplomatic gobbledygook is appropriate. Do you understand?" President Sampson had not yet varied her tone.

Thomson stood up ramrod straight and looked the president full in the eyes. "Yes, Madame President, I understand."

President Sampson stood, extended her hand, and said, "Thank you for your service, Mr. Secretary."

Thomson reached across the desk, maintaining eye contact, and shook her hand. "I wish you well, Madame President."

Chapter 59

"Congressman Wyman is on the line, Madame President," said her secretary over the intercom.

Once again President Sampson skipped the pleasantries. "Congressman, this call is about the BlackRock tax hearings you have scheduled."

Wyman emitted a self-satisfied chuckle and said, "Yes, Madame President, we have to keep a careful eye on the flow of funds to the Treasury."

In her now-habitual flat voice the president said, "I have checked with the Treasury Department, and they have no problem with BlackRock's taxes."

"Oh, I think they will by the time the press is through with them," Wyman said, with palpable smugness.

After a measured moment, Sampson said, "If you want to attack me and my administration, that is fair game, but I cannot have you harassing BlackRock for political purposes."

Wyman was unfazed. "Madame President, Congress is an independent branch of government. We do what we want—"

"Congressman, let me put it to you in a way you will understand. In the last appropriations bill you personally inserted about one hundred earmarks for your usual local supporters. The Justice Department may choose to investigate this connection. Furthermore, since your earmarks are not in the bills proper but in the committee reports, the executive branch is not required by law to release funds for those projects. Finally, my party will use all necessary funds to find and support an excellent candidate to run against you in the next election. Do I make myself clear?"

Wyman had been in Congress for forty years. If there was one thing he had mastered, it was when to hold 'em and when to fold 'em.

"Very well, Madame President. We have a lot of other business to conduct."

Chapter 60

Janet Sampson sat alone at her Oval Office desk with a pad and pencil in front of her. The elation she had felt when the bombs were disarmed and the terrorists killed had been short-lived. Her mood and the mood of the country had turned somber as the funerals for the victims took place across the nation.

She believed that her primary responsibility as president was to protect the populace. The terrorists were out there, and they weren't going away. More were being recruited every day.

She was reminded of a story her husband had told her not long before he died. In India a man and his son were strolling through their village and saw a big house on the hill. The son said to his father, "Someday when I grow up, I'm going to live in a house like that." A similar scene took place in Pakistan, and the son said, "Someday when I grow up, I'm going to blow up that big house."

Terrorism was conceived where there was no hope and no opportunity. She had to believe that, because if she didn't, it meant that civilization was on the brink of religious war.

Her reverie was broken by her secretary. Mike O'Brien and his wife had arrived.

Lisa O'Brien had been an on-air CNN anchor for five years and was far more than another talking airhead. She was everything a modern-day television anchorperson was supposed to be: beautiful, smart, and opinionated. Her Sunday evening week in review program was the highest rated cable opinion program on the air.

She had asked Mike to bring Lisa with him for two reasons. First, she respected the newswoman's opinion even if she did not always agree with her. Second, she would provide a good indication of how the media would react to her decision concerning Grant Meredith.

After a brief greeting, they settled on the sofa arrangement around the fireplace.

President Sampson got directly down to business. "I have asked you here to act as a sounding board for me concerning Grant Meredith. I have to decide what, if anything, to do about the case. Here is the situation as I see it.

"Three things are clear to me. First, the information Meredith extracted from the Saudi doctor saved untold American lives. Second, at the time he extracted the information, he had no idea he was dealing with a terrorist plot that had been launched in the United States while he was in Saudi Arabia. Third, he violated a poorly drafted statute for which he is being prosecuted.

"As I see it, I have four choices: pardon him now, pardon him after trial if he is found guilty, commute his sentence after trial, or do nothing and let the legal process run its course. I suppose I could order Fitzgerald to drop the prosecution, but that smacks of interfering with the impartial administration of justice; that is not an option as far as I am concerned.

"Lisa, how do you see the situation?"

"If you pardon Meredith, the left both here and abroad will crucify you for condoning torture. You will not be able to claim that his actions were done to protect the United States because, as you just said, they were not; they were done in connection with his business activities. He was not acting on behalf of the United States when he tortured the doctor, and there was no national security justification for what he did."

Lisa sat back and crossed her arms and legs as if daring President Sampson to disagree with her. Sampson looked to Mike O'Brien who had been sitting with his forearms on his knees staring at the carpet while his wife spoke.

"It's hard to disagree with my bride if one looks at things the way she does; so let's look at it another way. The problem is with the statute's definition of torture and the absence of any provision for extenuating circumstances. Congress has never defined torture except in general terms. Under the Detainee Treatment Act, torture must be something that shocks the conscience. If you define it that way, one can look at the surrounding circumstances. That is to say, what might be justifiable treatment in a ticking-time-bomb scenario would not be justifiable in a garden-variety civilian criminal interrogation.

"This doctor may be suffering from nightmares and such, but neither he nor anyone else was physically hurt. Meredith probably had no reason to think he was torturing the guy; scaring him maybe, but let's use some common sense here. The problem is that whether or not he intended to inflict severe emotional distress is a jury question several years and millions of dollars in attorney's fees from now."

President Sampson said nothing. She got up, walked to the window, and stared at the Rose Garden for a while. Turning, she said, "Lisa, this is classified and off the record, and I mean off the record. Do you agree?"

Lisa didn't answer right away. Mike reached over, put his hand on her thigh, and said quietly, "Lisa."

"Yes, President Sampson, I agree."

"Grant Meredith was responsible for finding the bombs. He risked his life and almost lost it going to Mexico and appealing to a certain powerful family for help. You don't know who they are, and I can't tell you. For some reason, one of them decided to help us and was able to locate the bombs. This country owes Meredith a great debt, but his role must remain secret."

Lisa sat forward, eyes alert, and said, "Do you mean the Sanchez family, as in Hector Sanchez, the president of Mexico? As in Carlos, the lord high smuggler of Sonora state?"

"All of this is classified," said President Sampson firmly.

Lisa's eyes grew wide, and she inhaled slowly, turning to her husband and saying, "What you keep from me is beyond belief."

Mike held up his hands in a defensive gesture.

President Sampson immediately interjected, "This is national security, Lisa. You don't have the clearance, and after all, you are a reporter with your own priorities."

Lisa sat back and again crossed her arms under her ample breasts. "What I said a moment ago still stands. Since you won't reveal what he did, no one knows, and you will be portrayed as condoning torture. There is simply no way you can defend what he did. Even now you aren't defending what he did; you are willing to excuse him because of what he did later. How can you pardon him without a reason?"

"You don't need a reason," said Mike. "Clinton did not have a reason, at least a legitimate one, to pardon Marc Rich. If you think it is right, just do it."

No one said anything for almost a full minute.

Finally, Lisa said, "You can pardon him in the interests of national security or offer no reason. If you use national security as a justification, the press will pull the CIA apart trying to find out why. If you refuse to give a reason, basically say 'because I can'; the press will vilify you for condoning torture. Pick your poison."

President Sampson turned a look on her adviser without portfolio. "Mike, any final thoughts?"

He stood and said, "President Sampson, whatever you do, there will be a substantial number of well-intentioned people who will disagree with you at the top of their lungs. It is impossible to please everyone. You can be a politician and stick your finger in the wind, or you can be the president of the United States and do what you think is right for the country. You have a value system which should be an anchor in times like this."

As the O'Briens left the Oval Office, Lisa turned to President Sampson and said, "Madame President, I don't envy you."

The next morning the White House press secretary issued the following press release:

"President Sampson has accepted the resignations of Secretary of State Robert Thomson and Attorney General Christine Simmons, both of whom have stepped down to spend more time with their families. She thanks them for their service to the country. Nominees to replace them will be announced shortly.

"President Sampson has also granted full pardons to BlackRock, USA; Paul Brandt, and Grant Meredith for their actions in interrogating a Saudi national while acting as security personnel for the Saudi government. The pardon was requested by the Saudi government and is considered to be in the best interests of US/Saudi relations."

Chapter 61

Grant and Stephanie were sitting in the late afternoon shade on the north porch of the ranch house. The last of thirty neighbors had left an hour ago, bringing an end to another year's branding party. Branding the calves was a Western ritual which usually involved all the neighbors. Those who rode helped gather the cows and calves. Men roped the calves, and Grant branded them so they could be turned out to pasture for the summer. It was hot, dusty work and usually great fun for Grant.

What enabled him to relax enough to enjoy some of the fun was the knowledge that he would not have to go to an extradition hearing. The end of that part of his personal mess was quite a relief.

When the branding was complete, everyone adjourned to the ranch house yard for a potluck lunch. It was Grant's favorite party of the year, and he was pleased that Stephanie had been able to come. She had been in charge of keeping the branding irons hot.

The sun, hard work, and margaritas had combined in such a manner that Grant felt like he was floating in a bubble. For a few hours he had been able to forget about the nightmare he had been living. The ringing phone burst the bubble as he dragged himself to his feet to answer it. It was John Coroner with the news that he had been pardoned. Grant rushed back outside, pulled Stephanie to her feet and led her in an insane dance around the porch. She obviously had no idea what was going on until he yelled, "President Sampson has pardoned me, and the nightmare is over."

She gave him a big hug and then forced him to continue with their insane dance. If anyone had seen them, they would have sworn they were crazy.

"Grant, Grant," she said, bringing them to a halt, "calm down, calm down."

Out of breath, he flopped down on the lush grass and looked at the blue Colorado sky. After a moment, he sat up and exclaimed, "We need to really celebrate. Let's take a trip somewhere, just get in the truck and figure out where to go while we drive to the airport. We can get clothes and whatever else we need when we get there. Let's go, come on, let's just do it!"

Stephanie stood over him and put her hands on his shoulders. "Grant, I've never seen you like this before. I like it."

Grant jumped up and ran off across the lawn. "Watch this," he yelled as he tried to jump in the air and click his heels together. It didn't work; too many margaritas. He ended up in a heap in the grass laughing like a little kid. Stephanie came over and dropped to the ground beside him, and they both lay on their backs looking up at the clear Colorado sky.

They lay there for a full minute. Then Grant jumped up and pulled her to her feet. "Come on, get your purse, and be sure to bring your passport and cell phone. Let's get going." They stopped at the barn to tell Tommy they were leaving to go somewhere; they didn't know where, and they didn't know when they would be back.

Grant was a free man again and on top of the world. He had the time and money to go and a beautiful woman to go with. By the time they got to the airport, they had booked a flight to Los Angeles where they would catch a flight to Tahiti with an open return ticket.

The short flight from Papeete on the island of Tahiti to the island of Bora Bora hit the runway and taxied to a tiny open-air terminal on an atoll unconnected to the main island. The island was almost completely surrounded by a coral reef creating a crystal clear blue-green lagoon in all directions. They got from the airport to the hotel by motor launch. Stephanie never looked more striking with her hair streaming in the breeze, color on her cheeks, and a smile on her lips.

They were greeted at the dock and escorted to their over-water bungalow. They could step outside on the private deck and climb down a short ladder to the water. After eight hours on two planes, they immediately put on their swimsuits and went for a delightful swim in the tropical waters amid a multitude of colorful fish. Now they lay on the deck lounges sipping from a complimentary bottle of champagne while the sun warmed their bodies.

"Stephanie," Grant said, "this has to be the most romantic island in the world."

"Grant," said Stephanie, making an X out of her index fingers, "don't get any romantic ideas. I'm beyond exhausted. One more glass of champagne, and I could sleep for a week."

Grant settled back on his lounge and began to relax. They were sharing the bungalow but had not discussed sleeping arrangements. She hadn't objected when the travel agent booked a one-bedroom bungalow; but other than one brief sexual encounter almost two years ago, their relationship had not been romantic. True, he had a few romantic thoughts about her; well, more than a few, since they had gotten reacquainted at the Sanchez hacienda. The fact was, he had no idea about her feelings toward him. This trip? Two friends sharing a good time? Maybe a little sex thrown in to help them relax? The beginning of a relationship? How was he to know? What did he really want, now that they were here?

It was all too much for him. He finished his third glass of champagne, watched a single cloud drift across the sky, and stopped thinking about anything.

Chapter 62

Carlos Sanchez paced back and forth in his library seething with anger. Ramon had suggested that Hector try to extradite Meredith for stealing the helicopter. It had been a dumb idea and had not worked. Meredith had humiliated him. Ramon, Hector, even Margarita had tried to reassure him that it was no big deal; Meredith couldn't hurt them.

What his children failed to understand was that a man in his position could not afford to appear weak. He ruled through fear and, when necessary, violence. If his enemies smelled weakness, they would strike like sharks smelling blood.

Six months ago a new chief of police in Nogales had refused to take a generous Sanchez family stipend. The man was an idiot. He refused to understand that his choice was *plata o plomo* (silver or lead). As the man left his home for his first day on the job, a big black Suburban pulled up in front of his house, and six men with AK-47s piled out and riddled his body with over a hundred rounds of high-powered lead. His wife and four-year-old daughter had been standing on the porch and saw him die. His replacement had been more than happy to accept the stipend.

That was how Carlos controlled Nogales. He saw himself as a generous man, willing to share, but he tolerated nothing but deference, nothing else at all.

Now there was Meredith. First the man was responsible for taking down the family's drug distribution operation in Arizona. Then the *arrogante hijo de chucha* came to his home and stole a helicopter. He knew people were going to talk, and he intended to give them something to talk about.

The next day a white Chevy Tahoe arrived in a cloud of dust at JJ's Cantina just outside Puerto Peñasco, Sonora. Two men armed with AK-47s and Glock pistols in their waistbands leaped from the backseat and moved warily inside the concrete-floored cantina. Two minutes later one of the men emerged and nodded. Carlos Sanchez emerged from the front passenger door and entered the cantina. The heavily armed driver stationed himself at the front door. It was 10 a.m., and the cantina overlooking Cholla Bay was empty except for a bartender warily polishing bar glasses with the speed of dripping molasses. He looked up, did a double take, and scurried into the room behind the bar. Outside on the patio two men sat at a concrete table waiting for Carlos. They both stood as Carlos approached their table. The bodyguards moved out of earshot and took up positions facing the beach and the Bay below.

One of the men wore blue jeans and a faded red T-shirt. He was of medium height and build with greasy black hair pulled back into a ponytail. He had a long, narrow weasel-like face with deeply pitted cheeks. A stringy black mustache and wispy goatee framed bloodless lips. His eyes were brown and shimmered with intensity.

The other man was tall with large bones and a heavy but not flabby build. Short brown hair topped a small head with a round face that sat on broad shoulders. He did not appear to have a neck. His eyes were too small for even his small head. One of them was milky white; the other was pale blue and never blinked.

These two men were *sicarios*, executioners for the Sanchez family. They and others like them enforced discipline within the organization. Their job was to torture, maim, or kill—and take care of the bodies. Many *sicarios* were drug addicts who operated under the influence of a narcotic to carry out their gruesome work. These two needed no such inducement; they were sadists who thrived on the pain of others.

Carlos sat down and motioned for them to sit. He pushed a nine-by-twelve brown envelope across the table and said, "His name is Grant Meredith. In the envelope you will find his picture, address, and a biography. There are passports and border visas for you. You will enter the United States legally. There is a Tucson address in the envelope. Go there to get your weapons. I want Grant Meredith killed in a very public way. I want his dead body on the television news and the front pages of newspapers. Questions?"

The two men looked at each other and shook their heads.

Carlos and his bodyguards left without another word.

Appendix

A. FOREIGN POLICY

1. *The Bush Doctrine did not usher in a radically new idea regarding American foreign policy.*

"We are pointing the way to struggling nations who wish, like us, to emerge from their tyrannies."

Thomas Jefferson
1790

"The authors of [the Declaration of Independence] set up a standard maxim for free society, which should be familiar to all, and revered by all; constantly looked to, constantly labored for, and even though never perfectly attained, constantly approximated and thereby constantly spreading and deepening its influence, and augmenting the happiness and value of life to all people of all colors everywhere."

Abraham Lincoln, June 26, 1857

"The objective I propose is quite simple to state: to foster the infrastructure of democracy, the system of a free press, unions, political parties, universities, which allow a people to choose their own way to develop their own culture, to reconcile their own differences through peaceful means. This is not cultural imperialism; it is providing the means for genuine self-determination and protection for diversity. Democracy already flourishes in countries with different cultures and historical experiences. It would be cultural condescension, or worse, to say that any people prefer dictatorship to democracy. Who would voluntarily choose not to have the right to vote, decide to purchase government propaganda handouts instead of independent newspapers, prefer government to worker-controlled unions, opt for land to be owned by the state instead of by those who till it, want government repression of religious liberty, a single political party instead of a free choice, a rigid cultural orthodoxy instead of democratic tolerance and diversity?"

Ronald Regan
Address to the British Parliament
June 8, 1982

The Obama administration's stance on the promotion of democracy abroad is somewhat different in rhetoric, but the substance of the American attitude has not changed. Compare the following to the Bush Doctrine set forth in the Prologue:

"To meet the challenges of this new century, defense and diplomacy are necessary—but not sufficient. We also need to wield development and democracy—two of the most powerful weapons in our arsenal. Poor societies and dysfunctional states can become breeding ground for extremism, conflict and disease. Non-democratic nations frustrate the rightful aspirations of their citizens and fuel resentment.

"Our administration has set ambitious goals to increase foreign assistance ... To advance democracy not through its imposition by force from the outside, but by working with moderates in government and civil society to build the institutions that will protect freedom"

Vice President-elect of the United States Joseph Biden
Speech at 45th Munich Security Conference
February 7, 2009

2. AMERICA AS A DANGEROUS NATION

"This gap between Americans' self-perception and the perception of others has endured throughout the nation's history. Americans have cherished an image of themselves as by nature inward-looking and aloof, only sporadically and spasmodically venturing forth into the world, usually in response to external attack or perceived threats. This self-image survives, despite four hundred years of steady expansion and an ever-deepening involvement in world affairs, and despite innumerable wars, interventions, and prolonged occupations in foreign lands ...

"This lack of self-awareness has had its virtues. It has sometimes made America's vast power more tolerable to large numbers of peoples around the world, for a nation so unaware of its own behavior may seem less threatening than a nation with a plan of expansion and conquest. But it has also been a problem. Americans have often not realized how their expansive tendencies—political, ideological, economic, strategic, and cultural—bump up against and intrude upon other peoples and cultures. They are surprised to learn that others hate them, are jealous of them, and even fear them for their power and influence. They have not anticipated, therefore, the way their natural expansiveness could provoke reactions, and sometimes violent reactions against them."

Dangerous Nation
Alfred A. Knopf, 2006
Robert Kagan
Pages 5–6

3. Two Competing Foreign Policy Philosophies

"Realpolitik refers to politics or diplomacy based primarily on practical considerations, rather than ideological notions.

"The policy of realpolitik was formally introduced to the Nixon White House by Henry Kissinger. In this context, the policy meant dealing with other powerful nations in a practical manner rather than on the basis of political doctrine or ethics ... Realpolitik is distinct from ideological politics in that it is not dictated by a fixed set of rules, but instead tends to be goal-oriented, limited only by practical exigencies. Since realpolitik is ordered toward the most practical means of securing national interests, it can often entail compromising on ideological principles. For example, the US under the Nixon, Carter, and Reagan administrations often supported authoritarian regimes that were human rights violators, in order to secure the greater national interest of regional stability. Detractors would characterize this attitude as amoral, while supporters would contend that they are merely operating within limits defined by practical reality."

Wikipedia, the free encyclopedia

"**Neoconservatism** is a political movement which emerged in the 1960s, coalesced in the 1970s, and has significant presence in the administration of George W. Bush.

***

"Critics take issue with the neoconservatives' support for aggressive foreign policy; critics from the left especially take issue with what they characterize as unilateralism and lack of concern with international consensus through organizations such as the United Nations. Neoconservatives respond by describing their shared view as a belief that national security is best attained by promoting freedom and democracy abroad through the support of pro-democracy movements, foreign aid and in certain cases military intervention ... Author Paul Berman in his book *Terror and Liberalism* describes it as, 'Freedom for others means safety for ourselves. Let us be for freedom for others.'"

Wikipedia, the free encyclopedia

B. Mexican Drug and Human Trafficking Organizations

1. Terrorists Can Enter the United States through Mexico and Canada.

"'Members of Hezbollah, the Lebanon-based terrorist organization, have already entered the United States across our southwest border,' declares *A Line in the Sand*, a January report of the House Homeland Security subcommittee on Investigations chaired by Texas Republican Michael McCaul.

"In Fiscal Year 2005 alone, 3,308 aliens got caught sneaking into America from nations the State Department considers state-sponsors of terrorism ... Of course, these are the folks the Border Patrol arrested.

"Federal law enforcement entities estimate that they apprehend approximately 10 to 30 percent of illegal aliens crossing the border ..."

As Immigration Bill Stalls, U.S. Border Invites Terrorists
Human Events.com, posted June 18, 2007
Deroy Murdock

"GAO investigators identified numerous border security vulnerabilities [on the US/Canadian border], both at ports of entry and at unmanned and unmonitored land border locations between ports of entry. In testing ports of entry, undercover investigators carried counterfeit drivers' licenses, birth certificates, employee identification cards, and other documents, presented themselves at ports of entry and sought admittance to the United States dozens of times. They arrived in rental cars, on foot, by boat, and by airplane ... In nearly every case, government inspectors accepted oral assertions and counterfeit identification ... and allowed them to enter the country. In total, undercover investigators made 42 crossings with a 93 percent success rate."

Border Security
Summary of Covert Tests and Security Assessments for the Senate Committee on Finance, 2003–2007
Government Accountability Office
May 16, 2008

2. MEXICAN DRUG TRAFFICKING ORGANIZATIONS ARE A THREAT TO THE US.

"US counternarcotics assistance to Mexico since 2000 has made some progress in helping Mexico [combat illegal drug trade] ... However, overall, the flow of illicit drugs through Mexico to the United States has not abated, and interdiction efforts in Mexico have seized relatively small quantities of illicit drugs ... Moreover, drug related corruption persists throughout much of

Mexico, and Mexican DTOs [Drug Trafficking Organizations] have increasingly become a threat in Mexico, which has seen an increase in drug related violence, and expanded their presence throughout much of the United States."

United States Government Accountability Office
Drug Control … Tons of Illicit Drugs Continue to Flow into the United States, p. 36
August 2007

"The Southwest Border Region is the principal entry point for undocumented aliens from Mexico, Central America, and South America. *Undocumented aliens from special-interest countries such as Afghanistan, Iran, Iraq, and Pakistan also illegally enter the United States through the region. Mexican DTOs collect fees from alien smuggling organizations for the use of specific smuggling routes. Among those individuals illegally crossing the border are criminal aliens and gang members who pose public safety concerns for communities throughout the country. In addition, hundreds of undocumented aliens from special-interest countries illegally cross the US–Mexico border annually. Available reporting indicates that some alien smuggling organizations and Mexican DTOs specialize in smuggling special-interest aliens into the United States. (*emphasis added).

"Violence associated with alien smuggling has increased in recent years, particularly in Arizona. Expanding border security initiatives and additional Border Patrol resources are very likely obstructing regularly used smuggling routes and fueling this increase in violence, particularly violence directed at law enforcement officers. Alien smugglers and guides are more likely than in past years to use violence against US law enforcement officers in order to smuggle groups of undocumented aliens across the Southwest Border. Conflicts are also emerging among rival alien smuggling organizations. Assaults, kidnappings, and hostage situations attributed to this conflict are increasing, particularly in Tucson and Phoenix, Arizona.

***

"Mexican DTOs are the most pervasive organizational threat to the United States. They are active in every region of the country and dominate the illicit drug trade in every area except the Northeast. Mexican DTOs are expanding their operations in the Northeast and have developed cooperative relationships with DTOs in that area in order to gain a larger share of the northeastern drug market."

National Drug Threat Assessment 2008
National Drug Intelligence Center
U.S. Department of Justice
October 2007, pages vi and 35

"Federal, state and local law enforcement reporting reveals that Mexican DTOs operate in at least 195 cities throughout the United States."

Situation Report
National Drug Intelligence Center
US Department of Justice
April 11, 2008

"Mexican drug cartels are engaged in an increasingly violent fight for control of narcotics trafficking routes along the US–Mexican border in an apparent response to the government of Mexico's initiatives to crack down on narco-trafficking organizations. In order to combat violence, the government of Mexico has deployed military troops in various parts of the country. US citizens should cooperate fully with official checkpoints when traveling on Mexican highways.

"Some recent Mexican army and police confrontations with drug cartels have taken on the characteristics of small-unit combat, with cartels employing automatic weapons and, on occasion, grenades. Firefights have taken place in many towns and cities across Mexico but particularly in northern Mexico, including Tijuana, Chihuahua City and Ciudad Juárez. The situation in northern Mexico remains fluid; the location and timing of future armed engagements cannot be predicted …"

Travel Alert
U.S. Department of State
Bureau of Consular Affairs
October 14, 2008

"In what could be one of Mexico's worst cases of drug-related corruption in a decade, Mexican officials alleged that a drug cartel infiltrated the highest levels of Mexico's attorney general's office, paying people there as much as $450,000 a month to get sensitive information about antidrug activities ... 'The investigation continues and we do not rule out that there are other people who could have taken part in crimes that will be called to account,' Mr. Medina Mora said. An adviser to Mr. Medina Mora said he hoped that with the arrests, officials had cut out '70% of the cancer 'in the institution ..."

Wall Street Journal
"Mexican Attorney General's Office is Reportedly Infiltrated by Drug Cartel"
October 28, 2008, Page A9

"The Mexican government revealed Nov. 27 that nearly half of all policemen tested for competency and honesty as part of President Felipe Calderón's national security reform have failed. Additionally, ... 90 percent of police in Baja California were 'not recommended' for police duties ...

"The tests—which consist of a background check, polygraph test, drug use analysis, psychological evaluation, and income audit— were designed to root out corrupt and/or incompetent individuals unfit for police work."

Mexico Security Memo: Dec. 1, 2008
Stratfor Geopolitical Intelligence

"The narcotics trade remains at the core of organized crime in the [Western] hemisphere. This is by far the most lucrative of illegal trades, generating hundreds of billions of dollars a year. Its immense cash flow, vast employment opportunities, and sophisticated networks feed other kinds of criminal activity and allow drug traffickers to adapt with extraordinary speed to governments' counternarcotics efforts. The drug trade is also singularly adept at corrupting judicial, political, and law enforcement institutions. In Mexico, open war between the cartels and all levels of government has killed 4,000 people so far in 2008 alone—about as many casualties as the United States has sustained in almost six years of war in Iraq. This violence already threatens to spill into the United States and to destabilize Mexico's political institutions ...

"However, current US counternarcotics policies are failing by most objective measures. Drug use in the United States has not declined significantly ... Falling retail drug prices reflect the failure of efforts to reduce the supply of drugs ...

"The only long-run solution to the problem of illegal narcotics is to reduce the demand for drugs in the major consuming countries, including the United States."

The Brookings Institution
Rethinking US–Latin American Relations
Report of the Partnership for the Americas Commission, pp. 24-26
November 2008

"Drug consumption and the resulting international trade in controlled substances remain one of the greatest man-made catastrophes of the past 30 years. Worldwide, the illegal drug trade totals $300 billion per year. The loss of human life resulting from the drug trade runs in the tens of thousands.

"Despite modest progress, continued US drug consumption is a root cause and a central driver of drug-related violence in Mexico."

Mexico, Drug Cartels, and the Mérida Initiative: A Fight We Cannot Afford to Lose
The Heritage Foundation
July 23, 2008

"As US ambassador to Mexico, I've tried to be honest with both Americans and Mexicans alike, and the truth is, Mexico would not be the center of cartel activity or be experiencing this level of violence, were the United States not the largest consumer of illicit drugs and the main supplier of weapons to the cartels."

Outgoing U.S. Ambassador to Mexico Lashes out on Drug War
Dallas Morning News
November 27, 2008

"For two years, Mexican President Felipe Calderón has waged war on powerful and violent drug cartels, deploying 20,000 troops and the full might of the state. Nearly 6,000 lives have been lost—more than all US casualties in Iraq. With no end in sight,

Mr. Calderón now says he can't win if the US doesn't do more to curb its drug addiction."

Mexico's Plea to Obama: Curb Drug Use
Christian Science Monitor Editorial Board
December 3, 2008

"Mexican DTOs represent the greatest organized crime threat to the United States. The influence of Mexican DTOs over domestic drug trafficking is unrivaled. In fact, intelligence estimates indicate a vast majority of the cocaine available in US drug markets is smuggled by Mexican DTOs across the US–Mexican border. Mexican DTOs control drug distribution in most US cities, and they are gaining strength in markets that they do not yet control.

"Violent urban gangs control most retail-level drug distribution nationally, and some have relocated from inner cities to suburban and rural areas. Moreover, gangs are increasing their involvement in wholesale-level drug distribution, aided by their connection with Mexican and Asian DTOs" (emphasis in original).

National Drug Threat Assessment 2009
National Drug Intelligence Center
US Department of Justice, December 2008
Page III

"MEXICO CITY—As drug violence spirals out of control in Mexico, a commission led by three former Latin American heads of state blasted the US–led drug war as a failure that is pushing Latin American societies to the breaking point ...

... the U.S. approach to narcotics—based on treating drug consumption as a crime—has failed. Latin America ... should adopt a more European approach, based on treating drug addiction as a health problem."

Latin American Panel Calls US Drug War a Failure
The Wall Street Journal.com
February 12, 2009

****